Alien Legacy

by

John C. Macidull

DORRANCE PUBLISHING CO., INC.
PITTSBURGH, PENNSYLVANIA 15222

ISBN # 0-8059-4589-X
Printed in the United States of America

First Printing

For information or to order additional books, please write:
Dorrance Publishing Co., Inc.
643 Smithfield Street
Pittsburgh, Pennsylvania 15222
U.S.A.

To my wife Janet, and my sister Madeline Leigh

Prologue

Azatlan (Modern-day Peru): 4179 B.C.

Two llama herders, dressed in ragged but gold-threaded embroidered robes of the high country, sat down by their small dung fire in the Andes Mountains and prepared a meal. One put potatoes into a clay pot of water while the other added spices of sea salt and ground red pepper. They talked of the Great Flood which had inundated all lands and civilizations five years prior and how another probably couldn't reach them at their altitude.

As they were talking, two short humanoid figures, dressed in grey body suits, emerged from the shadows and approached the fire. At first, the llama herders thought them lost children. But as they came nearer, the large heads, long and slender hands and fingers, and cat-like eyes were noted, and the herders were startled. As they stood up, one of the 'children' pointed to the sky. Both 'Indians' looked up and saw a beam of white light shining down on them.

It was an abduction. One could argue that it was a friendly abduction. In this case it could be considered an unfair trade. Unfair because two of the 'traders' were not given a choice or the free will to negotiate.

However it could also be argued that the sperm and tissue samples taken from them would not be missed or even noticed, and in return they were given a sample of technology that was many hundreds of thousands of years in the making. Like the Great Pyramid at Cheops in Egypt, it was a valuable gift to the pre-Inca civilization of what could be possible.

The next thing the llama herders remembered was standing in a cave. There was no roof to it, just misty white and purple clouds. In front of them were two disk-shaped objects and four of the grey 'children'. One pointed to the ground behind the 'Indians'. They turned and noted a line of glowing green leading off into the dark recesses of the cave. When they turned back around, they saw the 'children' enter one of the disks. It rose silently and disappeared into the clouds above. The other disk glowed faintly where it sat.

The 'Indians' inspected it but could make no sense of it. They tried to damage it by scraping its surface with stones. Then they beat on it with a nearby ten-pound rock. Finally they decided it was a gift from the sun god since it was mostly gold colored and seemed indestructible.

Eventually driven by hunger, they sought a way out and soon focused their attention on the iridescent green line. They followed it for over a mile between large boulders and stalagmites. It ended by a pool of water between two waterfalls. The one to their left rumbled loudly down into the darkness. The one to their right dropped like a curtain, reflecting small rainbows in the sunlight coming from the other side. There was a reed boat with paddles on the sandy shore . . . the same type used by their countrymen who lived down by the great sea and traded fish and salt for a living. Three hours later, they had paddled out from under the waterfall that led toward the light, across the lake, and were hiking down the mountain.

* * *

During the next year the five 'fathers' of the 'Indian' tribe visited the cave. After close inspection of the disk and attempts at damaging it, they all agreed that it was a gift from their sun god . . . and that tribute should be paid to it. First there was a twenty-year project to match the size of the disk with works of art in gold and silver. In this way, a new depository for religious endeavor was established. After a hundred years of more deposits, the cave's location was considered too important for more than one or two people to know of. And for the next few thousand years, its existence to the people was relegated to the realm of folklore and tradition, while the religious hierarchy had access to it for the purpose of elitism, a necessary prerequisite to ancient forms of taxation.

5,698 years later, Cuzco, Peru: 1519 A.D.

The morning sky was a blue dome, like the inside of a giant glass bell. Clear, cool air carried the sounds across the square. The ceremony in praise of the sun god was nearly over as plumed and colorful musicians and dancers ended their part of the Incan worship. Ten previous emperors and their wives, sitting on chairs, mummified, and covered in gold leaf, were paraded by. And then the ceremony was over.

The nobles stood in preparation to hoist the gold and gem-encrusted litter poles and carry their emperor, the Sapa Inca, from the temple courtyard to his stone palace overlooking the city.

As the drums and the deep pipes of haunting whisper-music stopped, a large eagle flew overhead, crying loudly. All eyes looked up and saw the great bird being pursued and pecked by several sparrows. Round and round it circled, flying higher to escape. Then, with a last call, it folded its wide wings and fell with a thump into the middle of the square. The sparrows flitted away, and a hush fell over the people. The death of this eagle caused by a few small birds was an omen that weighed heavily on all. Within three days the story was known throughout the Incan Empire.

Punta Aguja, on the Peruvian Coast: 1523 A.D.

The smugglers met at the appointed time, when the moon was full during the month of the ripening maize. A wide strip of desert lay between the Pacific Ocean and the snow-capped peaks of the Andes to the east. Stark and rainless hills allowed scouts to see for fifty miles. It was a favorite spot for the smuggling business, with little chance of ambush.

The Aztec from the North called his porters with silent, barely perceptible twitches of an index finger. They appeared from the shadows of the dunes and unfolded their burdens on the white sand under the bright equatorial moonlight, displaying the turquoise and opals from the land of the great canyon far into the northern desert. The man from the South inspected the unworked stones carefully and then called his men from a half mile down the beach. They led a group of five llamas, each with a fifty-pound load slung over its back that contained gold nuggets, lumps of silver, and feathers from the coraquenque bird. All such truck from the South was considered the property of the Sapa Inca and his family of nobles. The rare red feathers were the distinguishing insignia of royalty. For a commoner, possession of one carried the death penalty.

"I see there is not much of the blue stone this time," said the man from the South, from what is today Peru.

"Not important," began the Mexican from the North. "Remember what I said to you last trip, when you thought I was crazy?"

"Yes," said the smuggler from the South. "About the men with white skin that burned in the sun and the animals they rode. Animals twice as large as llamas. That they had metal skins they put on, and fire-sticks, and long sharp knives. Yes, I remember. You said they held the great Montezuma captive, and he died. Less than five hundred of these men against many tens of thousands of Aztec warriors. Then you said the white men and their giant dogs were forced back to the eastern sea without even their personal belongings. And I said that made less sense, that these men still had to see, and that a good stone or arrow in the eye would stop anyone, and that I thought you were crazy. That they couldn't have gotten away."

"Later," said the man from the North. "I wondered if perhaps you were right, my friend. That perhaps I actually was crazy or had dreamed it. But then, after a year, when I got back in the hills below the city by the lake of Tihuyacana, I found that the unwashed white men had not only returned, but had taken over the entire land, and they put the Aztecs into slavery. And so there was not much of the blue stone that had gotten through."

"I see, my friend," said the man from the South. "What do these men want?"

"As far as I can tell they want the yellow and white, but mostly the yellow. They have already gotten all that was there, melted it into bricks, and took it to the Eastern Sea where they have large vessels with broad white wings that move across the great waters like gods. Now they are making the people dig in the ground for more of the metal. And they kill at the least sign of resistance. They want the women also, but only for a while. They let them go when they are finished. But the men they work until they die."

"I see," said the man from the South, frowning upward, his smooth skin reflecting perfect half-circles of worry in the moonlight under his eyes. "And what else can you tell me? How do they live?"

"They eat like everyone else, but never do they work the soil or pre-pare food. They have many gods who look exactly the same, carvings of little men without clothing who are attached to cross-beams of wood by means of spikes pushed through their hands and feet and seem to be in bad shape. They carry them wherever they go and don't do anything of importance without showing them some kind of reverence. And there are special keepers of some of these gods. Men who wear black or brown clothing and never laugh. All the white men periodically go to these humorless god-keepers and, after much ceremony, eat and drink tiny quantities of special food and liquid they say is the flesh and blood of their god. They call it mass, holy mass. Then they go and treat women as bad dogs. Their silver clothing cannot be penetrated by even the itztli blade. And they have metal logs that shoot fire and thunder and can kill many men at one time. To attack them is pointless."

"They eat their god and drink his blood?" asked the man from the south.

"Yes, that is what everyone understands to be the case," said the Aztec.

"Then they are beholden to nothing and no one!" exclaimed the smuggler from the south.

"Yes," said the Aztec, "and their actions seem to prove it. They don't even bathe, and one has to breathe through his mouth when around them or vomit from the stench."

The man from the South stared at the ground while asking questions and listening, then looked up suddenly and began the business.

"Thank you for that information from the Aztec land in the North. How much yellow and white do you want for the blue stones and the fire rocks?"

The man from the North looked at him with warm eyes and said that he wanted no metal, just all the coraquenque feathers.

"None of the sweat of the sun! Or the moon?" exclaimed the man from the South. "Why?"

"Because it would be discovered. And after the white people discover any of the metal, it means torture."

"I don't understand," said the smuggler from the South. "If they want the yellow metal, and they get it, then why would they torture the person that gave it to them?"

"To see if the person they got it from has any more that he is hiding. The feathers are the only currency now," said the man from the North.

The man from the South stepped back in amazement, looking bewildered at his long-time smuggling partner from the North.

"Okay, my friend, I have thirty sheaves of coraquenque feathers. Divide the portion of the blue stone that it is worth to you."

He ordered that the fourth llama be brought forward, and the beautiful plumage was set down next to the turquoise. The man from the North looked at the opened sheaves, repeated that the feathers were the only currency now and said that all the blue stones he had were a fair exchange.

They parted company after agreeing that they would meet again in two years and that feathers and stones would be the primary trading items. The man from the South buried the sacks of gold and silver in the sand well inland from the sea at Punta Aguja, and let three of the llamas loose to go back to the mountains. He bent over and strapped his sandals tighter, then took some coca leaves from a special pouch tied to his belt and began chewing them, wondering why they weren't good truck for trading since they dissipated hunger and fatigue. Then he put the thought from his mind, gathered his men, and started the long trip back to Cuzco, the "Navel of the Universe" hidden in the mountains of the gods, amid the white peaks that no man had ever climbed.

Many times during the next month, he told the story of the white men in the North and of their power and values. Within a year every peasant in the Incan empire knew of these unwashed few. And over a million of the population died that year of a strange fever that no herb could cure. A porter from the South had touched hands and exchanged conversational breath with a porter from the North while counting out feathers, thereby bringing the first message from the Spaniards: *smallpox*.

Caxamalca, Peru: 1525 A.D.

The half-brother sons of the Sapa Inca had never been close. Huascar was the older. Atahuallpa, always the more ambitious, was a conniver with an underlying resentment at being second. Huascar was the diligent student of his culture and people. To Atahuallpa, Huascar inherited little vision from their conquering ancestor from a distant past, the great Tupa Inca. Atahuallpa was the man who would be the Sapa Inca, knowing with feeling, more than knowledge, that his courage of risk and show was what was important. He hadn't the slightest inkling that survival, often bred of conservatism, was the main pedestal upon which any idol could be maintained.

Before his death, Huayna-capac, the esteemed father of Huascar and Atahuallpa, had given Huascar the seat of government and Atahuallpa the more powerful army. It was the only bad political decision of his long and successful life. He left no undisputed heir, and in this way he divided the empire. Huascar ruled from the ancient capitol of Cuzco in the South and Atahuallpa from the city of Quito in the North. Both brothers claimed the title of Sapa Inca; Huascar because he was the eldest and in line, Atahuallpa because he thought he was better for the position and commanded the larger army. Both also had large popular followings, completing the necessary ingredients for a civil war.

* * *

Two hundred thousand men fought in the Battle of Cuzco in 1525. Over thirty thousand died. Their bones lay picked by vultures for months and then bleached white on the plain. Though the battle was won by Atahuallpa, Huascar escaped with most of his now much smaller army back to Cuzco. Atahuallpa, the clear victor, then moved north with his army, wearing the red-feather insignia of the Sapa Inca.

The country of Peru was in this state of affairs of stagnated civil war when Francisco Pizarro and his one hundred-seventy fellow Spaniards and their forty horses marched down the coast in search of gold and conquest.

* * *

Outside Caxamalca on the central plains of Peru, Atahuallpa and his men camped and waited. He looked at the town, his dark eyes evaluating the troop of approaching Spanish. Though a military commander, he also considered himself the head of state and would exhibit some diplomacy.

He sent word that allowed the Spaniards to enter the city and stay as guests. His plan was to reconnoiter in more detail this strange small band of men as any warrior-general would. His father and grandfather had founded the empire on such soldierly instincts. He envisioned executing only a few Spaniards, perhaps make the rest eunuchs for the court, and breed their giant llamas.

In a few days, Pizarro's men had made the houses in the center of the city an armed camp, with cannons carefully placed in alleys and their horses quartered and saddled in buildings for instant use.

It became an excruciating wait for the arrival of the Inca. A few of the Spaniards uncontrollably wet their pants when looking at the hundred thousand armed warriors positioned outside the city, silently staring at them.

Atahuallpa finally entered the city, seated on a golden throne atop a litter that was carried on the shoulders of nobles. A retinue of five thousand followed. They were all unarmed to show good faith. It was to be a ceremony of State. With a vast army close by, Atahuallpa had no concern. The litter was positioned in the middle of the courtyard and set down. Pizarro presented himself in a formal manner, then stood back and nodded for the charade to begin.

First, the Spaniards put on a show of horsemanship with an especially spirited Andalusian mare that often reared up. After several intricate maneuvers of military dressage, which ended with a charge toward a group of warriors, the horse stopped abruptly in front of them in a cloud of dust. Six of Atahuallpa's nobles stepped back slightly, and he made a note to have them executed for showing fear in front of possible enemies.

Next came a sermon by the Spanish priest, who read passages from the Bible. After the last translation, Atahuallpa became incensed at the references to ownership and the one true god. He took the Bible from the priest, paged through it, and said, "As for the Pope of whom you speak, he must be crazy to talk of giving away countries that do not belong to him. As for my faith, I will not change it. Your own god, as you say, was put to death by the very men whom he created. But mine," he said pointing to the sun, "lives now in the heavens and looks down upon his children!"

With that he let the Bible drop from his hand with a disgusted look on his face.

With that pretext, all Spanish eyes were now on Pizarro, waiting for the signal. Pizarro waved a white scarf in the air and the slaughter and hostage-taking began immediately and in earnest.

Two cannons fired into the confines of the courtyard at the five thousand unarmed Incas. Then the horsemen came from the alleys and began swinging swords.

In a frenzy of slashing and cutting, limbs flew off, backs were driven through, skulls were cleaved, and the gutters flowed for a while with blood over an inch deep. While shielding Atahuallpa, Pizarro cried out, "Let no one who values his life strike at the Inca," as he received a wound on the hand from one of his own men by parrying a blow that would have surely killed the monarch.

In a half hour, not including the cannons, each Spanish sword averaged killing fifteen Incas. Atahuallpa was secured in a room under heavy guard, all Indian nobles were dead in the courtyard, and ninety-five thousand armed Indians remaining stood on the hills outside the city, mute and leaderless.

Not one Spaniard was wounded except Pizarro himself, who had learned well from his countryman Cortez the method that had worked in extorting wealth from the Aztec empire. In almost exactly the same manner that Cortez had captured and kept Montezuma, Pizarro allowed Atahuallpa to keep his women and some servants and to continue the administration of the empire under constant armed guard.

Cuzco, Peru: 1525 A.D.

Huascar listened intently to the fragmented stories about his impetuous and haughty half-brother, the usurper Sapa Inca with a large, now worthless army. Then he left for his mountain retreat to meditate and hold council. Titu Ongo, his chief advisor, began his report.

"My Lord, Atahuallpa's Court of State entered Caxamalca in peace, but they were helpless without weapons. They could not fight against the Spaniards, against their metal skin, demon llamas, and fire-logs. Five thousand were slaughtered in the square within minutes. Perhaps we should give them what they want."

Huascar began speaking in a throaty voice that was strained with fatigue, frustration, and stress.

"Who is your Inca, Titu Ongo?"

"You are, my Lord."

"Then counsel me on what is, not what you think should be."

Titu Ongo bent low and backed away, his small frame and thin robe almost disappearing into the shadows of the room. Huascar, the scholar, the "mild Inca," watched Titu retreat and said, "Tell me, Titu Ongo, how long have you been my advisor?"

Titu answered in a subdued voice that he had advised for ten years, nine moons.

"And how many others have advised me that long?" asked Huascar.

"None," said Titu.

"And you know what all the people are saying?"

"Yes, my Lord."

"And since you have been hearing all this, is there one who knows more than you?"

Titu Ongo thought for a minute. He loved his Inca. But he didn't want to die. And he didn't want his family to die. Though he had over thirty years of valued service, no Sapa Inca had ever scolded an official without invoking the penalty of death. The only unknowns depended on how one acted after the scolding, whether it would be a quick or slow death, or a watching of one's wife and children suffer beforehand. There were many variables.

He could say that he had heard it all from the smuggler, but if the Inca found that he had even talked to a smuggler, things could go very badly indeed.

"There are only the persons I have heard things from that know more than me, my Lord. They know more individually, I know more collectively."

Huascar smiled. "Then who is more valuable to his Inca where time is of the essence, one who knows everyone's stories, or each individual story teller?"

Titu Ongo breathed a sigh and was glad for his long-time devotion to such a wise man. For several hours Titu Ongo told everything he knew about the white men's habits, all that he had heard about what had happened far to the north a few years before, and of the llama trains of gold and silver on the way to Caxamalca to ransom Atahuallpa.

"They want two rooms full," said Titu, "one of the yellow, one of the white."

Up to a point these people are similar to my great-great-grandfather when he dealt with the Talhyipas, thought Huascar. They didn't have obsidian blades or fast warriors with coverings on the bottoms of their feet. We don't have fire sticks or giant llamas or metal skin. But there is a difference. When my grandfather, the great Huayna Capac, won his battles, the conquered peoples were given things in exchange for their taxation . . . roads, a stable government, a way to sell their produce for a profit, warehouses for food when things went bad, bridges over the rivers, education of children, and care for the old. But most importantly, when a few of the outer provinces rebelled past all reason, my great ancestor left them alone. Today they live in jungles, eat tadpoles and monkeys, and shrink heads. But they were left alive and not bothered again. The difference is that these Spaniards could care less about whether or not we are around later, except to pay labor taxes. In the land to the north they have exterminated populations through labor in underground mines to get what yellow and white is to be had. All metal art they melted down into lumps. This is bad indeed.

"I now understand why they are here, Titu Ongo," he said. "And I know what kind of men they are. The worst thing for all our people would be for the Spaniards to know that there is any great quantity of treasure in the Empire. My half-brother has given them a small idea, only two rooms full. If gold were the sands of the beach, and I could eat it, I would. They will have no more."

After several minutes of meditation Huascar said, "So, they will get two rooms of metal. But it is like pouring milk from a breast into the mouths of gulls. When two are satisfied, ten more come . . . the more they get, the more they want, and soon they are eating the breast itself. I want no yellow or white metal left in Cuzco, except the little that is on the walls of the temples. They are not to get the golden chain that surrounds the city. They are not to get the works of art, the life-sized ones. And certainly they are not to get the Golden Disk of the Sun. But I do not want them to see any buildings there completely stripped of gold. Let them think they have gotten it all. You know where all the old palaces are. I want them uncovered and all the treasures of my ancestors retrieved. Everything will be hidden in the secret home of the first Inca in the mountains."

Titu Ongo was full of consternation at the thought of knowing the secret place of the Incas, a place whose existence was well known as a favorite folk tale during everyone's youth, but whose actual location could only be known by the Sapa Inca and his heir. Huascar saw the tremor in the face of Titu Ongo.

"I don't understand, my Lord," he said.

Huascar stood up and looked at the fire burning in the small hearth in one corner of the room. Incas never stood in front of people of lesser rank. And Huascar knew in doing so, he was giving an impression of weakness. But he had to get through to the best brain in his empire. He had to be able to use Titu Ongo's powers of imagination and calculation to carry through, even if it meant the risk of appearing less than the godly Sapa Inca everyone was educated to need. Abruptly Huascar turned around, his heavy, white, feather-robe with embedded golden bees flinging outward.

Titu Ongo's jaw dropped, and his eyes widened. Huascar paused for a breath.

"And so, you do not know what exactly to do, is that it?" he asked.

"Yes, my Lord," answered Titu Ongo. "What do you desire?"

Now I'm not talking to a worthless vassal, thought Huascar.

"What I want, General, is to gather and hide, for posterity, the eternal seal of all the Incas. In addition to our great Golden Disk of the Sun, you are to transport, within a few weeks, all the remaining yellow and white from the houses of my ancestors to the place of the gods in the mother mountains. You will need ten thousand men and twenty thousand llamas. And you are to use your imagination to accomplish this in secrecy. I will tell you how to get to the sacred cave of my ancestors. There is much room for everything in it and more. Memorize my directions."

He watched the concentration on the face of Titu Ongo while giving detailed directions. When he was finished, Huascar ordered him to repeat it. Then Huascar handed him a wide, golden, bejeweled bracelet. "Titu Ongo, you are now the only person, aside from me and my son, who knows where the cave is. After you have gathered and deposited nearly all the wealth of the empire, place this bracelet on the wrist of my father in Cuzco. It cannot be deciphered by the Spaniards and is too beautiful to be destroyed by them. It contains a map to the secret place that would be evident to our Rememberers today, or to any Rememberers in the future who know the land and the stars."

* * *

During the following week, Titu Ongo organized many thousands of men to collect all precious articles from living nobles and to break into the hundreds of buried mansions of dead nobles throughout the empire. At night the sacks of treasure were taken by llama trains, followed by litter-bearers with the heavier objects, to the most secret of ancient places.

Once they had arrived at their destination and stored the bounty, Titu Ongo let all of the workers who had been blindfolded go. The few others he dispatched with a stone swung on a lanyard, caving in the backs of their skulls efficiently and painlessly.

Huascar explained from memory the meaning of parts of the signs on the bracelet to his Royal Rememberers. One at a time and in private, he related a third of the map to his three best *quipos*. And he gave instructions that this information was to be passed on to other Rememberers in the future. *No need*, he thought, *to chance Spanish torture by any one of them knowing it all.*

Then Huascar reflected on what Titu Ongo had hidden . . . not counting what was already there for the gods, placed around their ancient sky-boat that had come so many years ago. He wondered what Titu Ongo had thought when gazing at the giant disk-shaped vessel of faintly glowing gold with a silver-blue bottom. His own father had shown it to him, saying it was a gift from the sun, and like the sun it could not be destroyed, but only worshiped. Titu Ongo had placed a sizeable addition into the huge room already full of delicately fashioned objects of gold and silver as well as thousands of pounds of gold nuggets and gold dust, heretofore waiting for the craftsmen.

"All of it, everything, the centuries of art, the treasures of my ancestors, the Spaniards would have melted down in a few weeks," said Huascar to himself. "Except the little bit left in Cuzco for the 'Sparrow Spaniards'," he added, satisfied, remembering the omen of the eagle dying in the courtyard years before.

Huascar thought late into the night. In the morning, in accordance with his religion, he confessed his sins to the sun god in his small chapel and bathed in a nearby stream to cleanse himself again of inherited sins. Then, for safe keeping, he sent his first-born son with a division of his best and

xvi

most loyal soldiers far into the mountains. To Machu Pichu, some said. After the prayers, he sat and thought for several hours. He came out of his concentration when his general arrived at dawn.

"Yes, Titu Ongo; you have done well, and you will live well," he said after the brief.

Titu Ongo looked at him in awe, wondering why Huascar was keeping him alive. Huascar saw his questioning stare and said that he was allowing him to live because of the massive feat he had done and for his loyalty. He added that because of these two things and the Spaniard's reputation for torture, only his power of speech would have to die. Titu Ongo, with immediate understanding, knelt before his Inca, quickly pulled an obsidian knife from his belt, and cut out his own tongue.

* * *

Pizarro told Atahuallpa that if there was any insurrection in the land, he would be held accountable. Atahuallpa gave the assignment to his elite guards. His half-brother had to be killed.

The twenty thousand elite arrived outside Cuzco at midnight. Small detachments, with larger backups, approached each of Huascar's warrior encampments. It was a coordinated movement. Each sentry was approached and told to bring up the local commander. The commander was told to wake his men. All were given the opportunity to join Atahuallpa. Many did. Those who did not were immediately dispatched by much larger backup forces waiting in the dark nearby. In this way Huascar's palace was entered without alarm.

Huascar was awakened and knew he was about to be killed when Atahuallpa's general gave him the courtesy of allowing ten minutes in his chapel to pray.

"Tell my brother," said Huascar to the general, after seeing a soldier nearby with a 'swinging stone', "that he is destroying the Empire's only remaining head, me. That his is already gone as I speak, and our god will not be kind to him."

Then he turned to pray. The stone swung from the strap of python skin, crushing the back of his head.

Two weeks later, without any evidence of an uprising in the land, an expedition was sent into the country by Pizarro to determine how great an insurrection there might be. A week before the expedition returned, Pizarro learned of the death of Huascar. Atahuallpa, now the last obstacle to Pizarro's consolidation of conquest, was then immediately tried for treason.

Atahuallpa laughed at the absurdity of it . . . of foreigners coming into his land and accusing him of treason. "Treason against nothing but their greed," he concluded.

After the trial Atahuallpa was given a choice: either be burned alive or accept the faith of the god nailed to the cross of little wooden beams and be garroted. Since it would not have been honorable for any Inca to be burned, he elected the latter, and in that manner was publicly strangled and buried as a Catholic.

* * *

Three days after Pizarro had his two rooms full of gold and silver, and after Atahuallpa was killed, an Inca noble requested an audience with the Spanish leader. Pizarro watched the man carry a large urn toward him, and he asked his adjutant if there was anything about which to be concerned. The adjutant said they had checked the contents and that it was, "Just full of corn, some kind of pagan ritual."

The man knelt before Pizarro and poured the corn onto the ground in front of him. Picking up a single kernel, he said, "This is what our Inca Atahuallpa gave you in good faith."

Then, pointing to the heap on the ground, he added, "And that is the amount he has kept, which you will now never see."

Pizarro had the man tortured, but no information came of it. He passed the incident off as a quirk of heathenism.

The following week, the Spanish expedition returned from Cuzco and the outbacks of Peru and reported the entire land docile and at peace. In this way the Incan people ceased to govern their land. They had been conquered by a handful of men through guile, murder, and treachery. The Spaniards thought they had taken all of value above ground in Peru. Then they began using the Incas as slaves to dig in the mines for what else there was. Many died. But the people knew about the treasure in the mountains, and they waited.

Chapter One

Kennedy Airport, New York: February 5, 1999

The Russian Aeroflot jumbo jet—Tupolev design with Rolls Royce engines, International Flight 324—like TWA Flight 800 in 1996, rolled down the runway and slowly lifted into the clear night sky. As it crossed the Atlantic coast heading east toward Europe, it disappeared from the FAA radar screens. Witnesses on the ground saw a bright orange glow in the sky, followed several seconds later by a large fire on top of the water just off Jones' Beach. Boats from nearby restaurants and yacht clubs quickly motored out to the area. But there were no survivors.

Los Angeles: February 5, 1999

Raul Rodriguez, Captain, U.S. Air Force, was on top of his world. He could barely contain his enthusiasm. After Desert Storm, he was immediately promoted and sent to Test Pilot School at Edwards Air Force Base in California. "Not bad for a minority," he kept telling his wife. Marisol shared his high spirits, and they looked forward to the birth of their first child. Life was good.

Later, when he was assigned to Groom Lake in Nevada for a year, she was not much concerned. They could keep their house in L.A. near her family, and he was allowed to come home on weekends. After a few months, however, Marisol was bothered when Raul wouldn't talk about what he was doing. All he said was that it was, "Perfectly safe, and quite amazing."

This latest mission at Groom Lake was especially intriguing, he thought as he drove back to L.A. for the weekend. The new Air Force simulator he flew that day, to him, was awesome. Earlier that evening, he 'took off' in the simulator, flew to New York in a flash, and then, according to the flight plan, pretended he was a missile against an airliner. He flew right through the front part of it. Of course it was a new simulator: There was as yet no programming for sound, as there was no sound of impact. And the flight back to Groom Lake was a little over-programmed in aircraft performance. He made it in less than a minute. *But that's what test pilots are for*, he thought. *To find the glitches*.

During this particular weekend evening, he drove down the hill from their home in Griffith Park to pick up some last-minute vegetables and condiments for the dinner his wife was making. He stopped at the main thoroughfare and waited for a space in the traffic in order to get onto Ventura Boulevard. A 4×4 van with a massive, hard-rubber front bumper pulled up close behind him.

Behind the next semi, thought Raul, getting ready to pull out. The timing was perfect. The van driver waited until the exact moment when no one could react. Test Pilot Rodriguez put his Toyota Camry into low and got ready.

When the semi was fifty feet away, the van turned off its lights, accelerated forward, and pushed the Toyota into the truck's path. There was a fiery crash. Rodriguez was killed instantly. The semi jack-knifed and rolled sideways into the oncoming lane. The driver suffered a concussion. Two other vehicles contained three fatalities and two serious injuries. The van backed up and turned around. Its lights came back on, and it slowly drove away.

CIA Headquarters, Langley, Virginia: February 5, 1999

Andrew Pitman, Foreign Office Chief, read the preliminary Aeroflot reports from the FAA and NTSB, then called his friend Admiral Nick Armitage. Armitage was the most ruthless professional Pitman had ever known. The man knew no fear except inaccuracy. Over the years Pitman had watched him politely pour warm water on the faulty arguments of Congressmen, Cabinet members, and the media. They seldom realized until later that they had, in fact, been politically scalded, then eviscerated. Armitage didn't like wasting time.

"Can you get me the military high-resolution east coast radar printouts of that aircraft?" asked Pitman. "This FAA Air Traffic Control data is awful."

A few minutes later Pitman was studying the faxed diagrams of detailed dots, codes, and symbols. Something didn't fit. These were tough airplanes with no history of breaking up due to mechanical failure. There was evidence of large pieces of the aircraft coming off. But there was no evidence of missiles flying up into it. *A meteorite?* he thought. *But that would have shown up and also have been seen from the ground.*

He called Armitage back.

"Thanks," he said. "I have another favor."

"Shoot," said Armitage.

"The National Transportation Safety Board, the Federal Aviation Administration, and the Federal Bureau of Investigation are not capable of, or budgeted for, salvage operations. They will try to contract some of it out, but they will end up using mostly the Coast Guard and the Navy. Think you could take command of the Navy salvage ships?"

"I'm already in command," said Armitage, "of the entire Atlantic Fleet. What exactly are you asking, Andy?"

"I mean on-scene command," said Pitman. "You know battle damage. It would be helpful for me to know immediately if anything unusual is brought up. Also, it would be helpful to the country if there were someone talking to the media with experience in these matters. This was an international flight with many Americans aboard."

"Thanks for your confidence, Pitman," said Armitage. "I haven't had a good cup of shipboard coffee on a pitching deck for over a year. But no promises. You know how unpolitical I can be."

"You are the most politically savvy person I know," said Pitman.

"I'll keep you informed," said the Admiral.

The Atlantic Ocean: February 6, 1999

Armitage was helicoptered to his small group of salvage ships on their way to the accident scene off the coast of New York. He set up a command center in one ship, and spent nearly all the first day concentrating on the media news. When he wasn't watching the tv he had installed on the bridge, he had the sound piped over the loudspeakers while walking the deck. And he was getting irritated by the minute.

What is with the news media? he thought. *Why are they wasting our time? For two days we have mainly heard complaints from a few Russians*

3

about the U.S. government not doing everything possible to recover the bodies of their loved ones . . . that only half the bodies had been recovered so far . . . only a hundred and ten bodies in two days from underneath two hundred feet of water. Well, perhaps they have a point.

When his small fleet anchored offshore at the scene, Armitage was motored in his Admiral's gig to the nearby docks and piers. He talked to several fisherman along the coast and told them that a Navy paymaster would be on the three major docks in the area during the next two days to pay a hundred dollars for every shark brought in, no matter what size, but that all boats had to have a radio and obey instructions to keep out of the way of salvage operations.

The next morning the sea was dotted with hundreds of small boats. That evening, on the news, the Russians again voiced their complaints. Then Armitage made his public statement to CNN: "I agree with our European neighbors from across the Atlantic. I saw that we were not doing enough to recover the bodies of their loved ones. And that is why there are all the fishing boats in the area that everyone has been asking about. We are now attempting to also recover all those body parts of friends and relatives before they have been entirely digested by sea creatures. Thank you for your ideas, help, and concern."

The Russians instantly disappeared from the news.

CIA Headquarters, Langley, Virginia: February 19, 1999

Two weeks later, Admiral Armitage visited Pitman at his office. He carried a large envelope of 8 × 11 photographs of recovered wreckage, a videotape, and lab reports.

"The results are conclusively inconclusive," began Armitage. "There is some evidence of external bomb-type damage, but no trace elements of explosives. The scanning electron microscope x-ray diffraction analysis results showed nothing at point of impact."

"Point of impact?" asked Pitman.

"Yes," said the admiral. "The metallurgical examination of the pieces of the fuselage just aft of the cockpit clearly . . . here, let me show you."

Armitage sorted through the photographs and pointed to two of them.

"These are of the skin of the aircraft on the right side thirty feet behind the nose. They clearly show high-impact bending from something outside the plane. The metal is bent inward. Also, microscopic analysis of this metal shows no heat damage, scouring, or pitting. Nothing like this has been seen before."

4

"Where did you get all this information?" asked Pitman. "You were only in charge of the Navy's part of the salvage operation."

Armitage smiled and said, "You know how it works with people you have helped in the past and who have helped you. Cashing in chits and such. The Chief of the NTSB Technology Department is an old fishing buddy of mine from many years ago when I was a Commander. You get to know someone after a while in the wilds. Anyway, he knows I would do no harm with such information."

"Any speculation on what caused the crash?" asked Pitman.

"No speculation. Just elimination," said Armitage.

"Go on," said Pitman.

"The evidence, including radar and the onboard black boxes, eliminates pilot error. It eliminates an internal bomb or external missile explosion or lightning strike. It eliminates an aircraft malfunction or collision with another aircraft. It eliminates being struck by a meteorite, unless there are invisible meteorites that can go sideways and slightly up at the same time. In essence, it eliminates all known causes of past aircraft disasters. Then there is the video."

"And what is on the videotape in your package, which you have obviously been saving for last?" asked Pitman.

"Yes, we were lucky and retrieved it on our first day of recovery operations," said Armitage, as he got up to place it in the VCR next to Pitman's desk. "And it is extremely odd. Well, part of it. One of the first bodies we recovered had a palmcorder zipped into the side pocket of a warm-up jacket the guy was wearing. The camera was smashed, but the tape, even though it was unwound, bent, and torn, was completely contained inside the pocket. All the pieces of it were there. I immediately sent my third in command with the tape to NTSB people who took it to a laboratory in Arizona which specializes in recovering tape from exposure to salt water and then piecing it together. After three days of soakings in different solutions, it was slowly dried and micro-glued together with lasers. Amazingly, when played, it was as if it were new. There was no distortion of images or sound."

Armitage put the tape copy in the VCR while Pitman turned on the TV monitor, hit the play button, and sat back down in his chair behind his desk. The first images were of a family. Two children who looked about ten years old, a boy and a girl, were packing small suitcases in a bedroom. The wife, or mother, was showing the daughter how to fold a small dress. The camera was handed to the mother, and the father was seen looking at his watch, then heard making comments about the taxi coming any minute. There was

5

some family banter in the cab on the ride to the airport. Long faces were recorded on the children when they saw the line at the check-in counter. It was obviously a normal family going on vacation. The next scene was of the children strapping their seat belts on. The husband was sitting next to the window taking the videos. One child was next to him, while the other was across the aisle next to the mother. The camera panned the cabin. The flight attendants closed all the overhead compartments; then, after the safety announcement, the cabin lights dimmed. Next the camera pointed outside the window, recording blue taxi lights and some snow on the tarmac, aircraft movement, and a bright, nearly full moon. The blue lights turned to white, and the aircraft accelerated down the runway. The city lights of New York could be seen getting smaller. The camera swung back inside and zoomed in on a flight attendant up the aisle pushing a cart. The next scene was back outside to the receding city and the rising moon.

Pitman suddenly leaned forward in his chair and grabbed the VCR remote from his desk. A shape was coming across the moon, its disk-like silhouette black and plain, heading toward the side of the airliner. Pitman backed the tape up, then played that part again in slow motion. It disappeared after crossing the moon, and Pitman set the VCR back to regular speed. There was a second of moon and stars before a loud explosive sound was heard. The picture returned to the cabin in time to record the sound of a few nearby screams amidst the thundering noise of fast air pushing into the cabin. No oxygen masks descended from the overhead and, all around where the food cart had been, it was now almost completely black. Inside the black circle, which used to be the forward part of the fuselage, there were many white dots.

Then the camera was turned up and back. In the dim light, it recorded the horrified but grim and determined face of the father. Eerily, with the high-pitched sound of the wind, one could see the image of the face disappear with the sound of a zipper as the father put the camera in his jacket pocket and zipped it shut. There was the continued but quieter sound of thunder, the ripping and popping of metal and rivets, and screams.

Probably muffled by the jacket pocket, thought Pitman.

After fifteen more seconds there was a loud 'crack'. . . . *Like hearing half a firecracker*, thought Pitman. Then all was silent.

"What about the stars seen through the front of the plane?" asked Pitman.

"They are clearly parts of the Constellations Lyra and Hercules," said Armitage. "Also, from the direction the plane was headed according to radar and FDR, Flight Data Recorder information, it matches the plane's location and altitude. It is conclusive that the front part of the plane was gone when those stars were viewed through the hole."

"What seat?" asked Pitman.

"The video was taken from 43-E," said Armitage, handing him a diagram of the aircraft's seating configuration.

"Have any idea," asked Pitman, "how the screams could have lasted all the way to impact? I would think an explosive decompression would have sucked all the air out of all the lungs instantly."

"Yes," said Armitage. "Normally that is the case at that altitude. But from the wreckage, radar, and this video info, the front end came off forward of the wings. The rest of the plane would have kept flying. The engines would have kept running for several seconds with the fuel left in the lines. The flight control surfaces, all still intact after the explosion, had been set for a wings-level climb. But with the front section gone, the air resistance—the drag—would have been increased tremendously to where the engines would not have enough thrust to compensate. The aircraft would have slowly nosed over and descended toward the water. At twenty-seven thousand feet, the loss of air pressure would have quickly caused unconsciousness, and the passenger oxygen masks would have dropped down from the overhead. But at five hundred miles an hour, I would guess that the air being pushed into the open front of what was left of the aircraft would not have allowed much of a drop in pressure and may have even increased it. Then when the aircraft dove and slowed down to where the pressure would decrease and become ambient, then it may have been at a low enough altitude where it wouldn't make any difference. The fact is that none of the passenger oxygen masks dropped. This would explain it."

"Possibly," said Pitman. "Very possible. Can I have a copy of this tape?"

"That, and all of this, is yours," said Armitage.

"Thanks," said Pitman. "I'll keep you informed and through you the NTSB of anything I may find."

After the Admiral left, Pitman sat and looked at the videotape over and over again for an hour.

Groom Lake, Nevada: February 20, 1999

General Johnston, U.S. Air Force, watched from behind the thick, plastic, bullet-proof window from the control room high inside the hangar. Below, the strange saucer-shaped craft drifted through the huge doors, floating barely a few feet above the cement floor, then gently landed. There was

7

no blast or fire from engines or retro-rockets. There was no debris flying around or hangar walls buffeting. There was no noise.

On railroad tracks, the giant hangar doors rolled closed, blocking out the night.

After the craft settled to the ground, an enclosed civilian-type airport passenger ramp rolled into place, covering half the craft. Inside the ramp, a hatch on the craft's side opened, and a single pilot stepped out and walked through the tunnel back to the ready room. No pilot had ever seen the outside of the machine. To them it was just a simulator.

General Johnston wanted to talk to him.

"How many times have you flown it?" asked Johnston after the pilot's verbal brief.

"This was my second flight," said the lieutenant.

"And how many other flights have there been?" asked the General.

"Don't know, sir. But I was allowed to read many detailed briefs on how to operate it. Judging by the different styles of writing, I would say that many have operated it before. It's quite *the* simulator, sir."

"And who gave you these written briefs?" asked the General.

"Why, you and the Colonel, Colonel Bobarski," said the pilot.

"That will be all," said the General.

Later, with Colonel Bobarski, the General related the latest decisions and evaluations. The pilot, of course, would eventually have an accident, like the others. They talked of the latest internal report from Air Force Intelligence, and the mission of the Air Force. General Johnston, over the years, had developed into what psychiatrists might call a manic depressive. He was full of bright enthusiasm at the beginning of his career. But with each promotion he became aware of less and less power and fulfillment.

General Johnston's initial rise in the ranks was accompanied by semi-conscious subterfuge. During the latter part of the Vietnam War his mind had snapped. He was a B-52 pilot, ordered to fly the exact same route to Hanoi day after day. After the North Vietnamese got their missiles in place, the route became a death trap. Many pilots quit and were immediately court-marshalled. Johnston's plane was hit but not destroyed. He made it back with shrapnel in both feet. In the hospital after Vietnam, he aggravated his foot wounds by secretly punching them with a pencil, stayed physically unfit for duty for a year, received his Purple Heart, and never flew another mission. And since being a wounded 'Nam vet in the Air Force was a rare thing, his career was made.

Soon thereafter he was assigned to a secret branch of the Air Force

Intelligence Command which investigated and kept records of UFOs, including those unreleased records and artifacts from the supposedly defunct Operation Blue Book. He had found his home.

When Johnston made General, with access to super secret information, it became evident that the U.S. Air Force had not had a unique mission for forty years, except for inventing the arms gap between the United States and Soviets during the 1950s. CIA U-2 photos clearly showed that there was a tremendous gap, but that of the U.S. over the Soviets. And though the evidence made Eisenhower feel more comfortable, the Air Force lobbied this hard information into oblivion . . . and the arms race began in earnest by both sides. Money in the scores of billions of dollars was given to the Air Force each year. But for what outcome during the next forty years? Their ICBM missiles were in fixed and targeted silos in the Midwest. The Navy had equivalent, sometimes better, missiles on nearly undetectable submarines. The Air Force had hundreds of B-52s for decades, ready to drop nuclear bombs on over seventy targeted Soviet cities. Many wondered at the time what Commander-in-Chief in his right mind would say, "Send the Air Force first. Their machines have some of our people in them." The Air Force had cruise missiles, but often had to fly bombers ten thousand miles to launch them. The Navy had cruise missiles on a hundred ships and submarines that could be launched instantly to anywhere on earth. The Air Force had jet fighters. But they could not be deployed except in friendly countries. The Navy could deploy theirs to any place in the world at a moment's notice. During all the conflicts after WWII, the Air Force was essentially a redundant Service with legions of Officer accountants whose jobs were to lobby the U.S. Congress . . . to show usage . . . to demand a budget as large as that of the Army and Navy. And most of this evolved after President Eisenhower's warning about the "Military-Industrial Complex." After forty years, however, the Air Force did obtain two exclusives: the SR-71 Blackbird which could fly from Idaho to China, take photographs, and return; and the Stealth bomber which was invisible to radar and proved its worth in Desert Storm.

General Johnston, like most fanatics who inexplicably gain a semblance of power, recognized the truth completely, then denied it completely.

After the comedian Jackie Gleason, an extraterrestrial enthusiast, got permission from President Nixon to view the alien bodies from the Roswell crash, Johnston knew he had both the power, and the mission, to keep all information from prying eyes. Nixon's order was absorbed so far into Johnston's newly created administrative paperwork requirements that it disappeared entirely and was eventually forgotten.

The Russian machine, however, was known to exist by all Presidents since FDR.

"Can you believe that President Clinton is thinking of giving the craft back to Russia in partial exchange for more nuclear disarmament?" said General Johnston to Colonel Bobarski. "He must think it is just some weird scientific thing that the Russians gave us in WWII as part of the Lend-Lease package . . . and that they probably built it themselves. Of course, we have not had a technically aware President, ever. Not even Carter. So he was not difficult to hoodwink. But we know better, Colonel. This craft has nearly unlimited energy. It is invisible to all known radars. Guns, missiles, and plastic explosives set off under and around it don't make a dent or a scratch. We can't guess what kind of gyro-stabilization system it possesses or cabin pressurization system. We haven't an inkling of how it anti-gravitates and propels itself. It can travel at unheard-of speeds, faster than the Space Shuttle, even through the atmosphere. It can also fly right through aircraft and some buildings, cutting with its saucer edge, and destroying them with no apparent damage to itself. It makes aircraft carriers obsolete. It defies all known laws of Newtonian physics. Essentially, though we can't duplicate it, it can, with proper operation, rule the world. And now we have to give it back. . . . Well, having and using are two different things. It's time to make our move. To speed things up a little, I think we should refer to our analysis of the maps inside the machine, specifically to the probability that another machine exists in Peru. That should get the Russians hopping."

"Makes sense," said Colonel Bobarski.

Old Town, Alexandria, Virginia: February 20, 1999

Jess Brandon exited the airport taxi in front of his pre-Civil War townhouse a block up the hill from the Interarms Company in Old Town. Though he owned a small percentage of Interarms, his interest did not extend beyond having access to their intelligence information on the seemingly endless brushfire wars going on around the world and the numerous new militia organizations recently formed in thirty-six U.S. states. Often this information proved useful by providing big-picture trends.

He paid the taxi, hefted his Tumi leather hanging bag, and pressed a button on his key chain to open the converted carriage-house garage door. The inside light came on as the cab drove away in the night drizzle.

Brandon had purchased his townhouse years before as just a place to "crash" when in Washington on business. But the more he used it, the more

10

attached he became to it. Soon he found himself painting, refinishing the hardwood floors, putting in bookshelves, having the chimney swept, and buying period furniture. He even put in a vegetable garden behind the place where there was plenty of sun between the large trees. And though Brandon always had money, he never showed it off. Since his father's murder during the Chiang operation, he had inherited more—many tens of millions more. But except for a private jet and an H-1 Huey helicopter kept at his farm in California, there was no show of wealth. Though he knew there were probably exceptions, he couldn't bring himself to trust the motivations of others after their observance of some of his wealth. Besides, he didn't need to live in the lap of luxury.

He called for his cat, Mina. Of course she would punish him for being away for over three days by remaining aloof. But she rarely wrecked anything—and always came around in a few hours.

Shortly after he met Jane and her father at a Pitman dinner party, he showed her the place. She was impressed with his attention to detail and at first erroneously judged him very domestic. The closer they became, however, the more she found an entirely different lifestyle . . . one that accompanies a secretive and sometimes dangerous career. She also saw his tenderness and vulnerability and felt that deep down he was a kind person. She liked to be around him. After a month, neither of them saw a need to see anyone else in a romantic or companionship sense.

He walked in, pressed the button again to close the garage door, and then entered his house though a side entrance. His housecleaner had stacked three weeks of mail neatly on a sideboard in the foyer. He set his Tumi down, picked up the mail with both hands, and went into the kitchen. On the counter next to the stove was a Stanley thermos full of scalding hot black coffee. He put the mail on the kitchen table, poured a cup, then leaned over the sink, and removed the dark brown contact lenses that usually covered his bright blue oriental eyes when he visited the Middle or Far East.

He placed them in a container of cleaning solution and dialed his fiancée, Jane, on the speaker phone while sorting through his mail.

She picked up on the second ring.

"Hi! How was your trip?" she asked.

"I'm getting too old for this," he said, "but I think it went well. I'll know in a week or so. Will be able to tell you about it in a decade or so."

Brandon had been up front with Jane about the secret nature of his business from the start. Jane had said things like, "I understand," and "I don't care, as long as it's legal." But during the past year she knew, and she knew that he knew, that she did care that she didn't know. It bothered her like a toothache that just kept throbbing in the background with no known dentist on the planet.

"So, are we still on for the boating and fishing weekend?" she asked.

"Still on. Why don't we go out to dinner tonight? We can leave from here tomorrow. I've some unpacking to do."

"Okay, dear. Anything I should bring for the trip?" she asked.

"The Pitmans are usually equipped with everything imaginable. But with your fair skin, a bottle of number forty-five sun screen might be a good idea," he said.

"I'll pick some up and see you in about an hour."

"Bye, dear," said Brandon.

Brandon unzipped the two dirty clothes compartments on his Tumi, one for socks, one for all else, pulled the clothes out, and set them on the stairs to the laundry room in the basement. Then he took the bag into his study at the back of the house. Though it could pass as a study, one section of the room looked more like a laboratory. There were three long tables covered with electronic devices, glass tubing, chemicals, and papers. In one corner was a powerful computer, 32-bit, over three hundred megahertz speed, twenty gigabytes memory . . . better than four Pentiums hooked together. In another corner was a scanning electron microscope, an SEM. On the wall above the SEM hung several large thin sheets of bronze, paper, iron, and steel. He looked at the dates on the label of each and smiled.

Yes, he thought. *It had been a fun trip. It would get more fun during the next few weeks.*

It was another of Pitman's brain storms. "Jess," Pitman asked the previous year, "do you know of any method where writing can be made on an object from a distance which wouldn't show up for a few weeks?" Brandon said that he knew ways of changing the molecular structure of surface matter with lasers from a distance which made the matter light-sensitive and which would then change color over a period of time, usually a few weeks. Brandon said that he would need some exotic and expensive equipment. Pitman had Brandon's 'lab' set up in a week.

The hardest part was getting exact samples of the paints and surface materials used on the giant pictures and statues of the heads of state of most of the Mideastern countries, China, and North Korea. The x-ray diffraction analysis done with the SEM provided an exact chemical composition of the materials. Then Brandon experimented with different crystal and gas lasers on surfaces of the substances. A ruby laser worked

12

well on water-based paint. Krypton gas worked on oils and some metals. Required exposure time varied from one to two seconds per one-inch wide foot of writing. The templates to guide the lasers were simple to make. The effect of atmospheric attenuation on the laser beams was negligible, even from a mile away. The whole package was installed in the framework of a Panasonic palm video recorder.

Pitman's plan was beautiful in its simplicity. The goal was to undermine the credibility of several leaders who passed themselves off as some sort of god with their giant images displayed everywhere while they were causing so much suffering, death, and disease. Pitman said it was better than the CIA plan to spike Castro's cigars so his beard would fall out. Brandon looked at it as an interesting scientific experiment, not dangerous at all, and wondered if Pitman thought him getting too old for real missions. Pitman said that, if successful, it would help the freedom of some depressed peoples . . . especially in countries that couldn't separate the functions of government from those of religion . . . including the religions of Communism, murder, money, and personal power. "Historically," Pitman had said, "it's a simple equation. The bigger the pictures of leaders' faces in a country, the smaller the existence of human rights."

Brandon looked at the paper sheets hanging on the wall. The test words he had lased on them before he left were now fully developed. They were written in the local languages, then in English underneath for CNN cameras. And they would soon be appearing on the foreheads of the huge pictures and statues of certain leaders in the Mid- and Far East. Brandon had covered many of the museums and plazas in nearly all the capitals and major cities. *The first should be developed during the next day or two*, he thought.

He read the words on the sheets. They had been chosen carefully. In the free countries of the world, a perpetrator caught doing such graffiti would probably have to pay for the damage and perhaps be required to do some community service. In those countries that Brandon recently visited, they would suffer immediate torture and execution. Brandon smiled as he read what he had lased onto the different icons. He limited the expressions to one or two for each forehead. They were translated underneath each into formal words like "Traitor," "Infidel," and "Fornicator with Sheep," and informal, local expressions like "Child Molester," "Cross Dresser," and "Goat Without Testicles." Of course it was ridiculous, he thought, but no less so than the images. The real message was not in the words. The message was in the power to put them there.

Assawoman Island, Maryland: February 20–23, 1999

Allie pulled softly on the yoke as the small amphibian flew slowly over the bay next to the Island. The sun reflected brightly off the water into her eyes, and she adjusted the baseball cap over her long hair. Her husband, Andy Pitman, read through the landing checklist.

"Ready for flaps?" he asked.

"Flaps full," she answered.

He put the flap handle down and watched her hands on the yoke. If there was any rotational movement on the yoke required for her to maintain wings-level as the flaps were coming down, it meant split-flaps, and he would raise the handle back up before she ran completely out of aileron control, and rolled them upside down into the water. This had never happened in this plane. But it had happened once during his early years as a Navy test pilot, and so watching for it became part of his habit pattern. He thought about all the survival habits he had developed over the years. It was a bag full.

Finally he checked that the landing gear handle was up and that the gear indicators showed all three up and locked, as she turned back toward the bay to land. She reduced engine power while turning and eyeing the waves for a read on the wind.

"Looks like from the northwest, about fifteen knots," she said.

Pitman said, "Yeah, about that."

She steadied out on a northwest heading and adjusted engine power to give her a safe rate of descent in case she hit the water sooner than expected. Without her radar altimeter or land or ships close by, it would be impossible to give good estimates of altitude over the water. She squinted at the horizon and the Island a mile off, checked her altimeter, and at fifty feet, she again pulled back slightly on the yoke, checked her airspeed, and added a tiny bit of power. The aircraft hull kissed the water smoothly.

She reduced engine power to idle and asked, "Are we down yet?"

"You're too much," he said, clapping his hands slowly, remembering her Soviet training in Aircobras and Mig-21s during her youth. "I can't grease it on like that even on a good day."

Though married for over twenty years, they still seemed to surprise one another . . . he, the ex-navy pilot intelligence guru, now running the foreign office at the CIA . . . she, the ex-twenty-year-old Soviet piano protege/spy, who defected while managing to maintain her cover. They were attractive and with compassion welded to minds of analytical ice-cold insight. A near-perfect match, they both thought at the time, and since.

After landing, she turned toward their weekend farm, or coop, as they called it. He lowered the landing gear handle and checked the indicators to assure that they were locked down. She taxied up the small cement ramp on the shore in front of their barn hangar.

In a few minutes their bags were in the house, she was unpacking, and Pitman was hosing down the salt buildup on the plane with fresh water. They were getting ready for a long weekend with company, fishing, boating, reading, and watching most of the ten videos she had rented. They expected Jess Brandon and his fiancée, Jane, the following morning.

After dinner, Pitman went out on the screened porch and stretched his tall, slim frame on a lounge chair, looking at the water while Allie did the dishes. Normally, the one who cooked was not the one who cleaned up. Over the years they could each gauge how good his or her cuisine was by the amount of belly-aching the other did afterward about doing the dishes. After a tender and succulent cordon-bleu, smoked baby oysters, and fresh steamed asparagus spears with a tangy hollandaise, Allie didn't say a word. She sat for a while sipping a glass of Merlot, then got up and fixed his scotch. He heard the water running in the kitchen as he gazed out over the bay, collecting his thoughts.

The Chiang gold operation the previous year had nearly gotten both of them killed. Sure, he thought, his bag of tricks had helped get them out of it. But just as assuredly, her mind had made it all a success. He was good at identifying intricate problems. She was good at solving them. His wife had the best analytical brain in the universe, he thought. And he needed it.

If it weren't for that mind, thought Pitman, *the Chiang clues would never have been deciphered. And Brandon lost his father during that operation. Most of it, however, was thrust upon us. We were forced into the game because of ancient ideas . . . thoughts which were beyond the time of our lives. Thoughts from before the Vikings discovered America. Thoughts which could influence generations. And perhaps that is what is important. They really are the only things that last for thousands of years. Thoughts. Caesar had gold and family and empire and fleets and palaces. But what is left of these things today? Nothing. Nothing except thoughts. Nothing except his Commentaries on the Gallic Wars and observations by others at the time. And how did these thoughts survive? The luck of writing. The luck of clay tablets and scribes, of papyrus, of pen and ink, of printing. The luck of folk tales and mythology. And we are here but for a snap. Mayflies in the Spring wind. Death and taxes are but fleeting sparks arcing from the big hearth in the sky.*

15

Pitman didn't notice Allie sitting next to him sipping a cup of tea and watching the changing expressions in his face. But she could see the sadness surface in the eyes and knew he was getting into his 'philosophic' mode. It usually didn't last long, but if let go, it often would make him lethargic and sometimes sick in bed for days.

"You know, dear," she said, "depression is only another form of intense concentration."

"Thanks," he said, never angry at being interrupted from one of those moods. "But it's not the 'philosophic' this time," he added. "Not the Black Dog."

"Well, good," she said. "Because I want to watch one of the movies we brought, *The Spurred Minion*. I'll let you know if it's any good."

"Before you do that, dear," asked Pitman, "tell me what philosophic thoughts you may have?"

"Good question," she said. "And so late in our relationship. My philosophy is pretty simple. I look at the night sky, sometimes through a telescope, and all the zillions of hydrogen bombs going off, being recreated, and continuing on for a few more billions of years, called suns. I really can't see that there is a shortage of energy in the universe. One of those dots of suns has enough energy to power Earth's energy needs for billions of years. That is the first thing. The second thing is, why any of it at all? Why not a vacuum? I mean, what is beyond our known physical universe. What could there be beyond the Hubble sightings of things that tend to describe our universe?"

"What do you mean, describe?" asked Pitman.

"Why are we all here, for starters? What is the essence of gravity? Electricity? Magnetism? Light? Our personal existences, especially for such short periods of time? It is such a bunch of crap. Being born. Going through all that adolescence stuff . . . how to dress, how to make love, how to get educated, how to be employed, how to gain power, how to live a long life, as if that were important. There has to be something else. That something else to me is just to live and enjoy the beautiful parts at every opportunity. Part of the enjoyment is helping to squash the bugs that do so much harm to innocent people, society, the economy, and the quality of human lives in general. And I suspect that is part of your philosophy also."

"Thanks, dear," he said. "You have killed the Black Dog of depression for a long time with me. And I will, if it is within my being, and should the need arise, do the same for you."

16

"*Au, contraire, mon ami*," said Allie. "You already have. You do it all the time. When I start getting depressed all I have to do is look around and at you. Why waste all this luck on a dark mood? Goodnight, my dear Andy."

Pitman kissed her goodnight and continued with his thoughts about antiquity. His hunches had recently provided some information that could be extremely important. But he didn't want to spring it on Allie until he was more sure about it. She had had enough on her mind during the past two years. And besides, he wasn't sure she could help with things like Peruvian art treasure, or the future ambassador to Peru who could be the next president, or the South American drug business, or a flying saucer, of all things. He would get more information first, he thought, stroking his grey pencil mustache.

* * *

Brandon and Jane arrived the following noon. They pulled up to the Pitman dock in a forty-two foot Marine Trader Trawler motorized yacht.

"Nice boat, and how are you?" asked Pitman, as he caught a line thrown by Jane and began tying it to a deck cleat.

"Thought we'd check it out," yelled Brandon, as he reversed the right screw and flipped the helm hard left. He cut the engines just before the boat settled against the dock rubbers. Jane jumped out and tied the stern line.

Brandon stepped onto the dock, shook Pitman's hand, and said, "We've been looking at it for months. Nice looking piece of work. No problems so far. May buy it."

Pitman said, "Speaking of nice looking, hi, Jane."

She gave him a quick hug, a 'political hug' as Pitman called them. It didn't matter to him. She was a friend of Allie's, who had introduced her to Brandon. The poor girl didn't know where she stood, if anywhere, in their cloak-and-dagger business.

Allie hugged both her and Brandon warmly.

"So, what's up?" asked Brandon as they walked up the dock toward the house.

"Nothing right now. Tuna fishing, as soon as we get the lunch baskets aboard my Bertram," said Pitman.

"Want to try my possible new acquisition?" asked Brandon.

"What's the name?" asked Pitman, not having a chance to see the stern.

"Morning Glory," said Brandon.

"How many owners before you?" asked Pitman.

17

"Two," said Brandon.

"And what was the first name this boat had?" asked Pitman.

"Morning Glory," said Brandon.

"Then it's fine with me," said Pitman.

"And I thought *I* was superstitious," said Brandon.

* * *

They packed Pitman's coolers, fishing gear, bait, and bedding aboard, untied the lines, and motored around the bend into the Atlantic Ocean. Allie noted the spot on the beach where she had been hauled into a rubber boat and taken to a Russian submarine nearly two years prior. Pitman noted exactly where he had been when the submarine had surfaced. Neither said anything about it.

After an hour heading east, Brandon studied the color of the water and said, "I think this might do. Looks like the Gulf Stream may have gotten this close to shore this time of year, and so we can go for both blue fish and tuna."

"Tuna reminds me of a joke," said Allie, as the other three rigged four lines with a herring, a small mackerel, and two with feathered lures.

"So what's the joke?" asked Jane, while letting out one of the lines.

"It's an intelligence test," said Allie. "What doesn't fit in this group of four things?

"Just a second," said Pitman, as he wrestled with an outrigger connection.

"Okay, what four things?" he said.

"Lobster, shrimp, a Chinese person who has been run over by a truck, and . . . tuna?" said Allie.

"Obviously it isn't the Chinese person," said Jane.

"Same here," said Brandon.

"Same here," said Pitman.

"Tell you what," said Brandon to Jane and Pitman, "let's each pick a part of it, and whoever is the winner gets five dollars from the other three. Allie gets the leftover choice."

"Deal," said Pitman.

"No deal," said Allie.

"Deal," said Jane, "but I want to be the lobster."

"Have any problem with me being the tuna?" asked Brandon.

Pitman said that he was too old to be hurt by labels, so he would be the shrimp.

18

Allie listened to them, wondering if some kind of conspiracy was brewing, and said, "So, have all the little chickens got their little parts? Am I to be the Chinaman?"

"Yes," they all said in unison, like school kids.

"Then, money on the table!" said Allie. "But since I know the answer, it's only between you three.

She put a lead sinker from Pitman's tackle box on two five dollar bills and an IOU from Brandon.

The lines were now out, the boat trolling on auto in an open ocean with an operating radar equipped with an audio beeper set to warn of any other vessels within three miles.

Brandon popped a beer and looked at Allie.

"And the winner is . . . ," she exclaimed, "Jess Brandon! Tuna!"

She pulled the money and IOU from under the sinker and handed them to Brandon.

"So what's the reason he won?" asked Jane.

"Because the other three in the category are all crushed-Asians," said Allie.

They all looked at her. She said, "You have to say it fast, as in crustaceans."

They all moaned. Brandon tore up his IOU and counted the two five dollar bills over and over. "Ah. Always knew I was the big tuna," he said.

This attempt at humor was met with an icy stare from Jane. She didn't like losing, even in games.

"So it wasn't an intelligence test at all," said Jane. "Just a play on words."

"A play on words!" exclaimed Allie. "*Just* a play on words? Words are very important, Jane. They are our main means of communication. If we can understand them better by *playing* with them, then we will better understand one another. How do you think Senator Dodd feels, knowing a hydro-electric dam can never be named after him?"

Jane smiled at the wry humor of it.

"Fish on!" yelled Brandon.

The line spun off the reel with a high, sharp ratcheting noise. Pitman got there first, increased the friction, and yanked the rod back to set the hook.

"My pole," said Jane. "I baited it."

Pitman handed it to her, bowing away deferentially, with Arabic arcing hand-signs going from his forehead to his nose to his chin and down in quick succession. Jane took the pole, was almost yanked overboard, quickly

19

let up on the reel's friction control, sat down in the marlin chair, strapped a waist belt on, and then reset the drag to a tighter setting. She was now ready. They all looked at her, then at the shape of a huge fish churning the surface before sounding.

"Wonder what kind it is," said Brandon.

"Tuna," said Jane. "Heading north, to Newfoundland. Bluefin probably. Definitely not a marlin or any bill fish. Could be over a thousand pounds."

She cinched her belt tighter and asked for the shoulder straps. Brandon hooked them to her lap belt and said, "So, what are you going to do? Sit here for twelve hours? This tackle can't bring him in."

"Perhaps it's a her," she said sarcastically while reeling in for the first round.

"Even worse," said Brandon, enjoying the excitement.

Jane reeled in, the line whined out. Brandon poured cool water over her shoulders. Pitman conned from the flying bridge and maneuvered the boat before Jane ran out of line when the fish sounded. Allie reeled in the other three poles to get them out of the way.

For two hours the four of them helped. The line went out and down. Jane reeled it in. The line went out. Jane reeled it in. Pitman maneuvered the boat. Brandon massaged Jane's arm muscles. Allie poured water on the reel when the fish dove. After another hour the fish was weakening. Brandon knew they would never get it. But it was important to Jane. He went below for his underwater camera.

The fish came up again, perhaps to get a look at its antagonists. Brandon put on a snorkel mask and leaped into the water. He swam away from the boat and snapped three pictures before the fish sounded again, then swam back and climbed aboard.

"What the hell do you think you are doing?" asked Jane, reeling strenuously.

"Just a swim," said Brandon. "Hot."

"Just can't stand it not to be your show," she said as the reel whined again.

Pitman maneuvered the boat. Allie poured more water on the reel and put a thermos of lemonade to her lips. They were both getting into it.

Brandon fetched a beer from the cooler and sat on the bait tank, watching.

"No more help from you I see!" said Jane, reeling frantically as the fish came in.

20

Pitman climbed down from the bridge and grabbed a gaff. The fish came along the side of the boat only ten feet away. Jane reeled slowly. Brandon watched, amused. It was a huge tuna. Probably over a eight hundred pounds, he thought. Its big black eye seemed to look at all of them. The feathered lure could be seen solidly hooked in its jaw.

"Just a few more feet," said Jane as she reeled in slowly.

When he saw the fish up close, Pitman wondered why he was even holding a gaff. A wrecking crane would be more appropriate. Then, with one quick jerk and swirl, the fish broke the line, floated lazily away looking at them again, and then slowly disappeared into the depths.

Jane threw the pole down, unhooked her harness, lay on the deck, and screamed.

"Ahhhhh," said Brandon. "A true fisherperson."

* * *

The next morning Brandon was at his laptop.

See Spot run, he typed, disgusted with himself after staring blankly at the computer screen for ten minutes. *See Dick's laptop, Jane. See the software. See the hard drive. See the floppies. Perhaps a bit-dump, then reboot, a beer, and a nap.*

Brandon mumbled to himself that he couldn't write another word, especially on Vietnam. Who was he kidding, he thought. He was no Herman Wouk writing *Youngblood Hawk*. He couldn't write himself out of a wet paper bag. Nevertheless he later read a few paragraphs to Jane.

"Nice idea," she said after hearing some of the Vietnam lines to her. She thought writing would help ease him out of his profession of espionage. She worried he was beginning to enjoy the violence. So far he had been completely professional. But she knew from previous discussion that he was thinking of taking out some frustrations by bending the rules, just a bit . . . to really hammer the geeks who caused so much pain and suffering to innocent others. And they both knew that it would be like some sort of dangerous candy. It could be fine for a while, but it broke the laws of diabetes, similar to police brutality. It always came back, someday, as some kind of smelly syrup that oozed into one's life, family, culture, and country.

He eased back in his desk chair and noted his small pot-belly developing, in spite of exercise and a muscular frame. And he had a few grey hairs, he recalled during a rare moment of vanity the previous morning when looking into the mirror. He fidgeted with a flap of rubber from the worn-out sole of his right Reebok and thought about Jane. *Well, at least I can write a little story about her,* he thought, while reaching forward to turn the machine back on. He typed:

CD\return

file Jane.fil\return

Jane MacEntire: legal consultant to the representative of Virginia, third district. Good career. Met her at a party. Tall, blond, not heavy, not thin. Hour-glass. Smart, articulate, incisive. Loving, giving, sexual . . . observant, rational, shrewd. Manipulative in a fair way. Love at second sight.

* * *

She placed a glass of orange juice in front of him.

He called up another file and turned the computer screen toward her.

She read, *There were the six clues for the six comedies from Shakespeare.*

"So?" She said, after reading, *1. Wet; 2. Dry; 3. Abortion; 4. Nine inches; 5. Six inches; 6. Three inches.*

"So, match them up with Shakespeare's six comedies," he said. "I'll bet my crushed-Asian money you can't get all six."

"Very clever," she mumbled to herself after two became clear to her. "Very clever indeed!"

Ten minutes later she had them all figured out and wrote the solutions down: 1. *Midsummer Night's Dream*; 2. *Twelfth Night*; 3. *Love's Labors Lost*; 4. *The Taming of the Shrew*; 5. *As You Like It*; and 6. *Much Ado About Nothing.*

He handed her the ten dollars.

"So how was your week, dear Jane?" asked Brandon.

"Interesting. Did some research on one of our Senators. Thought he was a VIP. Turns out he is only a MIP. Medium Important. Got the goods on him," said Jane.

"How so?"

"You know that parking lot county zoning debate that has been in the works for the past year? Well, I got the number on it."

"Let's see," recalled Brandon. "Your man, the MIP, wants them eight feet wide, to allow more cars. Average width of cars is five feet. Seems reasonable. Do I have it right?"

"Yes, your memory hasn't failed. But how wide do you think the average car is with its doors full open?" asked Jane.

"Don't know," said Brandon, "but would guess about eight feet."

"Close," said Jane. "It's eight feet ten inches."

22

"So how does this figure into the MIP?" asked Brandon.

"He owns nearly all the auto body shops in the county," said Jane.

"Still don't get it," said Brandon.

"With parking places nine feet wide, there would be virtually no dings when opening car doors or fender scrapes when pulling in and out. At eight feet wide, his family business would at least double . . . all paid for by insurance companies. That's where the real motivation came from. It took me a year to figure it out."

"Hmmm," said Brandon. "Our state representative is skimming from the populace. An old equation. What are you going to do about it?"

"Almost nothing," said Jane. "I've got the figures from other cities and his financially vested interest documented. This will be placed on his desk before the final debate next week, with a note that all local papers will receive a copy depending on the outcome. He'll vote for nine feet."

"And will you tell him who did this research?" asked Brandon.

"Of course," said Jane. "You know how I hate subterfuge."

"So why don't you run for high office, make yourself a MIP or even a VIP?" asked Brandon.

"Because I'm already a VIP," said Jane. "Most all of us are VIPs. It's when people get on the greed and power trips that they digress into MIPs and then LIPs and finally NIPs."

"LIPS meaning Lesser Important Persons," said Brandon. "I get the other one also."

"Exactly," said Jane. "They finally become owned by their environment, the press, the perks, the money. They seem to retain little that is themselves. They have no original thoughts. All about them is in the web of their delusion. They accept being kept in a silk cocoon by the spiders of the world, numbed, traded as commodities. They are the NIPs. We, the little people, are really the VIPs. We are the ones who get things done. We are the ones who live lives and drive trucks and raise children and make computers and cars and medical improvements and art and history. Of course there are many VIPs with the money who use it to help get these things done. It's called capital investment."

"Is this going to take long?" asked Brandon.

"Not long," said Jane. "I'll keep talking while I make you some tea. There's a spare tape next to the machine. Keep it going. I'm on a roll."

Brandon checked the tape machine, then went to a chair outside the hatch on the aft deck. He heard Jane talking as he rigged a feathered lure onto his pole and cast it over, placing the butt-end into the receptacle, and watched the pure blue and white foam of the ocean waves roil around him as the line went out.

That evening, drifting far offshore, Pitman listened to the radio for weather. Brandon, Jane, and Allie looked at the underwater polaroids Brandon had taken for her. They showed a bluefin tuna almost half the length of the boat. It was a beautiful fish. And Jane realized that it had been playing with her more than she with it. There was no way she could have landed it. Allie mentioned that she hadn't poured enough water on the reel . . . that it may have helped. Pitman said he was not familiar with the boat, and he could have maneuvered better. Finally Jane realized all the patronizing and said, "Okay, I get it."

* * *

After Allie and Jane went to bed, Brandon went topside and discovered Pitman pacing the bow. Pitman mentioned that Brandon's recent trip was beginning to pay off. Leaders all through the Mideast were placing guards around their huge public images. Crowds of people gathered around the guards. Then, when the words slowly appeared on the foreheads of their leaders, many took them to be messages from God.

Pitman said it was a fine, but small coup, seemed distracted, and abruptly changed the subject.

"Did you ever see the movie *Strange Encounters of the Third Kind?*" asked Pitman.

"Yes," said Brandon.

"How about *Cocoon* or the *X-Files*," asked Pitman.

"Yes, both," said Brandon. "Why?"

"What do you think of them?" asked Pitman.

"Farfetched, but not entirely implausible," said Brandon.

"How so?" asked Pitman.

"Are you familiar with the Air Force's Operation Blue Book?" asked Brandon.

"Not really," said Pitman. "Just know the name and main function. Don't recall any hard results. What do you know?"

"Well," said Brandon, "Operation Blue Book was shut down thirty years ago. The Air Force said it wasn't worth the money. But there were many snags in their evaluations."

"Like what?" asked Pitman.

"Like the Roswell, New Mexico crash in 1947, supposedly that of a spaceship. That has never been properly explained. First the Air Force tried to cover it up by lying to the public. Said it was a weather balloon. Then they simply refused to say anything or provide any official information. They are now fifty years into denial. But the witnesses, the people on scene, say otherwise. Books have been written about it. There was supposedly wreckage consisting of very strange materials and bodies."

"Yes, I know about Roswell," said Pitman. "There have been many dozens of eye-witness accounts of sightings, human abductions, and animal mutilations. Accounts by very reputable people. It's all fairly common knowledge."

"Why are you asking about all this?" asked Brandon.

"Just a hunch," said Pitman. "Do you think you could get some hard information from the Air Force on what they have?" asked Pitman.

"Not up front," said Brandon. "Perhaps covertly. May be possible to turn up something at Wright Paterson, or Groom Lake in Nevada, where these artifacts are supposedly being kept."

"My hunch," said Pitman, "involves some information I came across having to do with some strange business dealings going on in Peru. There may be something down there . . . maybe the proverbial flying saucer, uncrashed. You may need to go there."

"What exactly brought all this up?" asked Brandon.

"There has been some strange message traffic between our President and the Russians and among the Russians themselves. We may have had a space ship from another world in this country for many years. These communications are categorized as ultra-secret. Also, there is some information from Armitage on the Aeroflot crash. He recovered many pieces of structural and seat wreckage that look like they were sliced with a pair of cutting shears. Very neat and clean. Little bending. No heat. Can't really tell if it was from an explosion. And the FBI has found no evidence of trace elements from a bomb.

"The Peruvian connection is also vague. Not much to go on at present. There are several symbols, or letters, found on pieces of alien material from the Roswell crash. They were drawn for me many years ago by one of the Army investigators there. They are simple things, like a triangle with a bar on top, a sideways trident, a couple of interconnected circles, a cat-like figure, things like that. Our future ambassador to Peru sometimes wears a gold bracelet that has some of these same symbols embossed on it. Much more research to do in that area."

"Okay," said Brandon. "I'll get onto the Air Force business first."

"And I'll let you know about Peru as things develop," said Pitman.

"Also, we'll need to be at communication level One-A."

Brandon said goodnight and went below to get some sleep. He tossed for over an hour, then got up and went to the galley to make some hot milk and honey. For him it worked better than sleeping pills. Besides, he had an aversion to all pills except aspirin and vitamins. He had seen too many pill and drug casualties in Vietnam and had tried some himself. They caused too much relaxing not to be dangerous . . . and physically expensive.

Jane awoke and looked at the clock. Then she looked at his bunk, and got up to put on a sweat shirt. She found him sitting in the captain's chair staring out to sea.

"So what's up?" she asked.

"Oh. Nothing. Another mission or two. Couldn't sleep," he said.

"Nothing you can talk about, I know," she said.

"Not specifically," he said. "But I can talk in general terms. Care for some hot milk and honey?"

"No thanks," she said. "Just drone on. My ears should be good for fifteen minutes or so."

"Well," he said. "I've come upon an interesting question."

"And what might that question be?" she asked.

"The question is . . . what are the most stupid things leaders and men of power have said during the course of recorded history?"

"History is bunk?" she asked.

"That's one," he said. "But Henry Ford also did many good things in the field where there was no history for him to learn from. The Romans never built automobiles."

"So what statement is on the top of your list?" she asked. "Which one have you been thinking about?"

"'Ask not what your country can do for you, but what you can do for your country' has to top the list," said Brandon.

"How so? This man was a hero," she said.

"Heroism and fact do not often go hand in hand. Usually there is a difference between a drugged or suicidal act, and one which helps the overall cause. Virtually all of our Congressional Medal winners helped the cause, a war effort. And it doesn't take a genius to figure when a forty-knot PT boat was cut in half on August 2, 1943, by a seventeen-knot Japanese destroyer, the *Amigiri*, that there was not much there that helped our side in the war effort. And so the hero part, except perhaps for some of the rescue, was invented by a rich and influential father."

"The 'ask not' part?" she asked.

"Yes," said Brandon. "This is a nation of both asking and doing. When the top leader says not to ask, then he or she does not have a grasp on what it takes to make a fair nation. Every citizen here has a right to ask what their country is doing for them while paying taxes or required to do military service or both."

"So why is it stupid?" asked Jane.

Brandon got up from the captain's chair and brushed his hands through his hair, thinking.

"When anyone," he began, "who is in a position of authority says 'don't ask' as a matter of national policy, we are all in a lot of trouble. And so soon after Hitler and Stalin. Funny how it turned out though. After Kennedy was killed, entitlement laws were passed that allowed great quantities of asking, and getting, without requiring any doing at all. It nearly bankrupt America."

"So why is this important?" she asked.

"It's in relation to a job I have to do. The government . . . the military, the FBI, other organizations seem to think that it is fine for the taxpayers to provide their salaries, but not fine for the taxpayers to ask what they are doing or to ask for information that is not restricted by law from the public domain. Even under the Freedom of Information Act you get documents back with large sections redacted out with black ink."

"Where is this leading?" asked Jane. "My ears are de-tuning."

"Okay. You're a space nut. You have hundreds of books on NASA, space exploration, rockets, UFOs, and extraterrestrials. So you are familiar with the Air Force Operation Blue Book and the Roswell incident, right?"

"Yes," said Jane. "Go on."

"So what about Roswell?" he asked. "What's the main thing that sticks out in your mind about it?"

Jane thought for a minute, then said, "The interview with the army engineer."

"What engineer? What interview?" he asked.

"The one on TV ten years ago and then again five years ago. I don't remember his name. I think the interview was taped during the eighties. He was an old man then. He had nothing to gain by lying. He talked plainly. Said that he was ordered to the scene and given a piece of material about a foot long and several inches wide. He was to take it to a laboratory and evaluate it. He said that he could not drill into it, could not burn it, could not cut it, and that even strong acids he poured on it did no damage whatsoever. He said that, in his experience, it did not come from this world."

"So why does this stick in your mind?" asked Brandon.

"Well," said Jane, "if this material could not be destroyed, where is it? So, I see your point. But there could be a good reason behind not allowing it into the public domain. If this material is so indestructible, and it got into the hands of the Soviets during the Cold War, wouldn't that be a little dangerous? I mean, they might have figured out how to duplicate it for tank armor, lighter aircraft, and deeper submarines."

"That reasoning was excusable for then. Not now," said Brandon. "After fifty years, tank armor, aircraft weight, and submarine skin are still destructible, and this material is still invisible to the scientists of the world."

"Yes," said Jane. "Logical point. And thank you for giving me something to sleep on. Good night, Dear."

Moscow, The White House, and Groom Lake, Nevada: February 21–24, 1999

What was left of the KGB in what was left of the Soviet Union had verification that the device loaned to the Americans during WWII was operational. An encoded message sent to the Russian Embassy in Washington on February 1 by a U.S. Air Force general had finally been deciphered. Part of the message said to closely watch the results of Aeroflot Flight 324, scheduled to depart Kennedy Airport in four days, on February 5. On February 21, the KGB feverishly reviewed all their taped CNN news coverage on the tragedy and concluded it was their loaned machine that had done the job. A demand was quickly placed, through secure diplomatic channels, for its return, in exchange for Russia's destruction of three thousand additional warheads.

* * *

"It was on a formal loan," said the U.S. President to his NSC chief. "And you have given me no information of its value. Is it, or is it not, something we need for our national security? Does it operate? Does it fly? Is it from another world?"

"We have no information on it along those lines . . . just that it is made of some strange and seemingly indestructible material," answered the NSC chief. "The Air Force says that since the shut-down of Operation Blue Book during the sixties, it has been just an object of curiosity. There has been no additional funding for research on it."

"You mean, no funding that we know of," interrupted the President.

28

"Well, true," said the NSC chief. "As you know, Congress has given many of our agencies and military departments billions in non-discretionary, non-accountable funds during the past fifty years and continues to do so. But according to the head of Air Force Intelligence, General Johnston . . . here, I'll read what he said: *The subject item obtained from the former Soviet Union during the World War II Lend-Lease program was thoroughly evaluated for twenty years. The conclusion, from extensive analysis, remains the same today. The item, though interesting, has proven to be essentially worthless for any perceived military, industrial, or domestic use.*"

"But it *is* worth the destruction of three thousand Russian warheads," said the President, "and that is valuable! Also, there is an election coming up, and I have to think of the big picture."

The president ordered the craft returned to the Russians.

* * *

General Johnston and Colonel Bobarski then spent many days and nights destroying all flight and operational records at Groom Lake, while keeping one copy on a dime size micro laser-disk for themselves. The records at Wright Paterson AFB were safe enough for the time being. But they were next on the agenda to be destroyed.

"Can't take any chances," said the General.

They watched from the glass-enclosed office overlooking the inside of the hangar as the craft was shrouded in a black plastic box and hoisted aboard a flatbed for transportation to a ship at the Navy dock in Alameda, California. It was only twenty feet, three-and-a-quarter inches in diameter, and eight feet, six and five-eights inches thick. Yet it weighed forty thousand five hundred and three pounds, ten and three-quarter ounces. The middle of the flatbed sagged as it was set down on it. A huge sign on the back said, EXTRA WIDE LOAD. The semi was escorted out of the hangar by two Air Force police cars in the front and two behind.

Chapter Two

Conima, Peru: February 25, 1999

An Incan peasant led a small, sturdy horse from an old thatch-roofed barn in the high-mountain village of Conima. The animal was laden with bundles of sticks that covered a Marlin 30-30 carbine and an old set of leather saddle-bags filled with flashlights, ropes, a slicker, food, grain for his horse, three slings, eight sling-stones, and two bolas. He traveled toward the next town and occasionally chewed coca leaves to sustain himself at the high altitudes of the Andes.

His floppy hat identified him as one of the mountain people, and the few passersby gave him little notice. After a few miles the wind picked up, and it began to get dark. He lowered an alpaca poncho that had been draped over his shoulders. The dirt road he followed cut a thin brown line through a sea of stunted, pale-green brush.

He stopped, rubbed the nose of his horse, and looked for anything unusual behind him. The taut skin on his high cheekbones reflected the last of the twilight as he moved onto a trail toward the higher altitudes in the sacred mountains of the Incas.

Three days later he emerged from the mountains and retraced his steps back to Conima. There he went into the barn, released the ties that held the sticks, and tossed the now bulging saddle-bags onto the right seat of an International Scout four-wheel drive. In another five minutes he had transitioned from peasant garb into blue jeans, a parka, and underneath, a denim vest that held a wallet full of credit cards. Two days later he was in England.

Sotheby's Auction House, London: February 26, 1999

Malcolm Bloomquist was driven from his corporate offices in downtown Washington to his ornate house on Foxhall Road in Georgetown. He had been on the phone seemingly for days with members of Congress, the President, and Chairman of the party. These political duties prevented him from coming home and reading his junk mail for a week. He had slept in his downtown penthouse.

His butler opened the large oak door, took his coat, and watched as Bloomquist's six-foot-three frame walked across the Tuscan marble floor to the sideboard stacked with unofficial mail. When he got to a certain announcement, he pushed the rest aside, called his secretary, and booked the next first-class flight to England.

* * *

It wasn't just a rumor he had heard. Sotheby's was auctioning some rare pre-Colombian art, which was his passion. The following afternoon in London, he took his company limo directly from the airport and sat in the auction room, wishing he had known to come a day earlier to inspect the items in detail. He hoped for some pottery, perhaps a cup for drinking chicha.

When the first object was brought out, his heart began palpitating with excitement.

He was allowed to look at the large engraved dinner plate of solid gold closely with a ten-power jeweler's glass before bidding. There was no mistaking it. The markings were unique to the Huayna-Capac Inca nobles. When the bidding started at fifteen thousand, he was dubious. But perhaps, he hoped, these people didn't know the value of it. And, he reminded himself, Sotheby's would never hold him to a bid on an object that he personally couldn't authenticate. He raised his hand. At fifty thousand dollars the bidding stopped with him. He mopped perspiration from his upper lip and waited for the next object, which was even more beautiful than the first, a foot high ear of corn, with solid-gold kernels, turquoise leaves, and thin silver tassels. An hour later he was the owner of all five pieces and had spent a half million dollars.

On closer inspection afterward, he was more thrilled at the condition of the works he had purchased. They were all perfect. Not a nick, not a scratch. He also knew they could not be duplications. The minute tool marks were clearly Incan.

During the next two days, Bloomquist spent considerable energy trying to find out who the seller was and each inquiry was met with a stony stare. The people at Sotheby's had the same reputation for secrecy as Swiss bankers. On the airplane flight home he resolved to get to the bottom of it all.

Lima, Peru: March 5, 1999

A week later Bloomquist sat in an office at the corner of Avenidas Espana and Garcilaso de la Vega, the U.S. Embassy in Lima, Peru. It was still the hot season south of the equator. There was much automobile traffic outside the window.

"The streets are much busier during siesta hours than they were a few years ago," said the other occupant of the room, General Carlos Espinoza, puffing on an Arturo Fuente cigar. "Perhaps because of more air conditioned automobiles," he added.

Bloomquist, the newly designated U.S. Ambassador, offered him a drink. They had known one another a long time, but without friendship. Espinoza had received much money from him over the years to find pre-Columbian artifacts. It was what Espinoza called politics. But now that Bloomquist was the designated ambassador, Espinoza had to show even more deference and consideration.

"Just sherry, *gracias*, thank you," said Espinoza. Bloomquist poured two sherries, handed one to the general, and then sat on an opposite couch, his tall heavy frame sinking to where one might expect the springs to yell, or fabric to split.

"Any progress?" asked Bloomquist.

"Some. You were right about the traditional stories. They have substance. My cousin in Seville searched the archives there. A report to Pope Sixtus the Fifth, in the year fifteen eighty-six, confirmed rumors of vast quantities of gold that were hidden nearly forty years earlier. My cousin, Sanchos, worked on it for over three weeks!"

Bloomquist edged forward on the couch with frustration as he reached toward the table for his wine glass.

These pedestrian Spanish Hidalgos, he thought. *Does everything have to be a goddamn liturgy of relatives and hands soiled by labor, as if that were a sort of extreme-unction, some indication of ultimate loyalty?*

He smiled benevolently and asked if there were any details.

"Unfortunately the methods of extracting information were not refined in those days, and the persons usually died during questioning. And so we only know what was in one letter to the Pope those many years ago . . . what everyone seems to have known for a long time."

"And what did the letter say?" asked Bloomquist in a polite tone.

"That there is a huge quantity of golden artifacts hidden somewhere. That only the Inca knows where it is. And that only the Inca can get it back," said the general, smoothing a wrinkle in the side pocket-flap of his ornate uniform jacket. Bloomquist watched him and absently counted the number of rows of military ribbons on his chest. *He looks like a bantam Brezhnev*, he observed. *A little cock with bright feathers.*

"Is there still an Inca chief here?" asked Bloomquist.

"Yes, there is a Sapa Inca, or emperor. Of that we can be sure. And all the subservient Inca population know it. Why do you think they have remained unchanged for five hundred years? These are a patient people. They have survived in spite of working as slaves and being kept in poverty. No other culture has done this for so long and remained intact, not even the Aztecs. Well, perhaps the Hopis and Zunis from your country. There is something that has held them together this long. It may be the existence of the 'sweat of the sun and the tears of the moon', their gold and silver, or the air boat that their folk tales say is locked up in the mountains . . . a gift from their sun god."

Bloomquist sat upright in the soft couch. An ancient term, "Sweat of the sun, tears of the moon," pronounced by a Spanish Hidalgo. He studied General Espinoza's giant mustache, his long Castilian nose, his portly, short frame, and his shoes of fine Corinthian leather.

"Perhaps a Rememberer could help," said the General.

"A 'Rememberer'?" asked Bloomquist.

"Yes," said Espinoza impatiently, "A *requerdo*, a *quiposcamayo*. They use the strings with knots in them, the *quipos*, to remember the statistics in the empire. To keep track of taxes, crops, population, and historical events."

"So," began Bloomquist, knowing very well about *quipos* and Rememberers, "we either need a Rememberer or the Sapa Inca."

"*Si*," said the General, "But it might be difficult to find either."

"Why do you say that?" asked Bloomquist.

"We know there is a Sapa Inca. But we have no idea who he is. And we have no information that there is a current Rememberer, though their culture has remained so unchanged that one could conclude that the art of *quipu*-reading has not disappeared."

"Yes," said Bloomquist, impressed. "I have read that there has been no known Sapa Inca for several hundred years, though we know from their private religious ceremonies that they think one exists."

"One exists," said the General with finality while placing the goblet to his lips. Bloomquist's devious and accurate mind instantly calculated a solution, while his good eye absently focused on Espinoza's mustache.

The General stared at Bloomquist and thought he heard a slight hum, or purring. He looked at the television, then the stereo. Then the noise went away, and he looked back at Bloomquist's jowled face and studied the large black patch over one eye. Bloomquist voiced his plan.

"You have dedicated friends?" he asked more as a statement than a question.

"I do," said the General.

"And there are mummies of dead Incas that have been kept by you Conquistadors for hundreds of years?" added Bloomquist.

"Of course, you know it," said the General. "You have seen the photographs."

"Then let us get one of them and take it to the British Museum," said Bloomquist.

Espinoza looked at him aghast, as if it were a sacrilege. Bloomquist noted the expression.

"So, you think it would be some sort of abomination?" asked Bloomquist.

"First," said the General, "it would cause many problems. And *segundo*, I don't see the use in it."

"I don't see what problems it would cause," said Bloomquist. "You've had Francisco Pizarro's mummy in a glass case in the cathedral here in Lima for centuries."

"It's not the same. Pizarro was Spanish," said the General, wiping his forehead with a handkerchief. "We respect the memory of our ancestors. They worship theirs in today's time. You see, we have played a game since the Conquest. They pretend that they have been converted to Catholicism. We pretend that they have forgotten their ancient faith. It has worked with the mother country and Rome for five hundred years. There has been no serious uprising for three hundred years. And only one minor one since. And that is because of this unwritten agreement."

He snaked his tongue along his mustache and again wiped his forehead.

Bloomquist thought a moment, then said, "And they still wear the same clothes they did five hundred years ago. And they are still a threat to you. To the balance."

"Yes. Same clothes, but wearing broad-brimmed hats. Their way of making us think they are subjugated," said the General. "And they know a few of the mummies are with us. They know we brought the bodies of Manco Inca, whose bracelet I sold you years ago, and Titu Cusi from Vilcabamba in 1572, and burned them. And they know that we buried the last of Manco's sons, Tupac Amaru, and of course Atahuallpa. And that we have, well hidden, the mummies of the great Huayna-capac Inca, and his wife, the parents of Huascar. But they also know they are undisturbed, that our non-violation of them is part of the unwritten agreement."

"What would be the first thing they would do if one of the mummies was moved out of the country?" asked Bloomquist.

"*Por Dios!* Bad things would happen!" exclaimed Espinoza. "They made things very difficult for us three centuries ago when we burned a few. You see, we can make them work in the mines until they die, and we can make them sing Catholic hymns in Latin on feast days in the cathedrals, and we can take their children and their women, and spit on them in the streets, and they will do nothing. But they are a warrior race. And their Sapa Inca connects them with their god. And so we promised them this in the unwritten agreement. We would not harm another of their Sapa Incas if they submitted completely to us. To them, as a people, they gave up little to retain their identity. To us, we got what we wanted for nothing."

Bloomquist looked at the General in a new light, that of unexpected respect. The man knew his slaves. He rubbed his hands together for a minute, then popped the question.

"General, if one Sapa Inca mummy were perceived to have been taken out of the country, say to the British Museum for an archeological autopsy, what would happen?"

"The present Sapa," said Espinoza, "is the only Inca allowed to touch another Sapa's mummy. The present Sapa Inca would probably follow immediately. And the population would react. They would poison the water. They would set fires. They would cut telephone lines, smash transformers, sink boats in the harbors. And they would do it all at night, and go to their special places, caves, high mountain enclaves, during the day, where they could live for many months without being found. They would make the Communist *Sandero Luminosos* look like Boy Scouts. It would not be good."

"Yes, but how long after the Sapa Inca left would they do this?" asked Bloomquist.

"Within a few days," said the General.

"Well," said Bloomquist. "You control the newspapers. What if the transfer was announced in the press as a thing of science, something archeological? And then retract it a few days later?"

Espinoza quickly saw the plan and the wisdom of it.

"The Incan world would not react right away," he said. "And if the real Sapa Inca left to follow, we would know it. The Indian population could be fed photographs the next day showing that no Inca mummy had left, that it was a big editorial mistake, and that any group of ten of them could be allowed to inspect and verify. Then the others would simply wait for their present Inca to come back. But if the present Sapa Inca dies they all would quickly pick another Sapa and go on the rampage. I know from an Incan confidant that they never forgot Atahuallpa, who left no provisions for another commander to take charge in case something happened to him. It might be worth a try. Nothing to lose really. If Atahuallpa's murder and burial had not been public, they would have waited months before choosing another Sapa."

Bloomquist was floored. The Spaniard had actually used the correct term, "murder." He focused his eye again on the General's face, thinking it could be up to his standards of an aristocrat.

"There will be a photograph of it in the newspaper, a detailed photograph of the mummy being crated for shipping," said the General.

"And you will be taking care of the plane?" asked Bloomquist.

"TWA has a daily flight to London. I'll arrange to have it land en route on my airstrip in the Azores. It will be delayed only a few moments. And you will be informed of all progress. I have an ongoing deal with international professionals, or patriots, I should say. They have business interests here in Peru, several teams of well-trained zealots to do their bidding, and they owe me a great deal. The plane will not be a problem."

"I think we may be able to strike a handsome deal if we ever find this cache!" said Bloomquist generously, as he rose to shake hands.

That evening the General sat in his study and listened to the conversation with Bloomquist again, while constantly fidgeting with the ear-plug attached to the small tape recorder he always carried in his uniform pocket. He looked out his hacienda window at the mountains east of Lima and wondered about the present day Sapa Inca. Who could he be? He was certain of only three things. One: a large number of ancient golden Peruvian art objects had appeared on the world market during the past few months. The great brokerage house in London, Sotheby's, had auctioned off nearly fifty pieces without disclosing who the seller was. Two: Indians, some with traces of Spanish blood, were buying up large parcels of land in Peru. Where were they getting the money? Three: his drug operation in the high country was not running smoothly. He could handle the acts of violence. The *Sandero Luminoso*, or Shining Path commies, were under control. The pro-Cuban Tupac Amaru revolutionary movement killed thousands during the 1980s, and not made a dent in the business.

But now, he thought, *something is messing with the whole structure. The workers are not picking as much of the coca leaves. It is too much of a coincidence. And the Inca, if Bloomquist is right, has to be behind it. There is too much money buying up too much land by too many unfamiliar people. Any amount of Indian art could not be worth the trade in drugs that is both lucrative and lasts long after gold is gone,* he figured. *Though it may not be worth putting the coca business at risk, I can always use an extra hundred million dollars. I will watch the process closely. I will alert my London hit team, just in case there is a problem with the plane landing in the Azores. Also,* he finally concluded, *me having the extra millions is the same as the Indians not having it.*

He picked up the telephone and called his man in England.

Chapter Three

The Kremlin, March 5, 1999

The new Russian Defense Minister sat by the fireplace in the Grand Hall of the Kremlin with his aide, Popov, and reviewed the latest on the craft. Russians didn't have the foggiest idea how to operate the machine. Nearly all of their real experimental and visionary scientific talent had been either worked to death or liquidated during the various purges over the years. All they had left with expertise were some nuclear, rocket, and aeronautical engineers. The machine had arrived the previous week. It was being measured and weighed in great secrecy. But so far they hadn't figured out how to even get inside. All their previous records on it had been destroyed by Nazi bombs during WWII. But there was some encouraging news. The U.S. Air Force General's message had said that they had successfully flown the craft and had much information on its performance parameters and seemingly unlimited flight envelope. The reference to the Aeroflot Flight 324 disaster was especially encouraging. And five million dollars in gold, in his Swiss account, would buy instructions on how to get inside, adding that the flight operation package could be purchased at a later date after further negotiations.

"So what do you think?" asked the Defense Minister.

"Don't have a choice," said Popov. "Even if we already knew how to get inside, it would be worth the purchase. If this General's information is true, it could save us years of research trying to figure out how to operate it.

Besides, five million in U.S. dollars is less than the cost of one Mig-29."

"I agree," said Malenkov. "Have our intelligence people follow through with it. From what our janitor-spy at Groom Lake says, it not only has been thoroughly tested, but the test results have been kept so secret that it is doubtful even their President was informed of the potential of the thing. Circumstantially, this seems reasonable or he wouldn't have considered giving it back. To his administration, they were only returning an artifact that was lent to them for safe keeping during the war. Could be a major stroke of luck."

"And where did we get the thing anyway?" asked Popov.

"As you know, all our files were destroyed. But I've talked to some old-timers. It was found in a cave in Siberia several hundred years ago. Peter the Great sent a small expedition to investigate the rumors. They were true. It took a fairly large expedition and about five hundred horses to get it back to St. Petersburg. Later, Catherine had it moved outside the city, where it just sat in the open for many decades. It was a local curiosity in that it glowed slightly at night and that even during the harshest of winters, no snow accumulated on it. Peasants would often stand near it to keep warm. Word got around, though. During the early twentieth century, when the West was first experimenting with nuclear energy, Einstein mentioned it to Roosevelt, who made it part of the Lend-Lease package. Stalin could see no use in something that had been merely a curiosity for so long. And since he needed planes, tanks, and locomotives, it was like getting something for nothing. Now it seems, with this nuclear disarmament, that the U.S. government thinks it is getting something for nothing with it. Anyway, we have it now. It could be our ace for dealing with the West in the future."

Old Town, Alexandria, Virginia: March 5, 1999

Brandon placed the straight-edge razor in the ornate green marble sink, twisted the faucet off, wiped the remaining shaving cream from his face with a towel, looked in the mirror, and pulled on his eyelids. The brown contact lenses dropped one at a time into his hand. He stared at the contrast of his face. Almond-shaped oriental eyes with bright blue irises. He noted the smoothness of his olive skin over the hairless torso and well-defined arm muscles. His Anglo-American father and Chinese mother each got their 50 percent gene input, he thought.

He walked to his bedroom under a cathedral ceiling, sat down on the edge of the bed, and began reviewing contacts listed in his small hand-held electronic office manager. An hour later he arrived at Dr. Lilly's office on a side street of Old Town, Alexandria, and wondered if he had the right address. When he heard loud rock guitar music coming from behind the door, he was fairly sure of being lost. He rang the door bell and heard church-bells that overpowered the Grateful Dead. Dr. Lilly shut off the CD and went to the entrance. He warmly greeted Brandon and asked him to please follow him through the corridors of a large attached building.

"Sorry for all the noise," said Lilly, as he motioned Brandon to sit in a comfortable black leather chair in a dim room. "But that foyer back there is where I spend my spare time between clients. I don't like waiting and so fill up the between times."

"Am I a client?" asked Brandon.

"Perhaps Pitman is," said Lilly, "But no, you are not a client relative to my normal line of business, which actually is therapy, sometimes through hypnosis. But I can't move quickly from one client's story to another, like drilling holes out of doughnuts on an assembly line. I need to schedule down time for it. And since I have not yet learned the virtue of patience, I improvise."

Brandon liked the grey-haired, steel-eyed Lilly after those few words of introduction.

"First, I would like to know what you are," said Brandon.

"Just someone who can't be in the field. Never should have been. My nerves couldn't take it. But I do have loyalties and debts. Most cannot be paid because the recipients are dead. Pitman, however, is not. And I owe him a great deal. Not just because he saved my life, but he got me out of the main business and into the side of it that I can do well. So that's what I am. I help people much the same way as Pitman helped me, while retaining my ability to exercise my real expertise in a covert, but non-involved manner."

"Okay," said Brandon. "What gives?"

"Got Pitman's message and codes, and shortly thereafter, an opportunity presented itself," said Lilly. "Here's the layout. . . . An associate of mine has a patient. He's an Air Force Officer about your height and weight. A Lieutenant. And he's in security. Had some psychological problems after a tour in Bosnia. My associate recommended that he take a week off, travel, go on a cruise. We've taken care of that. Our people are near him at all times. He left yesterday. It will do him good. In the meantime, we obtained copies of his orders to Wright Paterson in Dayton. He has not been there before. As you know, in the military, one can come off leave at any time, and show up early at their next duty station. And if anyone there had known

40

a Lieutenant Bob Jones, it's a common enough name. Here's a key to a lock box at the D.C. bus station. The suitcase inside contains everything you will need for insertion, including uniforms, identification, orders, family history, latex pre-oiled fingerprints, the usual. You will have three days there before receiving priority orders out. The real Bob Jones will show up on time. There will be a flap about his prints matching yours. But different people will be checking him in and there probably won't be much of a to-do about it until later. And by that time you will be gone."

"Sounds okay," said Brandon, placing the key in his pocket.

Dayton, Ohio: March 5, 1999

Brandon first checked into the BOQ at Wright Pat. It was a late Friday afternoon. He then made his apologies to the people at the Duty Desk for showing up three days early. He said not to bother with calling the other places on base required for him to appear, that he would do the rest of his formal check-in on Monday and meet his new Commanding Officer, Colonel Farnsworth. He just wanted them to know he was around in case there was some security problem. After a few sighs of appreciation and welcome aboard handshakes, they took his photograph and fingerprints, and in a few minutes, a laminated temporary ID card slid out of the bottom of the computer. He snapped it onto his shirt collar.

Then he went back to the BOQ, cut through the bottom of his suitcase, and studied the package from Pitman which contained schematics on the layout of the place.

By midnight, Brandon had completed a routine security inspection of all the guards on the base. The famous hanger was impregnable. However, the administration and records buildings were not.

He spent most of Saturday going through the large aircraft museum. That evening, during another spot inspection, he merely mentioned to the guard on the floor of the records building that he would be touring the spaces on his own for about an hour. He signed the log while his photo ID was inspected.

"Sir," said the desk guard, "this is only a temporary ID."

"Sorry," said Brandon, while digging in his back pocket for his wallet, "Here is my permanent Air Force identification, which allows me into any classification 1-C building and below. This is a 1-D building."

The guard hadn't the foggiest idea whether it was a 1-D or 10-Z building and called for clarification. Main security said it was a 1-D building. Brandon was passed through. With Pitman's information, he knew where to go. He passed no one in the halls. *Probably because of the weekend*, he thought. In ten minutes he was in the right room and into the hard files. There were thousands of them on hundreds of shelves. It took another ten minutes to find those that dealt with Roswell and related subjects. He snapped away with his mini-digital cameras. Each of the four he carried on both sides of his ankles inside his socks could record a hundred high-resolution images. He rapidly went through the papers, reading only the subject lines. After forty minutes he was finished. Many of his recorded images were of photographs.

He casually signed out of the building, went back to the BOQ, and set up his laptop. He carefully hooked up his first camera to it. After twenty minutes, he had downloaded the four hundred images into the laptop's hard drive. Next he unplugged the phone from the wall, inserted the fax/modem line from the laptop, and dialed the secure number. At a Baud rate of 52,800, all scrambled photographs were transferred to Pitman's machine in Washington in thirty minutes. Then he replaced the phone jack, and redialed another of Pitman's secure lines.

"They're starting to print out now," said Pitman. "Good quality. If you don't hear from me in an hour, go ahead and erase all copies at your end. See you tomorrow."

Sunday morning at the Duty Desk, he checked out. The different people on duty looked at this Lieutenant somewhat quizzically. But the orders were clear and there was a plane waiting for him. Pitman had sent a CIA Learjet with markings and paint job similar to those of the Air Force MAC transports.

Georgetown, Washington, D.C.: March 6, 1999

During Brandon's flight from Wright Pat to D.C., Pitman called him on the aircraft phone and asked, "Can you catch TWA flight 450 out of Lima to London? It leaves in eighteen hours."

"Yes. What package?"

"Standard M equipment. A courier with a sealed envelope will meet your plane here," said Pitman.

"What about the photographs?" asked Brandon. "I'd like to study them myself."

"They will be in the envelope on a CD. Access code is 'Einstein'. You can study them at your leisure."

Pitman looked at Allie after he hung up. Allie didn't like it.

"That was Jess Brandon, wasn't it?" she said.

"You don't really think, my dear, that I could keep him sidelined for long. I allowed him to go so that he would miss the place he has to come back to. It will help him get things into perspective. His conscious mind sees an operation. His subconscious needs a home."

"Andy," she began while pouring tea in the breakfast nook, "you know perfectly well what he needs. And what he needs is here. Yet you send him off for reasons that are only in your best interest. You want a job done. So you send him. Don't give me this crap about 'in his best interest'. And you haven't told me a damn thing about it!"

"Okay, in our best interest, his and the country's. You think we can afford to compete with people who have large organizations dedicated, even competing with one another, to steal our technology? Granted, we have no need for such bureaucracies, but we have a vital need to know how much they have gotten. How much they have operational. The pincers of time and technological advancement, the two entities that have governed all battles and all wars in all history, continually squeeze out threats and conflict . . . and besides, it's what he wants."

Allie looked at him with her rare expression of utter displeasure. Her stare made people squirm. She stood and retied the silk ribbon holding her long greying hair in a ponytail. It was a sign Pitman had noticed on many occasions that meant strong feelings were incoming.

"Andy, we leveled a long time ago about things like this. You will not insult my intelligence. It is degrading to repeat the terms of an agreement. Now, I know about the technological stealing by the new Soviet states and the arms market. And that Jess is valuable. But he is finally getting his life together, and he is vulnerable . . . can't even talk about his past. And he's never trusted anyone in his adult life except you, his friend Jim, and his parents, all dead except you. And now you are taking advantage of it! Certainly there are others who could go to Lima. He's finally got a taste of a good woman and is getting his head on straight thinking about it, even getting some therapy, and now you send him off."

"You left something out, Allie," said Pitman, eyeing her carefully, and rubbing his mustache.

"What's that?" she asked.

"The part about you being left out," he said. "You feel unimportant or something. The fact is that this is a milk-run. A spontaneous airplane ride. And, as far as I know, it is unimportant. I wanted him to ease out of the business. To experience some of the boredom of it. It's nothing. I had some microphones planted in a room in South America, in our Embassy in Lima, with the approval of our current ambassador, soon to be replaced. The recordings on them were unusual, farfetched really. A couple of people talking over drinks. I would have shared it with you, but it's not important yet. And probably won't be. Crazy really."

"But crazy enough to send Brandon out," she said.

"Like I said, dear, I wanted him to ease out of the business. He has to unwind. At his age any woman needs to know what he was in order to accept him for what he is. Otherwise it won't work. And if he can't talk, she can't know. Right now he can't talk. And it's a milk-run, a milk-run, like the FBI garbage details. Part of the job he has never experienced. I want him to not want it so much."

"You forgot to mention one thing Mister P," said Allie. "Adventure of all types has followed Brandon since Harvard almost non-stop. He has never once picked through normal garbage. He has never paid his dues as a rookie like almost all operatives do at least once. But Brandon did pick through garbage that was worse than any regular garbage. He picked through the crap in his mind, of his thoughts, of his heart. When he found his friend Jim tortured and dead in Vietnam, do you think he would have gone through a thousand pounds of trash to make it different, to even be able to back up a single day to change things? He would have sifted through that garbage with tweezers. The fact is he paid those types of dues up front. And it almost ruined him emotionally."

Allie hadn't thought of her youth in Russia for many years. *There is speculation*, she thought, *and there is knowing. There is believing, and there is knowing. There is wanting to believe, and then there is knowing. And there is no mixing in the ether of the universe among any of them, and the knowing.* She knew then that she had perhaps forgotten some of the knowing. That there was a reason for her love. That the universe had dictated some of it, and she had dictated the rest . . . that all she and Pitman had together were words and senses and feelings and understandings and remembrances and children. And that they had been using these things to communicate. And that, as she couldn't do all of that all of the time, he couldn't either. Pitman said she was right, that perhaps he hadn't thought it all the way through. Allie got up, leaned over, and kissed him on the top of his head, then turned to walk up the stairs saying, "Well, at least he's the best. So I'm not worried this time. But let me know beforehand if there is a next time."

"I will, my dear," said Pitman.

He reached for his glasses in an small ancient Ming vase by the couch, placed them over his prominent beak of a nose, and looked around the living room of their house on O Street in Georgetown, thinking again that she was right.

Old Town, Alexandria, Virginia: March 6, 1999

Brandon leaned back in his chair and said, "Nice dinner, Jane."

She noticed his energy, and knew something was about to happen.

"What?" she asked.

"Mission to South America. Milk-run. I think Pitman is feeling sorry for me."

"So why the anxiety?" she asked.

"Don't know; don't like milk-runs. Listen, dear," said Brandon, "I know this is not easy for you, me doing these things. But it's something that I have a feeling will work its way out. *Is* working itself out. I feel an ending. But in the meantime, it has to be done. It is a part of me to do what I can for now."

"Well, I'm not going to shuffle and wonder long," she said. "I mean, I will wait a while for you. You're worth it. But I don't see just sitting around while you work these things out. Think I'll go out to your farm for the duration on this one. The horses could use some TLC, and your dogs miss both you and me. Chief Dancing Eagle can't do everything. And I can telecommute for my boss from there for a week or two."

"Good idea," said Brandon. "You want to go commercial to L.A., or should I have the Eagle pick you up in a few days?"

"That's a choice?" she asked. "Is it in my blond-hair genes or long legs that makes me the type to be spoiled? The Indian, of course, is the only reasonable alternative. Also, I like talking with him. He has a different answer every time I ask why you haven't yet smoked that catlanite and sycamore peace pipe he made for you. It has just been hanging on the wall for years."

"I'll call him right now," said Brandon, squeezing her hand.

He punched a button on the speaker phone, then another for automatic dial. The Eagle picked it up after the first ring.

"How!" said Brandon.

"Oh, everything's fine," said Dancing Eagle from Brandon's farm in Lone Pine, California. "Manny should be dropping a foal any time now. Good crop of grapes, maybe a thousand cases of prime vintage. Alfalfa is in. Windmill's still turnin' and pumpin'. Dogs chase rabbits. Life goes on."

"Jane wants some of it, and she wants it now," said Brandon.

"My wife could use the company," said Dancing Eagle. "She says that since our kids are gone, she enjoys being with pale faces that happen to be in the neighborhood. We warriors, however, are above all that. National Airport, Hangar Five, early next week? I can call her."

Brandon looked at Jane. She nodded okay.

"She says okay. Thanks," said Brandon.

The cat, Mina, suddenly appeared and jumped into Jane's lap.

"Hello pretty Siamese," said Jane.

Brandon looked at his cat and heard her purring loudly. "Ah," he said. "Females know all the punishment tricks."

"But what a nice kitty," said Jane.

"Yes," said Brandon. "She is the prettiest cat in the universe, with a wonderful personality to go with the looks. But actually she is a spy."

"A spy?" asked Jane.

"Yes," said Brandon. "A spy from another galaxy, perhaps another universe. My theory is that when she pretends to sleep eighteen hours a day, she is actually transmitting information to her home galaxy on an ultra low frequency of some sort. Otherwise there is no good reason for her existence."

"Really," said Jane. "Are you saying you don't get any pleasure out of having her around?"

At this point, Mina leapt from Jane's lap to the floor and rubbed against Brandon's legs, purring loudly.

"No," said Brandon. "I love this cat. She reminds me of the Sphinx, only prettier. She requires no grooming, no dainty canned diet, and no house training. Just dried food, water, and a litter box thrown out once a week."

Jane could see the affection in Brandon's tone and asked, "Anything you don't like about this cat?"

"Yes. She doesn't have prehensile paws and knows no tricks."

Georgetown, Washington, D.C.: March 7, 1999

The next day Andy Pitman came home from his CIA office distracted. He pecked Allie on the cheek, gave her an extra hug, and set his briefcase down while wiggling his nose into the crook of her neck. He stayed there a few seconds breathing in the perfume, then straightened up and reached into his pants for the usual manila envelope of work information for her to go over. She still had the best brain in the business, he thought. And even after the last operation with Chiang's gold, she remained wonderfully invisible, as merely the wife of an upper middle-class Washington bureaucrat.

Though Pitman, the pragmatist and collector of fine paintings and porcelain appreciated her tall shapely figure, sensitive, caring eyes, and Greek goddess face, he was awed by her mind. Shortly after meeting her in Brazil years before as a naval intelligence officer, he had discovered her unique powers of analysis. It was not just the dazzling variations on a theme she could do on the piano. It was how she could pull together myriads of seemingly disconnected information into a sensible whole . . . how she could make sense out of chaos. After the marriage, when she agreed to help him with his work, he felt as if he had won the lottery a second time.

She eyed him questioningly. They both had been acting differently ever since the Chiang operation. He spent more time on the phone with the kids. She spent less time at her bridge parties and more time piloting their small plane. Perhaps, she thought, they were both still recovering from the trauma and didn't need anything new just yet.

She put the envelope on the coffee table, went to the sideboard, and began mixing him a scotch, measuring every drop—a marriage-long ceremony that unexplainably gave him a feeling of comfort and acceptance. He put an ashtray on top of the envelope.

"What's up?" she asked. "No normal review of the latest in espionage?"

"It can wait," he answered. "I have a problem, actually two problems."

"Dear, dear," she said. "Hope they are at least pretty."

"Well, the first doesn't have hoof-and-mouth, anthrax, or AIDS, as far as I can tell at the moment," he teased, and took a sip. "The second has to wait for more information."

"But the first is probably just me," he said. "There's a person I don't like. And it's screwing up my judgement. I thought you could help me out."

"Not the new Director?" she asked.

"No. You know how I am with bosses."

"Yes, you work for the American people, they work for the American people. Politics and experience separate the twain, nothing else."

"It's my monthly poker game at the Metropolitan Club."

"Who," she emphasized, "at your monthly poker game?" getting impatient.

47

"Malcolm Bloomquist," he said. "The man I recorded last week in the Peruvian embassy, remember? The reason I asked Brandon to go on that milk-run."

"Christ, Andy! You sure know how to pick 'em. One of the wealthiest scions in the country, the next U.S. ambassador to Peru, the heir-apparent to the Republican candidacy for President of the United States. The darling of good-ole-boy power brokers. And by what ruse did you have the embassy bugged?" she asked.

"Not bugged," he said, "Recorded. The outgoing Ambassador, Wentworth, whom you know, and I had a talk a month ago. He said that he had made his office in Lima available to Bloomquist, though not yet confirmed as Ambassador, during the transition. After I explained my concern about Bloomquist's lack of diplomatic experience, he formally requested from the CIA that an automatic voice-actuated recording device be installed in his office for record keeping for the archives. When he leaves office he will take it with him. It's all legal. A person can hardly be held guilty of bugging his or her own office, can he?"

"No," she said. "But I don't suppose the recorder was in plain sight either, was it?"

Pitman threw up his hands and said, "Okay, it's *always* going to be something!"

She watched him stare at the Ansel Adams photograph of El Capitan Mountain on the wall for a few seconds, then asked him to get to the point.

"He cheats at cards. I mean, I think he cheats," said Pitman.

"I'm not following you, dear. Either he cheats or he doesn't. What are you saying?"

"I'm saying that I can't see anything. He wins when others deal also. But the odds of his winning are not in proportion to the winning. If he were the future U.S. ambassador to Russia, even now after the collapse, I would take my losses as a contribution toward the man's training and education. But he may be a future President, and it bothers me. Hell, Napoleon cheated unconscionably at cards, but always returned the money after the game. At least he had no illusions that cheating on your peers was as much of a game as the game itself, as long as no one came out the poorer. This is different."

She looked at him sourly, expecting some strange request.

"What do you want me to do?" she asked.

"How about playing some poker?" he said.

"You mean me? In that stuffy old Metropolitan Club? I'd rather eat a handful of dead flies. Besides, it's an all men's club."

"You know perfectly well," he said, his voice rising, "that the Supreme Court ruled on that several years ago, and that wives of members are also considered members."

"That doesn't mean I would be welcome," she said. "Most of them are a bunch of stuffed shirts that I've met at embassy parties. Half have silver spoons still pinched between their cheek and gum like Copenhagen snuff. No thanks!" she said with finality.

Too final, he thought, *Too abrupt. Our past bets and payoffs always involved some discussion before decisions were made.*

"Okay. What do you want?" he asked.

Her eyes twinkled at his perception and the corners of her mouth uncontrollably turned upward, the zeniths of a suppressed smile.

"I want a new airplane."

"A what?"

"A new airplane. Our old Lake Special is, well, old. Old radios, old seats, takes too long to get off the water, and it's starting to rattle a little. I think a Lake Turbo Renegade 470 would do nicely."

He took a sip of scotch and asked, "Why not just buy one yourself? You can afford it."

"Yes, but Andy Pitman gets attached to old faithful things, like me. I'm concerned that if I did, you would keep flying the old one, and I'd be flying alone on our trips together."

Pitman thought she was probably right.

"Tell you what," he said, "You play poker at the Metro. If you can *prove* that our esteemed future Ambassador cheats, I'll pay half of a new plane for you, and keep the old one for me. If you also find out *how* he cheats, I'll go the whole cost on your new plane, and sell the old one."

"Consider it a deal!" she said. "When?"

"Show up at eight-thirty tomorrow night. I'll send my message of regret five minutes before, at eight twenty-five. Charles, the titular manager of the place, will read it to the table. It will include an apology that feigns health problems, with a proviso that you will be taking my place. None will refuse. It will be a welcome change for them. New blood."

"I want you to give me everyone's name. Anything else?" she asked.

"Just a point to keep in mind. I know how well you manipulate cards. A regular mechanic, I'd say . . . a legerdemain. Just keep in mind that these guys may know the game very well, but none knows the physics of cards like you do."

"Thanks for the confidence, dear," she said. "What else?"

49

"What else?" he asked.

"Yes," she said. "Problem number two. You look like you just finished five games of racquetball, when three would be overdoing it."

"Flying saucers," said Pitman.

"Flying saucers?"

"Yes, there's something going on. I can't seem to get a handle on it," said Pitman.

"You mean flying saucers like in the Roswell case? Or perhaps Tunguska?" she asked.

His jaw dropped. Though she was a part-time editor in a publishing firm, he never suspected she would know anything about this strange area.

"Yes to Roswell. Never heard of Tunguska," he said. "What do you know?"

"Common knowledge really," she said. "It is thought one exploded shortly after the turn of this century. Flattened trees all around. Roswell and Operation Blue Book provide no hard evidence to the public domain though. What's the problem?"

"Part of the problem is that the government may have been covering up things for fifty years. I can understand it, though I don't respect it. They want an edge on technology for defense. And this technology is like giving bent-up parts of a submachine gun to Brazilian rain forest Indians. They may not know what it can do, but with a little heat and work, they can make the strongest arrowheads and fish hooks imaginable."

"So, what's the other part?" she asked.

"The other part is that there may be an intact, operable submachine gun around."

"Around where?" she asked.

"Peru, I think. Perhaps Russia also," he said.

"Okay, fill me in," she said.

Pitman told of how he had related some ancient information from college days to things in the *Celestine Prophesy*. And that it all led to the possibility of a space vehicle high in the Andes Mountains of Peru, long before the Spaniards got there. That the place could now be known. And that whoever got there first would have a machine that could rule the world, if they could figure out how to use it.

"Also," he added, "I have four hundred photos of documents and photos that Brandon took at Wright Paterson Air Force Base. I would like you to look at them. And what is Tunguska?"

"On June 30, 1908, in Siberia, something exploded about five miles

50

up. Part of a forest was levelled in a radial pattern for twenty miles around. Glass globules were found. Iridium was found. Tree ring growth patterns and local animal mutations were consistent with high levels of radioactivity. The Russians still perform annual scientific expeditions to the area. Some say it was a comet, some a malfunctioning UFO, and some an atomic bomb. That's all I know about it," she said, while picking up the hard copies of the photographs.

Pitman just stared at the floor in amazement for a while, then went through the ceremony of lighting his pipe.

* * *

An hour later, Allie heaved the four hundred photos of documentation and photographs onto the coffee table and said, "I want all the information on the careers and personal lives of these people." She handed him a list. Pitman read, *Doctor Roger Hapgood, Major John C. Reynolds, Doctor Edward B. Matthews, General Felix Osborn, Staff Sergeant Michael J. O'Tool, Lieutenant William H. Haversham, Lieutenant Cecil S. Hirshorn, Captain William Bender, Major John Chisolm, Captain Raul Maria Rodriguez, Captain Edward J. Smith, Lieutenant Larry Uppal, General Haynes Johnston, and Colonel William Bobarski.*

Pitman said, "Okay. What's your thinking?"

"These are the people stationed there who had top secret, level one clearances. The first five on this list were mentioned in the documentation as being involved with this project during the late forties and early 1950s. Then no one there had this clearance level for another thirty-five years. The others popped up during the 1990s with the same highest clearances. Why the gap? Why the resurgence in activity?" she said.

"Anything else?" he asked.

"If you can find out anything on the funding of this project, it could also prove useful. But I doubt you or anyone can. You know how the Air Force is."

"Afraid you're right on that one," said Pitman. "But I'll give it a try."

TWA Flight 450—Scheduled non-stop, Lima to London: March 8, 1999

It was a hectic schedule to Lima, but workable. Brandon only had time to make the connection. No hotel room. No good sleep.

He sat back in the comfortable business class seat on the flight to London, relaxed, ordered a drink, and thought of Lilly, the "shrink." Somehow he felt better. The guy was a pro. The Wright Pat operation went nearly perfectly.

He pulled his briefcase from under the seat in front and put it in the empty seat next to him. He opened it, placed a tape Jane had given him into his micro-cassette, and adjusted the earplug. Her voice seemed strange. He listened for several minutes, then turned the machine off and removed the earpiece. He didn't need to hear what he already knew. She was about ready to leave him.

He pulled the laptop from his briefcase and placed the CD from Pitman into the ROM tray, pushing it closed. Then he began reviewing the Wright Pat photographs of documentation. The Air Force definitely had possession of, and had been operating, a vehicle not likely to have been made on this planet. And they had been doing it for over twenty years. It was not the Roswell craft. The flight log dialogues and experimentation told of a technology far beyond anything here. The materials could not be analyzed, much less duplicated. No drills, acid, or heat caused the slightest damage or change. Early test flights were conducted inside the main hangar at Groom Lake in Nevada. Later, three other flights had been made outside during no-moon nights to elevations of over a hundred thousand feet. But the heights were only estimates. The craft was invisible on radar, and the altitude instrument inside seemed to be on a logarithmic scale with an unknown base. A one-man crew was always used. From the copies of flight logs, no crew member had been used on more than three flights. There was much psychological analysis information on each pilot. Actual flight histories and answers to questions were transcription of pilot notes and interviews. It was apparent to Brandon that from the questions asked, and answers given, the pilots thought they were flying a new type of flight simulator.

But there was something else in one of the photographs of the craft itself. Brandon zoomed in on it with the laptop mouse. There were some of the same symbols Pitman had described from Roswell: a triangle with a bar on top, two interconnected circles, three other simple shapes. Under them was a propped up sign on an easel that said, in large letters, CCCP, the initials for the former Supreme Soviet Socialist Republic, the USSR. The craft had come from the former Soviet Union. During the height of the Cold War, the United States had been working with them . . . *probably "for the benefit of all mankind," from the same government yokel mentalities that produced expressions like "in the interest of national security," and "plausible deniability," and "graduated response," and "to marginalize opposing forces,"* thought Brandon. The USSR had neither the technology

52

nor pilot skills to test or analyze it. They had yet to make their first vacuum-tube computer. Eventually they tried to manufacture silicon chips, but couldn't even build a "clean room," and the effort went nowhere. Stealing technology, information, and hardware was what they did best. So they "lent" the craft to the U.S. where the results of healthy educations could be so easily stolen anyway. The magnitude of the collusion struck Brandon. Now Russia probably had it back. It may have been one of the secret bargaining chips to end the Cold War, to dismantle thousands of nuclear warheads. *Perhaps Pitman has one of his accurate "feelings" about this whole thing*, thought Brandon.

The senior flight attendant placed a glass of water and a miniature bottle of whiskey on the small extended table to his left. He looked up and noticed her eyes. Small sparkles of happy blue over well made-up bags of deep caring. *Positive. Balanced*, he thought.

"Thanks," he said.

"Any time," she said, smiling and walking off.

He x-ray eyed her well-shaped fanny underneath a tailored dress as she glided up the aisle, then thought what an easy mission it had been so far. Getting to Lima in time for the flight was the hard part.

Look for some Indians, said the instructions in the envelope from Pitman. *Follow and protect them until they get back to Peru.*

They were sitting three rows behind him. Five men in business clothes. High cheek-bones, straight, black, nicely trimmed page-boy hair. Serious. Unsmiling. They seemed like nervous children. *Probably their first flight on an airliner*, thought Brandon, while reaching for the phone. He checked to see if Chauncy and his man Matlock had departed for London on time and to tell them about the Indians. Chauncy's miraculous save of the Pitmans in Vienna the previous year impressed Brandon tremendously, and they had become fast personal friends.

Brandon replaced the receiver into the seatback in front. Everything was comfortably under control. He went back to the photographs from Wright Pat. One of them showed an open hatch. He zoomed in on the area around it on the outside of the craft, looking for some kind of door latch. There was none he could see. But he did see something to the left of the opening. He magnified the area and noted five small depressions, slight dimples, on the surface. They were arranged in a circle. He next focused on the scale of the photograph shown at the bottom. The circle of dimples was about five inches in diameter, about the size of a humanoid hand.

He reviewed some more of the documentation. It was obvious that the

Air Force officer hierarchy wanted to keep this find to themselves. All papers just referenced the craft in general terms, calling it, "The Object." But there was a warning at the top of each page. *Ultra Top Secret. This File For the Air Force Intelligence Commanding General's Eyes Only. Other Readers Subject To Wartime Espionage Punishment Laws.* These laws, Brandon knew, carried the maximum penalty of death and were written for crimes against the United States, not against an Air Force General's office and filing procedures.

Brandon also noted that the President, the Secretary of State, the Speaker of the House, and the Secretary of the Air Force were excluded. He wondered how many other Ollie Norths and unelected others were running around inside "his" government making up national policy.

He looked at the water glass and whiskey, extracted the CD and put it in his shirt pocket, turned off and closed the laptop, put it under his feet, and went to sleep, thinking of Jane and wondering if he was up to living with her, or anyone, for long, considering his background.

A half hour later he half-woke with a start and looked around, listening.

First he thought he heard a foreign dialect. Not unusual on an international flight, but it seem overly loud and animated. Then he became wide awake, thinking of the last big lesson from his parents who disliked the idea of him becoming a Navy Seal. They wanted a law profession for him after Harvard or a career in chemistry, his high school obsession. But they were also realists and experts at survival.

"Use your imagination," his mother would say, "and prepare for what is the worst and best that you can imagine. Einstein often said that imagination is more important than knowledge. You have the knowledge. Cultivate your imagination as if it were a garden, a bonsai tree. You have chosen a dangerous profession. Wits, calmness, and knowledge are not enough. Use your imagination, your feelings. They will also be your friends."

As these thoughts went through Brandon's mind, he pulled a magazine out of the seat pocket in front of him and a pen from his shirt pocket and worked on a crossword puzzle.

While scribbling a letter onto the square of 34-down, he first heard, then looked up and saw, both the pilot and co-pilot talking with three men through the partially open door to the cockpit. One questioned the pilot in an excited manner, waving a small pistol, then turned his head back and talked to the two behind him in Farsi or Arabic. Brandon couldn't tell.

Brandon squinted, listened, and concentrated, trying to see both pilot and co-pilot's hands. After he was sure that none were on the flight controls, he had his confirmation that the aircraft was on autopilot. And, he reasoned, the cockpit door was left partly open to give some passenger a view of the proceedings.

He opened the face of one of his pearl cufflinks, dumped its powdery contents into the glass of water on his tray, and watched it bubble, sending sleeping gas into the plane's recirculated air. Then he set it on the floor under his seat next to the aisle. He pretended to be asleep while holding his breath and slowly getting a pen knife from his right pants pocket.

Thirty seconds later, he heard two shots in quick succession. *Probably fired in desperation just before passing out*, he thought, while opening an eye slightly and seeing the last of the three terrorists by the cockpit door drop to the floor.

He then rose from his seat, walked past the sleeping passengers to the forward flight attendant station, and opened the emergency first-aid cabinet. Inside was the standard portable oxygen bottle that all airliners carried. He strapped the mask over his face, tucked the bottle through his belt, and turned on the valve, reading the quantity gauge. Then he grabbed a plastic cup from the forward steward counter, filled it with water, and dumped the contents of his other cufflink into it.

Next he went to the cockpit, leaned over the center console, and read the altitude, geographical position, and engine settings displayed on three television screens, one in front of each pilot seat and another in the middle of the instrument panel . . . called a "glass cockpit."

Then he checked the pilots. One was shot in the left shoulder, the other in the back. Emergency escape ropes were in their usual airliner compartments in the ceiling panel over the two pilot seats. He retrieved one rope, tied up one sleeping terrorist, and killed the others with well-placed esophagal kicks.

The radio squawked questions about flight intentions. He gently carried the pilot and co-pilot to the first class section, placing them in two vacant seats, and locked their seatbelts on. Then, looking around, he checked that the several dozen passengers in his field of view were still sleeping peacefully. He put the tied-up terrorist in the captain's seat and strapped him in, placing earphones on his head. It took a precious minute to drag the dead men to the forward lavatory. After a quick body search, he took a pistol and two extra ammo clips from one of them and went back to the first class section. He sat down in one of the plush seats, looked at his watch, and unstrapped the oxygen mask, holding it on his mouth.

After a few minutes, groggy people started waking up. The first to move was a flight attendant on the floor in the forward galley. She staggered around, wondering what had happened. Then she looked at the pilot and co-pilot in two of the passenger seats and wondered who was flying the plane.

Brandon watched carefully. One of the passengers behind him got out of his seat and moved toward the cockpit. Brandon waited. The man was hesitant at first, then walked faster. When he was in a position to see the terrorist in the captain's seat and no one else around, he said something to him in Arabic. A second later, with no response, Brandon saw him pull a gun from his coat and turn around. Brandon shot him in the forehead.

Now many people were awake and screaming. Brandon got up and asked the flight attendant for some help, stating that things were under control and that they were all out of immediate danger. She looked at him wide-eyed, still in shock, not knowing whom to trust, as he pulled the third body toward the forward lavatory and piled it on top of the others.

Brandon said that he just needed her to show him where the switch was for the intercom phone in the cockpit and to tell the other flight attendants to open the bar for the passengers. She looked at the pilot and co-pilot unconscious in passenger seats, one groaning slightly, and now wondered who was going to land the plane. Brandon read her mind and said in a soft voice that it was a good thing he knew how to fly.

She followed him to the cockpit. The tied terrorist glared hatefully. She handed Brandon the public address telephone receiver as he said that he would like her to say something after he was finished. Then he turned to the terrorist and said he hoped he understood English, because if he made an interruption, it would be his last.

"Ladies and gentlemen," began Brandon. "My name is Brandon. I am a trained air marshall," he lied. "This aircraft, as some of you may have noted, was almost highjacked by terrorists after trying to put everyone to sleep with a non-lethal gas. So if you feel groggy from your short nap or wonder why you missed part of the movie, that is the reason. The highjackers are now neutralized. But some in front were injured. So, as they say, if there is a doctor in the house, it would be appreciated if you would come forward. The plane is being flown just fine. Expect arrival at Gatwick on time, a few minutes past midnight. Also, I've asked the flight attendant," he read her name tag again, "Judy, to make an announcement."

Judy said that everything was fine and that free drinks would be available to all.

"I'll lock the cockpit door after you've left," said Brandon. "Call me on the intercom if something comes up. And don't let anyone into the forward lavatory."

"Right, I'll do what first-aid I can to the pilots if no doctors appear," she said on her way out, just beginning to sense that things were going to be okay.

Brandon pulled the terrorist back out of the left seat and onto the floor behind the center console, then retrieved the escape rope from above the copilot's seat and cinched him even tighter. The man said in English, "You will be dead shortly."

Brandon rolled him onto his side, broke one arm with a sharp kick, rolled him over, and broke the other. Then he positioned him so that he could see the man's face from the pilot's seat. After a quick look at the instruments, he got in the pilot's seat, found the microphone radio control box and switched to CAS, cockpit area speakers, so he wouldn't have to fool with earphones. Then he placed the captain's lip mike holder on his head, adjusted it to his mouth, and again checked the instruments. Level at thirty two thousand feet, heading zero six five. He looked at the transponder setting and first switched it to code 1000 for highjacking, then reset it to 1111, the code for an emergency condition. The codes would be read by every ground radar station within hundreds of miles.

The radio squawked: "TWA 450, come in, over."

"TWA 450," said Brandon.

"Do you have a problem?" asked British ATC.

"Not a major one," said Brandon. "There was a case of food poisoning here. Most everyone is unaffected. But the pilots are in serious shape and will require emergency care on landing, perhaps a surgeon. I am an ex-military pilot and can land this aircraft if you tell me the numbers and switchology. These glass cockpits with the computerized TV screens for instruments are readable but unfamiliar to me. Please have a pilot who is qualified in this aircraft get on the radio. Right now we are on autopilot and maintaining heading and altitude with an ETA to Gatwick, according to the computer screen, of one hour, ten minutes."

British ATC said that 450 was being read loud and clear and to stand by.

Brandon transmitted, "While I'm standing by, could you send a message to the U.S. White House Communications Center. Tell them, 'Gemini 4'. That's 'G-e-m-i-n-i, f-o-u-r,'" he spelled out.

"Gemini 4, roger TWA 450."

"Thanks," said Brandon as he adjusted his shoulder harness and checked the passed-out terrorist on the floor.

Lima, Peru: March 8, 1999

General Espinoza reviewed the surveillance videotapes from the airport at Lima and knew he must have the Sapa Inca under his control. The still photographs made of all five Inca faces were faxed to the future ambassador. Bloomquist sounded excited on the phone when he received them, saying that he had seen two of the men before in London. Espinoza said that all was going according to plan on the plane and the Azores, that his teams were in place. Bloomquist hung up the phone and was driven to the Metropolitan Club in his limousine. In spite of his millions, he still needed this monthly poker game more than ever. It offered support for his shallow ego.

Washington, D.C.: March 8, 1999

Pitman pulled the unusually thick manila envelope from his pants and handed it to Allie. It contained the records of all the pilot officers and civilian engineers who were stationed at Groom Lake in Nevada during the past fifty years. She asked him to make her a cup of tea while she "perused."

He had not had the time or desire to review the documents. *Besides*, he thought while microwaving, *that's her area. Analytical brainwork.* Then he measured and added a half ounce of cream to her tea.

"And so we have some of it!" she exclaimed as he came into the living room with her cup. "Have you read any of this?" she asked.

"Not yet," he said.

"Well, this is a sick society," she added sadly.

"So what now?" asked Pitman.

"The 'what,' " said Allie, "is that they are all dead."

"How?" asked Pitman, surprised.

"Well, here we have a suicide," began Allie while flipping through the pages Pitman had brought. "Here we have an automobile accident, here we have pneumonia . . . there is a white-water rafting accident followed by drowning, a bar fight, two kidney failures, and an undiagnosed disease. But these things are not important. What matters is the pattern. They were all involved with the strange machine. And except for Osborn, who passed away in 1967, they all died, even the old retired ones from the 1950s, during the time this General Johnston was, and is, in charge of the project, starting in December, 1989. First, except for Osborn, the old ones died between 1990 and 1992. Then, from 1993 to this year the younger ones, the pilot officers, six of them, met sudden and strange deaths . . . all of them save Osborn, old and young, except the Commander and his deputy, Johnston and Bobarski, died while Johnston was in command."

"This may be circumstantial evidence," Pitman offered.

"Yes," said Allie. "The circumstances show that the actuarial probability of this many people involved in the same effort and then meeting their untimely demises during the same peacetime conditions, is perhaps one in ten trillion. The circumstances dictate loudly that these people were all murdered. And how is it that Johnston has stayed in command there now for ten years. I thought the maximum military tour of command was four years."

"In some cases it becomes political," said Pitman. "Admiral Rickover, the 'Father of the Nuclear Navy', for example, stayed in the same position for about twenty years."

"I see," said Allie.

"I'll talk to the Air Force," said Pitman. "But for now, you have a card game to play and, even with my poor hearing, there is a taxi honking outside." She hugged and kissed him before stepping out the door, vowing to give it a try.

The cab pulled up in front of the Metropolitan Club, two blocks northwest of the White House. She handed the driver a twenty and got out. Tipping was a thing with her. Pitman did 20 percent. She did double that, if it happened to be in her purse, which was usually the case. The time was 8:20 P.M. Charles met her at the door, expecting her, telling her that her husband's message had just been delivered, ready to accommodate her every wish.

There should be many more professionals like Charles in the world, she thought, as he escorted her through the high ceiling, lavishly mirrored, thick-carpeted main room to the round table of green felt surrounded by soft, elegant, wood-framed upright chairs, cigar smoke, and the strong smell of power.

Five men rose politely, almost in unison, as she approached. Two reached to draw her chair back.

What a chauvinistic place, she thought, wondering if this was going to be worth the airplane. She sat down and fidgeted with a barrette in her hair before speaking.

"Good evening gentlemen," she said introducing herself. "As you know, my husband has been coming to this game for many years. The fact that he sent me, so you wouldn't be short a player, should indicate how important it is to him."

At least the woman knows her place, went through the minds of three at the table.

"And, how is he?" asked Summers.

"Just a touch of the flu. I hope the three-day variety. Nothing to worry about. And he has told me your names, but not your faces," she added.

They introduced themselves, and a short period of silence descended as they sat back down. Then Burgess, the Undersecretary of State for Mid-eastern Affairs, asked if she might like something to drink.

"Charles is getting it, thank you," she said. "What I need is to know the game and the stakes. Though primarily a bridge player, I am familiar with the rules of poker."

Polite and agreeable harrumphs and murmurings, mixed with card shuffling and money counting, took the strain away from everyone. Allie was handed the cards. She could name the game for her deal. The ante was ten dollars. She shuffled, then put the deck in front of the man on her left for the cut, and said, "Montana Red Dog. Some call it Indian Poker."

None had heard of the game. She explained that it was just an ice breaker. Each player got one card and, without looking at it, placed it against his forehead and held it there so everyone could see it but him. Then with their other hand they could place their bets in the usual manner.

They looked at her in stony silence. She dealt one card to each. When the first reached, she said, "No. Each one of you has to place it while everyone else is watching. Mr. King, to my left will go first."

Soon, five men and one woman were sitting in the most exclusive private club in the most important city in the most important country in the world holding cards to their foreheads. Allie looked at the other cards. One ace. One king. Two sevens. One four. Everyone passed. She bet fifty dollars. Palmer, with the ace, folded. Bloomquist, who had a seven, called her fifty and raised fifty. The rest folded. Allie called him. Bloomquist put his card down. It was one of the sevens. Allie had a five. He eyed her expectantly while raking in the ten and twenty dollar bills.

She reached for her drink and took a sip while looking at her watch. Then they started playing "real poker." Mostly five card draw, nothing wild. Allie looked hard at Bloomquist as he dealt. The patch over his eye seemed to quiver when his naked eye looked around the table.

War wound? I wonder, she thought while asking for a hit. After three hours, Allie had accumulated five thousand dollars, Bloomquist seven, and she had found out nothing, the same as Andy. She looked at her watch and said, "It has been enjoyable, but my pumpkin time approaches. So perhaps one more lap around the court for me."

Summers, to her right, dealt. It was a good hand for four of the six players, which is a rare thing for five card draw and nothing wild. Allie had two pair, aces over queens, and took a card. A queen. The others placed drawn cards in hands while Allie concentrated on observing Bloomquist who, on the opposite side of the table, also took one card. Part of his left cheek twitched when arranging his hand. And his one visible eyelid fluttered sporadically for a second.

She was the first bettor and pushed out a hundred dollars. Bloomquist's good eye stared at her for a second, utterly cold and unblinking, like a fish, sending a slight shiver up her spine. Everyone folded except Summers, who called with three jacks. *Okay Allie*, she thought. *Don't mess it up. It's your first and last chance tonight.*

Her total concentration was on Bloomquist's cards. He had thrown them face down on the table when folding. She memorized the positions. Summers methodically pulled them together in one small stack, like a trick in bridge, and placed them under the remainder of the deck he was holding. Before raking in her pile of bills she quickly turned her cards over and pushed them toward Mr. Summers. Then she placed the new money to her right, pretending to add the numbers on the bills, while seeing her cards go directly under Bloomquist's cards, and then announced, "Same game, five card draw, nothing wild."

As they all murmured approval, she almost grabbed the deck out of Summers' hand, and began to shuffle, cards cupped, all barely touching, only the top half of the deck meshing.

She read the cards as they flashed between her thumbnails. Three, ace, seven, nine, jack, ace, ace, queen, queen, queen.

She looked around the table while again meshing the top halves of the split deck. Then she did it again. Spade, spade, spade, spade, spade, ace, ace, queen, queen, queen. No mistake. Bloomquist made his ace-high flush, but had folded against her unknown full-house.

She took a large swallow of her drink and motioned Charles to get her another.

"I think I'm in for the duration," she said while dealing. "Well, at least until half past."

Everyone was glad of it. For the next fifteen minutes she didn't care what her cards were. She drew to nothing. Folding early gave her more time to observe Bloomquist. And he kept winning.

Andy was right.

My poor Andy, she thought. *This is driving me up the wall in one evening. He took it for over a year.*

Two hands later, Bloomquist turned toward Charles and placed a finger in the air for a drink. Allie noticed that the bottom lobe of Bloomquist's left ear was of a grey color. When he turned back, she could see that the shape of both lobes matched perfectly, but that the other was pink. Thoughts of heart conditions, different vascular pressures, and perhaps some sort of ear cosmetics, whipped through her mind. Then suddenly his head jerked slightly to one side. A small jerk. Something that she wouldn't have noticed had she not been looking directly at him.

Perhaps just a quirk, she thought, *that a lot of older people develop.*

After the next hand, Bloomquist made a quick apology, and nervously, thought Allie, rose from the table, made his apologies, and left the game. Allie played until the game ended, thanked the table, and stuffed her winnings in her purse. She got home at eleven. Pitman was up reading.

"Could you fix me something?" she asked while hanging up her coat.

"Sure," he said, placing his book on the coffee table. "Anything in particular?" he added. "Sandwich, tea, drink . . . all three?"

"A drink, not too strong, surprise me," she said while going up the stairs to get out of her clothes and into a robe. He fixed a kind of hot toddy . . . tea from the microwave, a little bourbon, and a cinnamon stick. He put it on the coffee table and picked up his book. By the time she came down it was cool enough to drink.

She sat down, took a sip, and said, "You were right. The man cheats. Though I couldn't catch him, I think he is catchable. Not what I would call a sophisticated cheater, though it might be difficult to prove if he cheats at all."

"How so?" he asked. "I would think the difficulty of proving it would make him sophisticated."

"Well, no. Anyone can cheat if they know the other person's cards some of the time," she said. "If they know the other person's cards all the time, then I would say a sophisticated cheater would still allow himself to lose at least once in a while. This guy never lost one single damn time when he bet after the draw. I caught him folding after drawing to, and getting, an ace-high flush. I had a full house, also with a one card draw. Now what kind of a ninny poker player would do that?"

"I see what you mean. He never lost when betting after the draw that I can recall either. But I find it difficult to believe that someone with his background could be that dumb. I mean, just the politics of it could be considered inane, and he is a political animal."

"You're separating dumbness from politics? As if they are mutually exclusive?" asked Allie.

"Point taken. Where do we go from here?" asked Pitman.

"Okay," she said. "If I'm going to earn a whole airplane, I'll have to have more information."

"Like what?" he asked.

"Like who the hell he is. I mean who *and* what. A history and profile."

"That should be easy enough to get," he said.

"No," she said. "I mean everything possible to get that's not in official records . . . a chronology of his life, going back as far as possible, every trip, every mistress, if any. For starters I want to know what the story is on that goddamn eyepatch. I can't believe it's from a Korean war wound. It twitches too much. Eye movement muscles atrophy after many years of non-use like any others. There must have been witnesses to the operation, doctors who worked on it, who may still be alive today. And his left earlobe is a slightly different color than his right."

"This will take some time, dear," said Pitman. "My people should get the base information within the week. Brandon is out of the country, as you know. And it'll take longer without him if there are any major snags. We should know if Inca Indians are going to be kidnapped by then."

"Brandon may be out of the country, but Chauncy is in. Did you forget that?" she asked as she rose from the couch to peck him on the cheek before retiring.

"Chauncy's out too," said Pitman fidgeted with a button on his shirt. She noticed.

"Helping Brandon, I suppose," she said.

"Now that I'm almost retired, in accordance with your wishes I might add," said Pitman. "Chauncy works more for Brandon than me. Anything else?" he asked.

"Yes. Did you notice any unusual jewelry worn by Bloomquist?"

"Yes, he was always wearing something strange, unusual gold tie clasps, lapel pins, huge rings," he said.

"Always gold?" she asked.

"Mostly. Sometimes turquoise imbedded in gold. Why?" he asked.

"Any bracelets?"

"Yes," said Pitman. "He did occasionally wear a bracelet of one sort or another."

"Well," she said, leaning over and giving him a rub on the back, "he was wearing a bracelet tonight. The half I could see from under his shirt cuff was thick and wide and gold and old. The engraved designs were exquisite, and the inset jewels were rough-cut. They looked pre-Colombian . . . maybe Incan, which means Peruvian."

* * *

The telephone rang just before midnight. It was from the CIA duty desk to Pitman. He rolled over, pressed the receiver into his ear, and looked at Allie who was staring at him intently in the dim light.

"It's a message from London," he said, reaching up to turn on the lamp. "Probably about Brandon," he added.

Allie felt apprehensive. Pitman appreciated her not rubbing it in about sending him in the first place. When Pitman heard the word "Gemini" he exhaled with relief. It meant that a life-threatening attempt had been successfully overcome. The number 'four' was another code for "continuing on to the scheduled destination, or with the scheduled plan."

A minute later the Duty Office confirmed that Brandon was aboard a London bound TWA flight over the Atlantic, heading toward England, with an ETA of one hour. Pitman turned to Allie and said, "Gemini four. Highjackers probably."

Allie breathed a sigh and rolled over saying, "Foiled highjackers, I think."

Chapter Four

Lima, Peru: March 8, 1999

General Espinoza received a call from the Azores. The plane had not landed. There had been no radio contact from his people on the aircraft. The pilot had requested that a message called "Gemini Four" be sent to Washington. Nothing else unusual. He called the airline.

"Yes, it's on time, sir," came the bright answer from the reservationist. He then called Bloomquist's pager, wondering if any information was available from his end. A few minutes later Bloomquist called him from the Metropolitan Club.

Bloomquist knew nothing and was agitated. Espinoza said not to worry, that he had men in London who would take care of it at the other end.

After he hung up the phone, the General called the Savoy Hotel in London. His team would be at the airport. The Indians would be taken care of, information extracted, and death for all, regardless of information received. He couldn't afford any interference with the drug business. If Bloomquist is right, thought Espinoza, and there is that much gold, and if somehow it got in the hands of these Incas, they may then have the financing to shut him down. The possible threat had to be eliminated. He would, he decided, play along, and continue to manipulate Bloomquist, until this threat to his drug empire was over.

TWA Flight 450—Scheduled non-stop, Lima to London: March 8, 1999

Brandon got the "hard numbers" from a Boeing 777 pilot at London ATC Center: "Stall speed 'dirty,' with flaps and gear down, slats out, is ninety-six knots. Approach speed with the wind here gusting to ten knots is a hundred thirty-five."

"And what's the stall speed gear *up*, flaps and slats down and out?" asked Brandon, checking.

"Ha!" said the 777 pilot. "Same speed. Ninety-six knots. Didn't know I was talking to an aero-engineer."

These numbers Brandon would watch like a hawk on the computer-generated pictures of instruments on the TV screens in the cockpit. The rest would be a walk in the park, he thought: select the ILS (instrument landing system) approach into Gatwick on the computer and the airplane would automatically fly to the runway. As instructed, Brandon punched the APP button on the center console to engage the automatic approach function of the autopilot. Then, given choices on the computer screen, he selected Gatwick Airport.

ATC talked him down to ten thousand feet, thirty miles to the airport, and gave him the go-ahead. Brandon watched the TV pictures of the attitude gyro and airspeed indicators in front of him. Nothing happened except the letters *LOC* and *GS* were printed in white letters at the bottom of the screen. He noticed no change in aircraft movement and transmitted, "Nothing much is happening."

The 777 pilot on the ground asked if he had the letters *LOC* and *GS* printed on the screen in white letters with Gatwick selected.

Brandon said, "Yes."

"Then the system is set. The aircraft will automatically intercept the Localizer and Glide Slope. If you do nothing else, the aircraft will land itself, deploy the spoilers on the top surfaces of the wings to destroy all lift on touchdown, and apply wheel brakes. It will engage the anti-skid system, maintain heading, and bring the aircraft to a stop in the middle of the runway. If any of these things don't happen, and you've flown heavy equipment before, not to worry, it's a beautiful airplane to land by hand. If something looks wrong, and you don't feel you have time to discuss it, jam the throttles full forward and go around. We can talk about it more then. Dispatch shows you have an hour of reserve fuel."

The deep, soothing voice of experience made Brandon feel better. He was glad the man on the ground had used the word "beautiful." An unnecessary word under the circumstances, but one that lent him confidence. A pilot's word.

"Thanks," said Brandon. "I've flown some heavy equipment, though nothing this big. Anything else I should know?"

"Stay on automatic for now. The controls may move around more the closer in you get, but don't worry about that. Concentrate on the speeds and configuration. If you need to miss any other traffic, you can manually override the automatic system with muscle power. But we're clearing all other aircraft under our control from your route."

"Roger," said Brandon as he watched the screen. The engine power decreased and the aircraft turned toward a spot in the sky east of Gatwick Airport. Then a tiny rectangle appeared at the top of the left TV screen. He didn't know what it was, and made a mental note to ask about it later, while concentrating on the other TV instruments. All looked good. The airspeed dropped smoothly below two hundred. The aircraft banked nicely to intercept the course to the runway centerline. Rate of descent was rock-steady at seven hundred feet per minute.

He looked again at the rectangle on the left screen. It had gotten larger and was a different shape, more of a trapezoid, strangely getting larger. As the airspeed dropped below a hundred and fifty he noticed something in front of him through the glass outside the windshield . . . a trapezoid similar to the one he had seen a minute before. He looked back to the trapezoid on the TV screen. They were the same size except for the coloring. He thought about how the one on the TV screen could be reflected onto the windshield of the aircraft and looked behind him for a mirror of some sort. Something was wrong, he thought. Then he saw some color around the trapezoid through the windshield. Little blue taxi lights. He looked again at almost the same image on the TV screen and back again through the windshield, and it dawned on him. The TV trapezoid was a computer-generated picture of what the runway should look like at Gatwick from the cockpit. The trapezoid through the windshield was the runway at Gatwick. The real runway.

Not bad, thought Brandon as he monitored the instruments. "Not bad at all. Maybe too good," he mumbled as a reminder to keep vigilant.

He checked the airspeed, landing gear, and flap indicators, then noticed a slight movement on the floor. The terrorist, bound tightly, with both forearms broken, was awake, and eyed Brandon maliciously. The man had a string in his mouth and was methodically pulling it in from the lapel of his shirt collar. Brandon looked further down. The pant leg was drawn up a few inches above the sock. And the "flesh" of the hairless leg gleamed back.

Plastic, his mind knew instantly, realizing he couldn't unstrap from the pilot seat and move to the man in time. He pulled the pistol from his coat pocket and fired. The bullet went through thickest part of the highjacker's forehead, *Where Hindus paint their red dots*, he thought. He wanted to keep one of them alive to question later. But the expression on the man's face and actions precluded taking that chance.

He punched the release buckle on his lap belt while placing the pistol on the center console and leaped with knife in hand. Surgically, he cut the man's pants up to the waist. The leg was covered with plastic explosive. The thin lanyard drooping from the man's mouth may have triggered something. Brandon followed it down to a standard grenade-type blasting cap: a small, sealed container that leaked acid onto a copper wire that held back a strong spring. Once started, it could not be deactivated. When the wire was eaten through, the spring-held firing pin would instantly set off the blasting cap, which in turn would detonate the plastic, blowing the entire cockpit to pieces.

He had about five seconds, he thought, as he ripped the blasting cap away from the plastic leg and threw it into the captain's leather map bag while kicking the cockpit door with his foot. As the door sprung open, three flight attendants looked at him apprehensively. He grabbed the bag, barreled through the doorway, set it down in the middle of the floor outside the cockpit, and then leaped toward them spread-eagled, trying to cover as much of their bodies with his as he could.

The noise was deafening. Leather and maps from the bag went everywhere, helping to dissipate the explosion. Brandon lay on the floor with the three flight attendants under him. He held them tightly in a group trying to keep his voice calm while saying over and over, "Everything's okay now ladies, everything's *really* okay."

Soon they squirmed from under him, looking around. Then the entire aircraft was sharply jolted, and two of them dove back under him. The senior flight attendant, Judy, heard the sound of healthy engines at full thrust and stood up for a second, then was forced forward, falling painfully against wall. The full reverse engine thrust and wheel braking had caused a sharp deceleration in the forward motion of the plane. Brandon waited until there was no more aircraft movement or loud engine sound, then got up on his knees and said, "Ladies, we have just landed at Gatwick Airport.

Please assume your duties and inform the passengers of where we are and that there will be a short delay in getting off the plane."

Judy helped him onto his feet, and after looking out the nearest window at the familiar Gatwick terminal, she stood on her toes to where her calves ached and kissed him on the mouth harder that she had ever read about anyone kissing anyone. He held her, wide-eyed with surprise as the cockpit radio asked him for a status.

* * *

While the fire engines and evacuation people were pulling up to the aircraft with sirens and lights blazing, Brandon inspected the body in the cockpit, cutting the cloth from the arms and chest. He noticed a small tattoo of crossed cutlasses below the right nipple. "Another terrorist group, probably," he said to himself. The forward door opened, and the British Secret Service entered, calmly and professionally sending for medical help and arranging for an orderly, controlled, and closely observed deplaning of passengers and crew.

Georgetown, Washington, D.C.: March 9, 1999

Allie woke late. Pitman was at work in conference, she thought. Didn't want to bother him. Her question could wait. She put a robe on and went downstairs to brew the coffee he always left under the bean grinding machine. Sipping it silently while looking out the window, she wrinkled her forehead in concentration, and again connected with what had transpired in her concentration shortly before completely waking up.

Perhaps it was nothing. But it was a thought. *And thoughts*, she mused, *were the only things that lasted in the history of human experience*.

Then she took out a pad of paper and started writing things in sequence.

Item: A call in the middle of the night about Brandon.
Item: Bloomquist twitching at eleven-thirty Washington time, then leaving the game.
Item: The time difference between Washington and an hour west of London.
Item: Nothing more on Brandon. Big highjacking attempt on the news.

She looked at the list, deducing, remembering about what time Bloomquist jerked his head and left. It could have been pretty close to right after the actual time of the unsuccessful highjacking. She slowly balled up the paper and burned it in a nearby ashtray. Then she heard the fax machine start humming in the library.

Gatwick Airport, London: March 9, 1999

Brandon identified himself and was immediately escorted off the plane under guard. After twenty minutes of questioning and going through his carry-on bag, Brandon said he did not now have time to go through normal customs procedure and handed them a telephone number. They made the call to the Prime Minister's office and let him go without a body search.

"It's a big story," said one inspector as Brandon left the room. "Four terrorists-highjackers killed by a passenger. Then you landed the plane miraculously."

"Give the credit to the people who built the plane," said Brandon. "The plane landed itself. Boeing is where the credit goes."

He walked out of the terminal just as the BBC News crew was going in a few doors away. Chauncy and Matlock were there watching everything outside the terminal. They hadn't followed anyone because they didn't know who to follow. But Matlock had videotaped everyone who left and zoomed in on all the car and taxi license plates as they departed the terminal.

"Any Indians?" asked Brandon.

"Great instructions," answered Chauncy. "Let's see, there were twenty-three Indians from India, all wrapped in colored sheets with red dots painted on their foreheads and wearing sandals. Or did you mean Indians with feather head-dresses?"

Brandon said to never mind; they would go over everything in the hotel.

"Why are all these ambulances and news trucks here with people wheeling large cameras inside?" asked Chauncy.

"Just believe that, though the flight was on time, Chaunce, it was not a normal flight. Tell you about it later."

They spent the next hour in their hotel suite looking at the videotapes.

"That's them!" said Brandon.

"Indians in suits?" asked Matlock.

"Yes, Indians in three-piece suits," answered Brandon. "Indians from Peru. Incan Indians."

"Nice shot of the back of the cabbie," said Chauncy to Matlock as he watched the Incas enter the vehicle. "Looks like plate number CD 819."

"Yes," said Brandon. "Why don't you two trace it with the cab company

70

while I set everything up for a quick exit with the Air Force. But don't do anything without calling me first. I'm the one with a gun," he added, pulling the plastic Glok pistol with silencer, and two cartridge clips from the back of his pants.

"Jesus, where did you get that?" asked Chauncy. "You know unregistered guns are illegal in England."

"One of the passengers on the plane was obliging enough to give it up. I would have gotten another, but figured it would have pushed my luck with Scotland Yard if they decided on a search."

The Kremlin, Moscow: March 9, 1999

The Russian President read the report from his chief scientist. There were crude maps inside the craft. One of them showed that two other similar vehicles may exist, one at the bottom of the Atlantic Ocean, the other in the Andes Mountains in Peru. He issued orders to activate his best double agent, Wanda, and to plant 'information seeds' with one of his organization's secondary operatives, General Espinoza. And hour later he was informed that Espinoza had already contacted Wanda.

Chapter Five

Georgetown, Washington, D.C.: March 10, 1999

Pitman came home finding Allie excited. He handed her his packet of papers and mentioned that he hadn't had much luck uncovering anything more than what he had faxed her earlier.

"Just a bunch of data," he said.

"What kind of data?" she asked.

"Well, the manifest of passengers on that flight for one, and why are you so excited?"

"Does it show that easily?" she asked.

"Your eyes are as big and shiny as brand new silver dollars. And I've known you a while. I would say you are excited."

"Let me fix you a scotch while I talk," she said while placing the papers on the coffee table and heading for the sideboard. He sat down and watched the pouring ritual while absentmindedly untying his shoes.

"The information you sent this morning is good," she said. "I got some more this afternoon. Half an airplane's worth, I'd say. The second half."

"Good God, you figured out *how* Bloomquist cheats?" exclaimed Pitman.

"I've got enough information now, I think, to prove how he does it. Enough circumstantial evidence to get a new airplane if I'm right."

She handed him his drink and began talking before sitting in the opposite chair. Pitman leaned forward slightly to catch every word.

"The information consists of some things that I remembered from the poker game, the detailed report you sent on Bloomquist's background, and some things I got from my friend Thelma at the Washington Post.

"Bloomquist," she began, "came from a fairly wealthy family with new money, clothing industry money. He had some sort of falling out with his gold-bricking stepmother in the middle of his doctoral work in engineering at MIT. He joined the Army, and was sent to Korea, where he got the Purple Heart for taking some shrapnel in the face and side of his head. A medical discharge followed for losing sight in one eye, hence the big black patch.

"Shortly after his return to the U.S., his father died and left everything to him and a small but comfortable stipend to his stepmother. There were no other siblings. He took over the business and, in a few years, sold it piecemeal to buy interests in several other companies, all outside the United States, all technical. He probably hated being called a clothier. He never went back to school. He married an Eurasian, a beautiful half-English, half-Bali woman from Repulse Bay, over the hill from Hong Kong proper, in the late fifties. No children. Then he settled down in California and began contributing heavily to the political scene. His ambassadorship was bought by years of steady and strong financial support and by holding several appointed positions that no one else wanted. But they showed the loyalty he constantly cultivated. Vice chairman of his party at the state level was the first. The list is long.

"In the early eighties he began buying interests in American companies. But he never sold any of his other businesses. He probably thought he had a chance for some high political office, but couldn't be considered if he exhibited little faith in the American system. And he had to leverage himself highly to do it without actually selling any of his foreign assets. Then the market crashed in 1987. He had worked out a margin deal with the banks that gave him a few years to spring for the cash. And he may have run into some problems there, like borrowing more with one hand to fend off the latest creditor with the other.

"Now comes the interesting part. . . . In college, he first majored in ancient history, then he switched to engineering. But get this, his doctoral thesis was working in electro-optics!"

She looked at him smugly.

"I don't follow. I don't see what that means," said Pitman.

"Sorry," she said. "I haven't given you all the information yet. I'm trying to get the order right in my mind.

"During the poker game, I watched him carefully. His one eye would twitch around the table, then stop suddenly, staring at a player for what seemed a long time. Then it would rove again, and stop on the face of a different player. The eye would do this to all at the beginning of each hand, and after each draw. I thought he was just trying to read something in the expression of the other players when they got their hands and drew cards. And I didn't think any more on it. But once, while I was watching him, his eye focused on me as I was looking at him. We stared at one another for a good fifteen seconds with no change of expression in his face, then his eye looked, not just away, but to a different player, staring the same way. My feeling at the time was, 'How mechanical.'

"Now for the final piece. Guess what his largest and oldest foreign company is?"

"Mitsubishi?" asked Pitman.

"Close," said Allie. "Country close. It's an ex-subsidiary of Fujitsu Corporation. It is called Kamasi!"

"You mean the makers of the most advanced cameras and optical equipment in the world?" asked Pitman.

"The very same," she said, while handing him a photograph of Bloomquist taken in a hospital in Korea in 1952.

Pitman looked at it carefully and said, "I've seen this in the newspapers. There was a write up on him last year, I think. It's in the public domain."

"The reproduced photograph is in the public domain," she said. "My friend Thelma got the original from the National Archives. This is just the original *published* newspaper picture," she said, pointing to it.

"So how is it different?" asked Pitman.

"See any little bottles hanging from the stand by the man in the hospital bed next to Bloomquist?"

"Yes, barely."

"Can you read the letters on the labels on the bottles?" she asked.

"No," he said, squinting closely.

"Now, look at the original 1952 photo from Thelma," she said, handing it to him. "It's larger and has more definition."

"Yes, I can see them on this one, but they don't make any sense," he said, adding, "They spell T-A-W and A-M-S. Don't know what they mean, but the S is backward."

"Exactly!" exclaimed Allie. "Not only is the S backward, but that means the other letters are backward also. The letters T, A, W, and M would look the same either backward or forward, but not the S. Which means that two half-words, T-A-W and A-M-S, are also backward and should correctly read W-A-T and S-M-A."

"And what words could they be part of?" he asked.

"Probably this," she wrote on a pad of paper: *WATer* and *plaSMA*. "Water and plasma," she said. "The complete labels, wrapped around the bottles, would have said, 'BLOOD PLASMA' and 'SALINE WATER'."

"Amazing," said Pitman.

"But the important thing," said Allie, "is that the photo was released by him years ago, and it's backward."

"Yes," said Pitman, finally getting it. "It shows that his patch is in the wrong place today. His right eye is the bad one, the one without the patch. If the original photograph were reversed, it would show that the bad eye in the Korean hospital is actually his 'good eye' today. And that his good eye today is covered with a patch!"

"C'est magnifique!" exclaimed Allie.

"And so," said Pitman, much pleased and impressed with her, "Bloomquist has been looking at people with a dead eye all these years, while his good eye has been hidden behind a seemingly black patch."

"That's right, Andy. And I'll bet my new airplane that there is an optical-electronic device behind that patch that is so refined that he has telescopic vision and could focus on a gnat's wing at a hundred feet."

Pitman paused to light his pipe, then asked, "So how does he cheat? That's the other half of the bet."

Allie concentrated. She wanted that new plane.

"He telescopes in," she said, "and focuses his good eye through the patch onto the other player's wet and reflective eyes or glasses, usually while they are looking at their own cards and holding their heads still. He sees their cards. He focuses on their cards while *they* are focusing on their cards. That's why he stared at me so long without blinking. He didn't even know I was staring at him. He was reading my cards being reflected off my own eyeballs!"

Pitman slapped his leg with admiration, then reached over and hugged her hard.

"Well, I'll be go-straight-to-hell!" he exclaimed, while letting her go and rising to get his checkbook from his briefcase.

Wright Paterson Air Force Base, Dayton, Ohio:
March 10, 1999

General Johnston and Colonel Bobarski sat on a sofa in the BOQ VIP suite at Wright Pat and reviewed the situation. There was mostly good news, but some discomforting things. Bobarski had destroyed all the records related to the craft in the administration building. But he had noted a difference in the order of two files which he had placed there himself. This prompted him to review all recent personnel activities and sign-in/sign-out logs on the Base. After careful analysis, subsequent interviews of duty personnel, and finally pulling up from the computer all photo IDs, he found that there were two Lieutenants named Robert Jones. They both had the same fingerprints. One had checked in and out for a weekend, followed by the other checking in on a Monday. The second was still there, and seemed to know nothing. The first had gained admittance to the administration building, then disappeared without a trace. Colonel Bobarski said he was worried.

Johnston said that even if someone else had gotten the documents, the Wright Pat records were incomplete. There was not even anything in them to show how to open the hatch, much less to actually operate the machine. Flight records were all transcripts of destroyed tapes, and even those were in the form of carefully blurred generalities of advanced computer simulation. "Kind of like the information we release under the Freedom Of Information Act," he added. "Besides, I have some good news."

Colonel Bobarski said he could use some.

"The Russians have contacted me," he said.

Bobarski sat up in his seat. This was indeed welcome. Their whole plan was based on a secure contact.

"How and when?" he asked.

"Recently, through the number code," said Johnston.

He had sent an envelope to the Russian Embassy. Inside was a list of two hundred seventy numbers, followed by the words, *New York Times, Two, Two*. The first number was twenty-nine. The twenty-ninth letter in the February second issue of the *Times* that year was R. The second number was 1,062. The one-thousandth sixty-second letter in the issue was E. The entire message told of what General Johnston had and what it was worth.

"So what did their message say?" asked Bobarski.

"Their envelope contained a list of over a thousand numbers. Then I got a phone call that said simply, 'Every other word beginning. Most recent *Ladies Home Journal*.' Sure enough, the first letter of every other word in the latest issue was the solution. It took me all night to count words and numbers. There is not a single missing letter. Of course I burned everything afterward.

"They have not only come close to meeting our monetary demands, but suggested a complete covert defection. They need our expertise. 'Documents can only provide so much,' they said."

"But we have never flown it," said Bobarski.

"Makes no difference," said Johnston. "They don't know that. Besides, there is no one else alive with any first-hand knowledge. And we can always use the Aeroflot airliner disaster as an example. Nice bit of flying too, even though the pilot was slightly drugged. Kind of a shame we couldn't use him again."

"What do they mean by a 'complete' covert defection?" asked Bobarski.

"Very interesting," said Johnston. "Their message said that we would be supplied first with close to the millions we asked for, in foreign accounts or however we wanted. Then, if we agreed to it, they would supply not only accidents, but bodies and identifications of us. We would live anywhere we wanted, but would have to travel on-site into Russia occasionally during further testing of the machine."

"What do you think?" asked Johnston.

"I think," said Colonel Bobarski, "that there is someone else out there, another person who had a pseudonym of 'Lieutenant Robert Jones', who has much information as we do that can be sold."

"That's a stickler," admitted Johnston. "But there was no indication of it from the Russians, and you know how much they like to bargain. Besides, we have the nuts of the information. The Wright Pat info was surface stuff that only proves the existence of the machine, not how to operate it."

"Yes," said Bobarski. "It would make sense for us to cash in and check out as quickly as possible."

"Then it is agreed," said Johnston. "I'll send them another message and tell of our non-acceptance of their offer. If we didn't ask for a few million more than our original offer, based on recent security developments, they wouldn't take us seriously."

London Suburbs: March 10, 1999

Chauncy called from a small shopping center on the seacoast at Devon. He had an address and could see lights in the house. Matlock was on the premise doing a reconnaissance. Brandon said he would be there in a half-hour.

Matlock kept in the shadows and trees by the road which ended at the door of one of several houses overlooking the ocean. He donned his night goggles, checked his equipment, and surveyed the house. All curtains were drawn. There was one man sitting on the front steps smoking a cigar and holding a radio. Matlock backtracked and crossed the road out of sight. In half an hour he had worked his way along the dunes by the beach and climbed under a part of the house that jutted over the cliff. There he carefully made three small holes under the floor with a small, silent, electric drill in a triangular pattern about a yard apart. In each hole he inserted a mini-microphone attached to a switch box and a set of standard earphones. He placed the earphones on his head and adjusted the switches on the box.

In five minutes he knew that there were five or six people in the house. They were well-grouped in the living room and dining area. Two people were definitely sitting at a table by the front window, one was standing by a sink close by, probably near a kitchen sink. He could hear water dripping and the garbage disposal came on once with a deafening noise through his sensitive earphones. The remaining two or three were in the middle of the room, one standing and one sitting in a squeaky chair. They all spoke Spanish except the one sitting in the center, who spoke a strange dialect that he had never heard. He connected a remote to the microphones, pulled the antenna out full length, attached it to the bottom of the house, and retraced his path along the dunes. By the time he got back, Brandon had arrived.

Brandon crouched into the back seat of Chauncy's car and listened intently to the conversation inside the house through the small headset. After a minute he said, "I don't think there is enough time to set up a normal extraction. They just killed one. Now they're starting on another. So I will go in, since I'm the only one with a gun. Wait five minutes, and then come in if you don't hear from me."

"You sure?" asked Chauncy, handing him his belt of stun grenades, tear gas, darts, and mace.

"Yes," said Brandon as he stepped out of the car, cinching the belt on tightly underneath his shirt. "Five minutes, unless you hear my radio mike keyed first. Then come in blasting."

Brandon walked up the side of the road, keeping in the shadows. The snug 7.62mm Glok fit neatly, almost invisibly even with the silencer, into his palm. At the front porch, next to a tall bush, Brandon casually walked out into the dim light, limping slightly and singing the song Molly Malone in a soft voice and English accent.

The guard started to rise inquisitively. Brandon's hand came up in a fluid motion, producing a 'phutt!' sound, and the guard slumped sideways, a small black hole in his forehead bleeding slowly.

Brandon tried the door. It was locked. He quickly went through the pockets of the dead guard and came up with a key ring. He looked at the lock and examined the keys. A choice of two. The first one turned the bolt in the door. *Best be fast*, he reminded himself.

He thrust the door back on its hinges and, with a quick look for obstacles, threw a stun canister into the living room, memorizing the positions of everyone. Then he closed his eyes, knelt down, and fired once. Five million candle power of light flashed in less than an eighth of a second into every crevasse of the house, followed by four rapid, ear-splitting booms. The man by the sink was dead during the flash. Bullets pounded the wall above and behind Brandon as he shot the second man and came up on one knee while opening his eyes. A third man was ducking to his right when Brandon's next two shots took off most of his right cheek and cheekbone and the fifth bullet went into his left eye. The fourth man was standing by one of the Indian hostages with a syringe in his hand, in shock, staring at one of the dead men. Brandon shot him in the temple and then replaced the nine shot ammunition clip in his pistol with the remaining fresh one.

Four of the Indians lay dead on the floor. The fifth had been bludgeoned but not yet drugged and no bones were broken. His eyes were swollen shut. Brandon keyed his lapel mike and called for Chauncy to come in, then checked for any further movement or sound inside the house while retrieving all the keys and wallets from the dead men.

Chauncy arrived while Brandon was untying the live Indian. He helped him to the sink to wash off his face. Chauncy checked the bodies and said, "Jesus Jess, these guys are armed! Look at this stuff! I'm glad the word prisoner wasn't in your vocabulary tonight."

Brandon washed off enough clotted blood from the Indian's eyes for him to see and then asked questions. All he could get was that his name was Tamac.

Lima, Peru: March 10, 1999

Espinoza paced the floor of his office. After the report from his people in the Azores, there had been no hourly report from his highjackers on the airliner. He called his assassin in London, Wanda, who had a reputation for loyalty to a contract, high fees in advance, and an almost perfect success record. When unsuccessful, or choosing not to follow through, the money was immediately returned to the client. Espinoza had used him on fourteen previous occasions and, after the third, gave him a million dollar retainer toward future employment at a moment's notice.

Espinoza asked Wanda to check the house in Devon where his team had gone from the London airport, where the Indians were supposed to be. An hour later Wanda called from his cellular phone a mile away from the house. He reported that the entire team and four Indians in the house were dead. Also, the local news media was reporting that several armed terrorists were found dead on the TWA airliner.

Espinoza asked if there was any information on what group or government could be responsible. Wanda said there was no sign at the house, but the news reported that several flight attendants and passengers had described a man that seemed to be in control and had flown the plane.

"*A* man?" seethed Espinoza. "*One single man?*"

"That's what they are reporting," said Wanda.

Espinoza snaked his tongue irritably over his graying mustache and nervously slicked down his jet-black dyed hair with his right hand. He felt the presence of a professional who was operating against him or perhaps against Bloomquist.

"Find out the goddamn name of this man," he said calmly. "And a description. Go to the customs people, airplane manifest, whatever. Call me when you have this information."

"Is that all?" asked Wanda.

"For now," said Espinoza. "But we need to talk in person soon. There are other problems developing."

Espinoza hung up the phone and punched at his computer keyboard. Half the wall next to his desk revolved and a giant screen appeared, a gift from one of Bloomquist's Japanese electronic companies. He gazed at his portfolio, noting the latest worth of his controlling interest in Telephonica del Peru and Banco Wiese. He typed other code numbers and new statistics appeared on the screen. The land transactions during the past year still bothered him. Huge tracts had been purchased for cash by native Peruvians unfamiliar to him. Many old Spanish families had cashed out and moved elsewhere in the world, some back to Spain. He had had several parcels investigated. All roads leading into them were blocked, some chained, some gated, two with moats and bridges. But his ground spies found no unusual activities inside. Just farming. It was too neat.

Georgetown, Washington, D.C.: March 10, 1999

"I came across something more during my research, Andy, that might be a connection," said Allie.

"Really?" Pitman answered, while seating himself at the table and unfolding his napkin.

"There's a footnote in an interesting history book," she said. "One that is such good journalism that it seems written yesterday."

"You mean a well-written history?" he interrupted.

"Well-researched and unbiased first," she said. "Then well-written. Over a hundred and fifty years ago. It reads like a current event. Ever heard of William Hickling Prescott?" she asked.

"No. Don't recall the name," said Pitman.

"Well, evidently some of the founding fathers at the Library of Congress agreed that he deserved to have some recognition for his work."

"And how did they do that?" he asked while watching her spear a slice of cucumber.

"They painted a picture of him with his name over one of the archways in our Library of Congress."

"You don't say," said Pitman. "What did he write?"

"Several histories having to do with Spain and the Spanish Conquest during the sixteenth century. His three main works are *Ferdinand and Isabella*, *The History of the Conquest of Mexico*, and the one I read last weekend, called *The History of the Conquest of Peru*."

"Sounds interesting. Does it shed any light on why virtually all the countries that were first taken over by the Spanish Catholics are in terrible shape today?"

"A little," she said. "Mostly an insight into their attitudes, which haven't changed much and which may prove useful in developing plans. They were a greedy and cruel bunch. All one has to do, now that you mention it, is look at most of the Central and South American countries and the Philippines today to see the same attitudes. Marcos was a fairly representative example, though there have been hundreds more like him. All trapped in that negative power equation. . . . Take to survive. Give and you're dead."

She stopped to finish her salad.

"And so," asked Pitman, "I suppose those papers you have next to you are notes from this history book?"

"Yes. You know that mummy photograph in the Lima newspaper and the bracelet on Bloomquist's wrist? Well, I have a feeling that bracelet

81

came from the body of that ancient Inca king. The wrist was deformed. The skin is depressed in the photo from a band about two inches wide, about the same width as the bracelet Bloomquist was wearing."

"Seems like a long shot. What makes you think that?" he asked.

"Well, first, let me read you this Prescott footnote, written nearly four hundred years ago."

She reached for the book and checked the page number, 749, against her notes.

"The Peruvians secreted these mummies of their sovereigns," she began reading, *"after the Conquest, that they might not be profaned by the insults of the Spaniards. Ondegardo, when corregidor of Cuzco, discovered five of them, three male and two female. The former were bodies of Viracocha, of the great Tupac Inca Yupanqui, and his son Huayna Capac. Garcilaso saw them in 1560. They were dressed in their regal robes, with no insignia but the llautu on their heads. They were in a sitting posture, perfect as life, without so much as a hair or eyebrow wanting. As they were carried through the streets, decently shrouded with a mantle, the Indians threw themselves on their knees, in a sign of reverence, with many tears and groans. . . . Ibid, ubi, supra. Some mummies were subsequently removed to Lima; and Father Acosta, who saw them there some twenty years later, speaks of them as still in perfect preservation."*

Allie paused and said, "The body clearly shows the imprint of something heavy and wide on that right wrist, probably for a long time. And that wrist was also in a state of 'perfect preservation.'"

"Very long shot, but a shot. Anything else?" he asked.

"Just something about gold. Here it is. After Atahuallpa was killed and Pizarro had his two rooms full of gold and silver, an Inca noble poured a bucket of corn in front of him, picked up a single kernel and said, 'This is what our Inca has given you in good faith.' Then, pointing to the heap on the ground, said, 'And that is the amount he has kept'."

Pitman asked, "Well, we can probably get Bloomquist's bracelet. But why would they hide all that treasure?"

"Because they had no use for it other than ceremonial," she said. "There was not much trade in gold. No scientific use, like shielding spacecraft windows from the sun's radiation or making circuit boards. It was only for noble and religious purposes. And after the Spanish came, it made bad things happen. Each Inca noble was responsible for obtaining his own treasure. There was no passing down heirlooms from father to son. Nothing was inherited. And by all accounts, each accumulated a considerable amount.

When they died, their treasures were sealed in their favorite mansions, which were then covered with earth. There must have been many hundreds of these buried houses.

"And all emperors and their wives were mummified and put in the great temple of the Sun at Cuzco, seated in gold chairs, next to the mummies of their fathers and mothers. Two rows, men mummies seated on one side, women mummies on the other. These were removed by the Spaniards and most have not been found. The five mummies referred to in this footnote," she said while tapping on the pages, "were found in a cave. A cave that contained no gold or silver. Even the robes they were wearing were devoid of the gold and feathered insignias of rank.

"I think," she continued, "that they had gotten word of what had happened to Montezuma after the Spaniards got all of his gold. And they certainly knew what happened to their Inca, Atahuallpa, when he fulfilled their ransom demands. I think they saw what happens after giving gold and silver to the Spaniards, and they then went into the hundreds of buried houses in the empire, removed all valuables, and destroyed most traces of those palaces. I think there is a vast treasure that has been hidden for centuries. And I think Bloomquist is on to it."

"Sounds reasonable, dear. Anything else?"

"Just that they, an Indian people, have retained their cultural identity intact. And they left no written records, just tufts of strings with knots tied in them . . . their form of both writing and calculating, a script made of yarns of different colors that we don't have the foggiest idea how to decipher.

"Most of the Indians of our West have some oil money or mineral rights or salmon rights or water rights or gambling rights. But it is not enough. They want their Black Hills back, their religious sacred lands back. And they should have some of these lands back in accordance with signed treaties. But they shouldn't do their arguing while wearing watches, driving cars, and not living on bison, pinion pine nuts, and dwelling in tepees. The Toltecs, Olmecs, Mayans, Arawaks, Chachapoyas, Aztecs, and all the northeastern Indian cultures are extinct as peoples, not all due to white people. The Incas, Sioux, Blackfeet, Nez Perce, and others have survived and have remained nearly inviolate in race and custom. They know, I think, who came first and who will leave last. The Cherokee, on the other hand, assimilated well into white culture. They had towns, lived in houses, wore suits with starch collared shirts. Had laws. Farmed. Became literate. And the whites, after the discovery of gold in Georgia, couldn't stand it. And the

Cherokee were forced, on drummed-up charges, to relocate west of the Mississippi."

"The point?" asked Pitman.

"It's a power point," said Allie. "If you are an American citizen and have something of great value that can be stolen, then laws will be made or interpreted by those who have the power to do it . . . by those who can back it up with physical force. The only protection from it is secrecy. Now, the Inca secrecy has backfired. Their treasures are now also secret from them."

"Hmmm," said Pitman, eyebrows knitted in concentration. "Wonder how much the treasure could be worth?"

"No telling," she said. "Certainly much more than the gold and silver in it."

"How so?" he asked.

"Well, they were mostly works of art. The few pieces from Atahuallpa's household, the ones that made it back to Europe in the sixteenth century without being melted down, confounded the goldsmiths there as to how they were done. The intricacy alone was beyond anything comparable in the Old World. The Conquistadors were like museum thieves who sent entire collections of Rembrants back in the form of kindling. Have you seen any of these surviving Inca art works? They are haltingly beautiful. But to answer your question, there is no telling how much they might be worth. First, we don't know how many pieces there are. But say each household had a hundred plates and statue-like things and say there were about two hundred houses. That would be twenty thousand pieces of art. One Picasso recently sold for fifty million dollars. If each of twenty thousand pieces went for five million each, that would still be a hundred billion dollars."

"So," said Pitman, "that would certainly give motive to a man like Bloomquist who is worth only a few hundred million, wouldn't it?"

"Yes," she said. "Especially if he has margined his companies beyond his ability to service his debts."

Pitman was silent for a minute, then said, "There is the other reason to solve this enigma."

"The flying saucer theory?" she asked

"There may be a saucer to be had. A space ship. Very ancient," he said.

Allie rolled her eyes up and then got up to make some tea.

London and Washington, D.C.: March 11, 1999

Brandon, Chauncy, Matlock, and the Indian, Tamac, boarded an Air Force C-141 Starlifter out of Mildenhall, England, later that evening, bound for the United States. Tamac became more coherent from Chauncy's medication as the flight progressed and spoke almost perfect English.

"Who are you, and where are we going?" he asked.

Brandon said that he and his men were friends and they were all going somewhere safe in the United States. This seemed to relax Tamac, and he sat unmoving for the rest of the flight.

Brandon had his own "safe house" near his "picket fence" residence in Alexandria, Virginia, that only the Pitmans, Chauncy, and Matlock knew of. They arrived in the morning. Tamac was given a bedroom and told to try to get some sleep. Then Brandon called Pitman.

Pitman asked how the survivor was.

"Safe," said Brandon. "He'll be okay for talking in a few hours but is still coming out of shock."

Pitman said that he would be over later that afternoon and that Brandon should get some rest . . . there was no more to do now.

Brandon hung up the phone, checked out a window to see Matlock in the van across the street, and looked at Chauncy in a chair by the front door. Then he went into the bathroom and took off his clothes. He stayed longer than usual in the shower, letting the hot water wash away all thought emanations that seemed to waft from the back of his head. It felt good.

Perhaps there is something to baptism, his brain flashed for an instant, the water quenching even that thought.

He turned the water off, stepped out of the tub, and reached for the towel. He dried his hair and thought about the killing he had done during the past twenty-four hours. One part of his brain said he had to be sane to think it was all insane to begin with. The other part said that if one weren't responsible for their family and friends, then the world was insane anyway, and it didn't matter. They, whoever they were, would soon know the killing on the airplane was done by him alone. And they would assume the job at the house was also a lone job. And they would probably come after him personally. They have been insulted. As 'gang bullies', they would gang up, if possible, to try and get even. Of that he was fairly sure.

He hung the towel on the rack and felt his old sickness coming back. He needed it more this time. He needed the challenge; the killing was secondary. He sat on the edge of the bed for a minute to think through the information they might have on him. Surely they would get his name from the manifest, or a flight attendant. If they had any connection with the CIA or State Department, they would have much of his history. The Chiang operation alone would be enough.

An adrenaline rush came. He got up and went to the phone and called Jane to say that he would be away for several days. When he hung up, he decided that he couldn't have it both ways. It wouldn't work and besides, it wasn't fair to her. After this operation, he would tell Pitman farewell and retire. It is a drug to beat, he concluded, and said to himself, "I am addicted to the game of hard ball espionage."

Chapter Six

Gatwick Airport, London: March, 11, 1999

The English tabloids were now full of the stories about the terrorists. A press conference was held by the airport manager and the Chief of Scotland Yard. They were Mideastern terrorists all right. Tatoos identified them as being from an "international mercenary fundamentalist group for hire." And they were all dead, subdued by an American. The United States said he was a special agent and did not want his identity released because it would impact future operations.

Wanda, in the press conference as a newspaper reporter, got a handout of a copy of the manifest. It wasn't difficult getting the address of the senior flight attendant from the phone book, a Judy DeHavilland. *She would certainly have been on duty in the forward cabin,* thought Wanda.

He took a cab to the Kensington District and knocked on her door. After identifying himself with his newspaper credentials and noting no ring on her wedding finger, he politely asked if he might get her story to add to an article he was writing. At first she was hesitant, though his slightly pudgy, middle-aged face and greying hair seemed trustworthy enough. When he mentioned that he had already talked to one of the other flight attendants for a thousand pounds cash upfront, Judy said that no one had told her not to and invited him in for tea.

He handed her a thick envelope of ten pound notes before sitting down. She took it and went into the kitchen to boil some water.

After a half-hour of questions, Wanda had a detailed description of Brandon and an understanding that the man had to be extremely dangerous and experienced.

I'll have extra fun with this one, thought Wanda.

He then asked if Judy could show him her flight attendant wings as verification of her position.

"It is required in my line of work," he said.

"Sure," she said. "I'll show you my uniform also."

When she had gone to her bedroom closet, Wanda pulled a small vial and a rubber finger prophylactic that doctors use from his side coat pocket. Quickly and expertly, he rolled the little prophylactic onto his right index finger, put a drop of clear liquid from the vial onto it, and smeared a thin layer onto the rim of Judy's tea cup, noting that it was over half full and still hot from a recent pouring. He returned the vial and rubber to his coat pocket a full thirty seconds before she returned.

"Thank you very much," he said after inspecting her uniform and wings.

"And if I could use your bathroom before leaving, I would appreciate it."

"Certainly," she said, paging through the money in the envelope. She put the envelope down, picked up her teacup, and started to make a list of things in her mind to buy with the windfall cash.

From the bathroom, Wanda heard the teacup crash to the floor and returned to the living room while rolling small rubbers onto all his fingers and both thumbs.

Judy was lying on her side on the floor, staring blankly toward the wall. Wanda picked up the broken pieces of cup, the saucer, and the envelope of money and placed them into his left coat pocket. He slid his teacup and saucer to her side of the tray and mopped up the spilled tea from the table with his handkerchief. Then he went into the kitchen and rummaged through her cabinets and pantry.

"This will do," he said, selecting a can of tomato soup.

In a few minutes he had a pot of it warming on the stove. He poured it into a bowl and put a spoon in it. Then he again pulled the vial from his right coat pocket and squeezed one drop into the bowl and one drop into the empty soup can. After stirring the soup, he poured it in the sink, flushed it down with water from the tap, and placed the bowl back on the counter with the spoon in it. Then he dropped the soup can into the kitchen garbage can, looked around, and silently let himself out.

Old Town, Alexandria, Virginia and Washington, D.C.: March 12, 1999

Pitman arrived at Brandon's house the next evening with a sheaf of photographs and papers. First he showed Brandon the London newspaper article which was headlined, TWA FLIGHT ATTENDANT ON TERRORIST FLIGHT FOUND DEAD.

Brandon felt a pang of sorrow for Judy. He said to Pitman that she didn't seem the type to be careless with food. And the timing was too close.

Pitman agreed and said he would contact Scotland Yard to find out the particulars. Then he sat down and asked a few questions of Tamac concerning the present Sapa Inca. The response was stony silence.

He showed him the picture of the bracelet. Tamac's eyes widened, but he only said that it was a picture of a piece of jewelry. Pitman said that it was a bracelet that may have a map on it. Tamac tensed again, but said nothing.

Pitman said, "Listen, Tamac. You would be dead now like your friends if we hadn't helped. We are not interested in your treasure. We are interested in stopping the drug trade in your country. If you have the key to this map, then you don't need us. If you don't have the key, then you do need us if you want to find your national treasure and finance your fight to get your land back and the bodies of your ancestors, the Sapas."

Pitman thought he found the right word, the raw nerve, "Sapa."

"Mr. Pitman," began Tamac, "we followed our revered ancestor to England because it is our way. The bracelet he wore disappeared three hundred years ago. But its message was, and has been, alive with all the Sapa's and their sons since. We knew it had an important message or map on it. And you are right, your people did save my life, and we may need help with a map. Before Inca Huascar died, he left different parts of the map with Rememberers, who left their parts to their heirs throughout the generations. Two of them, and the Sapa, died in London yesterday. And now we have but one Rememberer left who knows part of it."

It was too easy, thought Pitman. *He is telling the truth, but is holding back something important.*

Pitman could almost smell the electricity, the ozone, of being so close to something.

"Well," said Pitman, "what you say fits with what we know. Except for the fact that if you don't have the solution to the map, then where did all the items come from that were auctioned off at Sotheby's during the past year?"

Tamac repeated that the Sapa Inca and his heir knew where the place was, but added that they were both killed in London along with two *requerdos*. Pitman then asked him what it would take to work as a team in finding the Inca treasure. Tamac thought for a minute, then asked shrewdly, "If Pitman is willing to help his people, then why wouldn't he just give him all the information he knows about the solution to the map on the bracelet?"

Pitman said that it was because of history and fact. The history was that only the Sapa Inca and his heir were to know. The fact was that Tamac, and his dead friends, Sapa Inca or not, didn't know the first thing about surviving in the world of espionage, as proven by the incidents on the airplane and in England.

Tamac looked startled at this and asked if there was anything else Pitman would like to relate.

"Yes," said Pitman. "We will get you back to Peru after you are well. I think you know where the new Sapa Inca is. If so, tell him that we will get the missing bracelet back to him as proof of our dedication in this. And I will give you a radio with which you can communicate with me directly."

"We have radios, Mr. Pitman," said Tamac with strained patience, "and we have other means of communication and defense. We are a warrior race, Mr. Pitman. Please don't underestimate us just because of a few hundred years of non-violence. I will give you a frequency and a password for my contacts in Peru. They will want to know about all this as soon as possible. Anything else?"

"Just where did you learn to speak English so well?" asked Pitman.

"UCLA," said Tamac, suppressing a slight, painful smile from his face wounds. Pitman noticed a change in his tone.

* * *

Pitman gave Chauncy a choice. Either steal the bracelet from Bloomquist's high-security house or buy it. Chauncy decided to do neither. His men posed as everything from telephone men to garbage collectors around Bloomquist's daily routine—from home to office to lunch to office and back home.

On that same day, it was confirmed that Bloomquist was wearing the bracelet. It was snatched from his wrist so deftly by a passerby on a crowded Washington street at noon that Bloomquist didn't notice it missing until he got back to his office.

"Pretty slick," he said to himself while rubbing his empty wrist that had been sprayed with some kind of lubricant. Bloomquist now sensed that something big and sophisticated was involved. Something that could directly affect his chances for the Presidency in 2004.

It has to be related to this passion of mine, thought Bloomquist. *Old South American art. Can't tie it with Espinoza even in an unofficial capacity. The man is a drug tsar. Only embassy business can get out. Otherwise, my chances for hearing "Hail to the Chief," for me, are done. Wouldn't have a chance in 2004 or anytime.*

Bloomquist decided to bring in his long-time Asian subaltern, Fong. During the past thirty years, he had only used him for industrial espionage, mainly in the field of optics. But this was also a job along his lines of expertise.

Mark Fong's organization was based in Taipei. But it was financed by Bloomquist through an elaborate, multi-layered schematic of money transfers from Bloomquist International through off-shore banks and into the Fong Corporation account in Hong Kong. Fong picked up the Bloomquist hotline on his desk at the first ring.

"Yes sir," he said.

"Mark, I need some data, and I need it fast."

"I'm all ears," said Fong.

"I want a phone tap and a shadow on two people. They are Andrew Pitman and his wife Allie. They live on O Street in Georgetown. Surveillance round the clock. All contacts and activities. Give me the timing."

Fong paused for a minute while looking at his schedule, then said, "I'll need to be there to coordinate detailed research, but will activate initial gathering within the hour. Figure a complete setup within twenty-four hours. I'll be in the area within fifteen hours and will contact you then."

"Okay," said Bloomquist.

* * *

Bloomquist studied Fong's photographs of Tamac, the Pitmans, Chauncy, Matlock, the Incas flown in from Peru, Jess Brandon, the house in Washington D.C. where they all gathered, and the transcripts of the recordings of conversation that took place inside. He smiled at the thoroughness of the job. Long-range cameras and laser pattern differentials that 'heard' inside conversations from the minute vibrations 'seen' on the surface of windows from the outside.

So, he added to his thoughts, *The CIA guru Pitman is involved. Maybe even his wife. The coincidences are too far-fetched otherwise. Her playing poker. The failed highjacking. The debacle in London. Then, the next day,*

91

my bracelet stolen. Espinoza has to get a handle on it. I will call him and send him this information. I need my art!

London, England: March 12, 1999

Chief Inspector Smithson of Scotland Yard reread the lab reports on the soup remnants in the bowl on the sink, the soup can left in the garbage can, and the autopsy fluids from Judy DeHavilland's body. They all showed matching traces of a deadly strain of botulism. It seemed conclusive. But a call from the American, Andrew Pitman, requesting this information, gnawed at his gut. Pitman suggested that there may be something else to it. Smithson pulled on his handlebar mustache and frowned, thinking botulism. The soup company had been notified. His assistant had checked out the canning factory with a Health Inspector. Tight quality control was at the top of the company's list of priorities. A clean, sanitary operation was observed. Similar soups of different brands on the shelves of various markets around London had also been tested with no findings of botulism.

Smithson called the lab and asked that the soup can be brought to his office. Then he pressed the intercom for his secretary.

"Get me Wiggins, please. Thank you."

Wiggins was his personal doctor, a general practitioner, who seemed to know more than he ever actually said. Smithson also knew that Wiggins had started out as an epidemiologist, the type who discover how diseases get transmitted.

"Wiggins on line two," said his secretary.

"Wiggins," said Smithson, "can you come to my office this afternoon? I think I may need something for heartburn, and I want you to look at something."

"Two in the P.M. okay?" he asked merrily.

"Fine," said Smithson.

* * *

Wiggins took Smithson's blood pressure and temperature while answering questions about botulism. After several minutes of finding out nothing new, Smithson asked Wiggins to look at the soup can and documentation.

Wiggins studied it carefully, read the lab reports, then asked, "Where is the lid?"

Smithson, with irritation in his voice, called the lab again. The lid was delivered in five minutes.

Wiggins laid the lid on the desk, leaned over, and peered at it closely at desk level.

"No," said Wiggins. "Definitely no."

"No what?" asked Smithson.

"No botulism in this can," said Wiggins.

"How can you tell?" asked Smithson.

"This strain of botulism—a deadly strain, I might add—gives off gas, a lot of gas, before it becomes deadly. Even before it becomes deadly, the gas inside will distort the can, puff out the lid a little. When it does become deadly it will puff it out to a more noticeable degree. Always, when deadly, in a sealed can, the lid will be raised a bit in the middle. This lid is perfectly flat."

"Thanks doctor," said Smithson. "That helps, and I think I'm okay now."

Just to make sure, Wiggins took his blood pressure again. It was back to normal.

Immediately, Chief Inspector Smithson called for his car and team of experts and returned to Judy DeHavilland's apartment. This time they combed every square inch with magnifying glasses.

One found what looked like a small tea stain on the carpet. Another found a tiny chip of porcelain. Smithson looked around at places where the first team had dusted for fingerprints. Then he thought of the soup can and had a flash.

He went to the kitchen and opened a drawer. Spoons, forks, butter knives, a garlic squeezer, a wine opener, and yes, a can opener. He pulled a pen from his pocket and lifted it by its hanging hook while asking for a magnifier and duster.

"See anything on the handles?" he asked.

"Part of a palm print on the side of the top handle, only smears elsewhere."

In two hours Smithson confirmed that the palm print was not from Judy DeHavilland. In five hours a package arrived by special jet from Lyon, France. He had confirmation, through Interpol, that the print was connected to a person that the Europeans, and Smithson had been looking for years. A professional assassin. A man referred to as Wanda.

Smithson read through the file. *Five-feet-seven-inches tall. Medium length hair, sometimes dyed black, sometimes grey.* He looked at three photographs that had been taken from hidden surveillance cameras over the years, then read, *Likes to operate alone, but usually has extensive groundwork done by trained accomplices. Almost always uses the element of surprise. Does not consider innocents that might be in the way. Specializes in small, shape-charge explosives for final dispatching. Also very adept with firearms, remote devices, electronics, drugs, and disguises. Was observed once with the infamous Carlos, and may have been trained by him. Age estimated to be between forty and forty-five. Full set of prints obtained by chance after the Swedish ambassador to the UN was assassinated.*

Smithson paged through the rest of the vague description, then turned to the UN assassination. The Ambassador had three video and one infrared micro-camera in his office which covered every angle. The signals fed to a two hundred-forty hour constant loop recorder in a small room on the top floor. The cameras and tape ran all the time and the past ten days were always on record, constantly recording over itself.

Clever, thought Smithson, *Don't ever have to change tape. But it's there if something happens.*

Three nights prior to the assassination, the tapes showed a cleaning man come in and vacuum the rug. Two of the cameras showed him very quickly take a photograph of the Ambassador's desk. One camera could not have confirmed it. The man seemed to just be adjusting his ballcap. But from the angles, it could be seen that a small camera was held in his palm. The night prior to the death, the same cleaning man had replaced the fountain pen in the fancy marble-based holder with another. Then he twisted the top of it, probably to arm it.

There was no reason, thought Smithson, *to have an exact copy of the pen. The Ambassador could have either pulled it out to sign something or to inspect it. It made no difference.* The room, including the Ambassador from the chest up was destroyed. The prints were lifted from the handle of the vacuum cleaner.

He paged back through the file. *It is suspected that "Wanda" has connections with several terrorist groups . . . "Wanda's" escapes seem to be enhanced by flying business aircraft from subject countries . . . "Wanda" seems to have, or be associated with, a legitimate cover occupation which requires travel.*

Smithson called Pitman with a fairly complete description and profile, then faxed him the entire file.

Wanda! thought Pitman. *Another level. We're not dealing with unprofessional politicos.*

In fifteen minutes he had the entire CIA file on Wanda. During his review, some anxiety surfaced. The man was an experimenter. He wasn't an assassin who just killed people. No. The killing was usually done by trying different methods, most of them new and unique. If the first method didn't work, he would try another.

Pitman picked up a pencil and began jotting down notes from the file. After a half-hour he leaned back in his chair and studied them. Wanda had probably been responsible for thirteen killings during the past seven years. Of the thirteen victims, nine had been killed on the first try and four on the second try, all by unusual methods like poisoning during a formal state dinner with no one else being poisoned; car-bombs using sophisticated shape-charges where no one else in the car was injured; abductions of relatives to lure the victim into remote areas where he was abandoned to let the elements do the job; ultra-long range sniper rifles; using surrogates to do torture and extract information first and leave the actual killing to him.

Pitman concluded that to Wanda it was a pathological game, a learning experience, something to be savored as 'special'. Also, he figured, the man— after London—would quickly identify Brandon the key adversary.

Pitman first called Chauncy to cover Brandon for the next week or so. Then he sent a courier with the entire package to Brandon in Alexandria with a note: *Jess, read the package. This Wanda will be after you, and he won't give up. Plan on flying Allie's plane with her to Peru in a few days. I'll take care of things on this end. Pitman.*

Paris, France: March 12, 1999

Wanda had his own equivalent of the Interpol network in his spacious Paris apartment. Aside from hidden closets full of explosives and weapons, his study was a modern network of telephones, small satellite dishes, ready cash, passports, identification papers of many types, and computers containing contacts. All devices and closets were rigged to blow if the right combination of numbers was not entered into each locking device or computer code.

In twenty minutes, he had enough information on Brandon to arouse his concern. Newspaper articles about the Harvard hero from Vietnam. Service records. And the famous Chiang Gold operation that had been all over the media the year before.

Through international databases, some very private and expensive, Wanda knew Brandon was the key. Or was it the challenge? He decided it could not be a personal thing on his part. A person like Brandon would best be dealt with on an emotional level, Brandon's emotion. He studied the pages and data carefully and found one original document with Brandon's full signature on it, *Jesschuan Pierpont Brandon*. Carefully, he placed it into his fax machine, then picked up the phone. His handwriting expert called back in an hour.

"The loop under the 'J,'" she said, "is much larger than the one above it. There is much more under the surface than what he shows. He knows things from antiquity. The slants are uniformly vertical. Can't tell much from that. All loops are closed, even the small e's and a's. But the dot over the 'i' is unique . . . more of a small check mark than a dot, and high up and to the right. The man is a highly balanced contrast between being aggressive and stable. The fax shows no pen pressure. A real copy would be needed for a complete analysis. One can see and feel the pen lines underneath the original paper. On the surface, he's a serious person, probably mixed between his personal and professional endeavors," she said. "But I can't do a complete analysis without the originals . . . without matching the pen pressures with the individual letters."

"Don't have time for that now," said Wanda. "What's your advice with what you know at this time?" he asked.

"Compared with my writing analysis on you," she said, "don't mess with him."

Though Wanda thanked her, he hung up the phone with irritation and again studied the data carefully, cross-referencing many possibilities from different sources. Evidently, a person called Jane Mildred Mathas had used the same address as Brandon's Washington residence on a traffic ticket a year ago. Credit card number records showed they frequented many of the same gas stations and stores. And she had used her phone charge number many times recently from Brandon's ranch in Lone Pine, California. Also, there were recent credit card records of Brandon buying gas for an aircraft. Via modem, he checked the card purchase numbers with the detailed database records in San Francisco. From those records, he got the FAA registration number of the aircraft that was fueled. With the FAA N-number, he went to a different database in Oklahoma City and found what kind of aircraft it was, where it was located, and who owned it. It was a supercharged Lake Renegade Special 490. The owner was Alexis Pitman. It was located at Manassas Airport, Virginia.

If feasible, he thought, *better to snuff Brandon in the bud.*

Also, he would send Borgia to Brandon's farm to obtain any files there and kidnap Ms. Mathas if she were there. She could be the cheese for any psychological trap that may be needed.

In his mind, he again reviewed the Brandon information while exiting his back room and then changing clothes in his bedroom. The man had defeated two of his best teams. One on the TWA flight, the other in Devon. *Defeated was not the right phrase*, he thought. *Wiped out* was more accurate.

Wanda exited his flat and walked down the street to his legitimate import business on Rue de Napoleon. His secretary, mistress, driver, and sometimes co-pilot, Naomi, handed him the accountings for the past week. A shipment of two million plastic combs of every description from South Korea had come in, and were on their way to a thousand retail stores in the EEC and Eastern Europe. Ten thousand marble chess sets from Mexico had gone to Russia. The four hundred jade carvings from Singapore were still in his warehouse, but an offer had been made.

Wanda had purchased Naomi through the Byzantine underground slave market when she was ten years old. First he sent her to the best private schools in France for an undergraduate education. Then she had received extensive instruction at specialty schools around the world in high technology security, engineering, hand-to-hand combat, international finance, and piloting business jets. The more she progressed, the more he became attached to her, and over the years, he changed his mind about her role in his assassination business. He may want to retire with her, perhaps even marry her. Now her role was exclusively to run the import business in Paris and to fly co-pilot on his international flights. She knew that he had another occupation . . . the large amounts of money she invested for him during the previous ten years could not possibly have come from imports. She had all the books memorized. When confronted, he only said that he had another source of income which was none of her business. This did not bother her, as she was forever grateful to him for rescuing her from the auction block. She could easily have been sold several times during her youth.

After she had him sign a few papers, Naomi drove them to his private hangar at Orleans Airport outside the city. On the way, she picked up the car phone and ordered that both his British Vampire fighter jet and his business jet be towed out. Then she checked on the caterer.

Stunt flying always calmed him. During his hour of aerobatics, she pre-flighted, inspected the baggage she always kept in his long-range Gulfstream G-4, and filed a flight plan. A few minutes after he landed, they took off for the United States. Flights like this were the only times she had him completely alone and all to herself. To her, the routine was delicious. She did the takeoff. He handled the radios. After an hour, at altitude, cruising on autopilot at night over the ocean at over thirty thousand feet, she excused herself and went to the cabin. There, she put the final touches on the catered French cuisine, candles, music, tablecloth, napkins, and flowers.

When all was ready, she poked her head in the cockpit and said, *"Bon appetite!"*

He switched the radio and mike back to the cabin, checked the flight instruments, and then unstrapped. In the middle of the dining room table was a glass digital TV screen. In the middle of it was a remote radar display. On the side toward the window was a display of the cockpit instruments, and on the wall another radio microphone for communication with the International Air Traffic control system. They toasted one another before going into the bedroom. The sort of love making, while hurtling through the atmosphere at over five hundred miles per hour, with no one actually flying the plane, gave them both a feeling of added excitement. Though not really dangerous, it was slightly more dangerous without anyone in the cockpit. There was the one-in-a-million chance that some mechanical malfunction would occur that would require immediate attention. A collision course with another aircraft that hadn't been picked up by their Collision Avoidance System, was even less of a probability. After dinner he glanced at the screen in the table. They were at nearly forty-thousand feet over the middle of the Atlantic.

Even so, afterward they showered in shifts, with one always monitoring the cockpit flight instruments and radar on the TV. Thirty minutes before the scheduled descent they were both strapped back in the cockpit drinking coffee. She asked about this mission, sensing some concern. He said it was a strange one, but that all she had to do was be herself and do her job; just keep the plane ready to go, and if he didn't return in three days, she should fly out, with or without him.

Virginia and Washington, D.C.: March 12, 1999

After Pitman asked Brandon to fly to Peru with Allie in her plane, Brandon practiced. First, he strapped a double bag of heavy duty garbage bags full of rocks in the right seat to approximate the weight of Allie. Then, over the skies of Manassas, Virginia, and the peaks and valleys of the Appalachian Mountains, the Lake Turbo Renegade was put through nearly every twisting performance maneuver possible, using the test pilot skills he had learned at Pax River. After a break for lunch, reviewing the published manufacturer's flight manual, and a re-fueling, he concentrated on finding the edge of the plane's envelope in the vertical. He flew straight-up climbs and straight-down descents, while turning the supercharger on and off and trying various angles of flaps, with the landing gear up and down. He tried different roll rates and established the speed for both slow-speed stalls and accelerated stalls in the various aircraft configurations. After two hours, he felt comfortable and headed back to the Manassas airport. At five thousand feet, he cut the engine off and watched the prop feather automatically. Then he glided down and made a dead-stick landing. On roll-out, he restarted the engine and taxied in.

The tower operator asked if he had any engine problems, that it looked like his prop wasn't turning on landing. Brandon said, "No. Everything's fine. Might want to check the prescription on your glasses."

* * *

After landing at Washington Reagan National Airport in D.C., Wanda listened to a recording of a phone tap his expensive contact had placed on Alexis Pitman. State-of-the-art it was . . . no FBI hard wiring; no court order; just a simple, barely visible device stuck onto the phone line twenty feet from where it came out of the Pitman house in Georgetown. It sensed minute changes in electromagnetic fields or, in this application, telephone conversations. Brandon was mentioned. Wanda called Espinoza.

"The man is planning to fly down in a civilian prop plane, a Lake Turbo Renegade 470. So I have a plan in motion here, using other sources. If they prove unsuccessful, I will know while en route to Peru and will need access to your Peruvian Air Force to do the job there."

"Be here, and you will have it," said Espinoza. "However if he does come, and it is a small civilian plane, he will be stopping for fuel at least once on the way, probably several times. I can arrange to have him delayed on the ground en route. Would that be better?"

"Yes," said Wanda. "If you can arrange it in Mexico, it would be much better. I have hard contacts there."

"I'll cover Mexico and keep you informed via your aircraft phone and fax," said Espinoza.

* * *

On the drive back from Manassas Airport, Brandon was fairly sure he was being followed. One car was regularly replaced by a different one between eight and ten car lengths behind at every other intersection. He decided to drive into D.C. and walk around.

* * *

Brandon parked at a meter on Maine Avenue near the Capital Yacht Club. He put two quarters in and then began looking back through reflections in restaurant windows. When Wanda crossed the street, Brandon stopped and watched to determine his direction, then compensated to remain ahead. Sometimes it was impossible to anticipate accurately. If an escape was available, Brandon positioned himself to follow immediately, to keep the person in sight, and pass unnoticed to another forward position. And all the while he noticed small things. Did the person look behind himself very often? Did he stop to read for more than fifteen seconds? Wanda looked behind himself every five to ten seconds.

Good, thought Brandon. *He's always eyeing the wrong direction. The pro I'm after.*

The side street narrowed and came to a tee in heavy traffic. Wanda crossed over to Brandon's side, and Brandon slipped around the corner. A paper boy came up from behind and asked him for a sale while two heavy men jabbed guns in Brandon's side and led him to the back of an ice truck that was parked ten feet away.

The heavy door reeled down with a slam, and the paper boy sang in a loud voice, "Papers, twenty-five cents!" as if nothing unusual had happened.

* * *

"Brandon has disappeared," said Matlock into his cellular phone. Chauncy answered in disbelief, asking, "How could that have happened? Didn't you have both a front and rear tail on him?"

"He was being followed by someone. Someone very tricky and slippery. Jess tried his own front tail. They must have had someone else in front of him. He rounded a corner down by the fish market and just disappeared."

"You think he wanted to disappear?" asked Chauncy.

"Could be, but I doubt it," said Matlock. "This character following him headed back the way he had come as soon as Jess rounded that last corner. It was a setup, pure and simple. Brandon would have seen through it. The corner led to a side street full of noon traffic. Our people covered both ends of the block in about ten seconds. They had all that time to abduct him into a car or fish truck. And we couldn't stop the traffic or tail all the vehicles."

Chauncy ground a cheroot between his two front teeth and asked if there was any good news. Matlock said that his men still had a tail on one of the characters. "He is staying in the Mayflower Hotel. All exits are covered."

"That's a start," said Chauncy. "Have our helicopter stand by. Day and night equipment aboard. When this guy moves, let me know. You fly the chopper, I'll be on the ground. If there is a. . . . " Chauncy stopped when Matlock held a finger up for silence and cupped his earpiece.

"He's moving now," said Matlock. "He just got in a cab and is heading south toward 14th Street Bridge."

"Good," said Chauncy. "Keep the chopper at least three miles away. Don't want any helo noise to make him nervous."

"Later," said Matlock as he left the room.

* * *

Matlock had a good description and license number of the Yellow Cab and quickly acquired visual contact.

"He turned off on GW Parkway, heading south," transmitted Matlock.

Chauncy sped up and crossed the 14th Street Bridge a few minutes later.

"He turned off on Slaters Lane. He's out of the taxi at the Marina Towers Apartment complex. Got him in sight," said Matlock peering though powerful helmet mounted gyro-stabilized binoculars while flying at a thousand feet, miles away, out of sight and sound. "Grey coat, grey pants, black hair," said Matlock. "He just walked through the bushes toward the generating plant next to the apartment building by the big black pile of coal next to the river."

"Good," said Chauncy.

* * *

From engine noise and gear shifting, Brandon calculated the distances during the cold trip to wherever to be about five or six miles. On arrival, the door opened and he was led by the two men to a chair in a darkened room, where he was tied securely with self-locking rope straps. The harder he fought, the tighter they got. Brandon soon stopped struggling. His blindfold was removed. A man sat in front of him and waited in silence. Then another man walked from the shadows and stood in front of him. It was Wanda, the man whom he had been following. He pulled up a chair, and asked who Brandon was.

"A naval officer," said Brandon.

"You military people are all the same," said Wanda. "You operate big toys and play global cop games, but can't think. You're what I call 'tiny mercenaries'. I wonder what Jane will think when she hears about your demise?"

Brandon appreciated the attempt to get under his skin. *Very professional*, he thought.

"So what's next?" he said. Wanda saw the see-through. Brandon knew he had made a mistake and should have made some show of emotion.

"Next is for you to answer some questions," said Wanda.

Then he seemed to listen to an earpiece speaker, nodded his head, and added, "Have a good death, Commander Brandon," as he disappeared back into the shadows of the room. Brandon heard a large door close and lock.

* * *

When Chauncy was a mile from the Slaters Lane turnoff, Matlock reported, "Medium size power boat exiting a treed area behind the power plant."

"Break high cover and investigate," said Chauncy.

The helicopter nosed over and down.

"Heading cross river," said Matlock. Though there were many other boats in the area, Matlock kept it in sight, reporting its position every few seconds.

Chauncy pulled into the Marina Towers parking lot. He could see Matlock's helicopter speeding toward the middle of the river. Chauncy crossed through the bushes through a hole in the fence and onto the power plant property. His second car had arrived, and he ordered his men to close in. From both sides, they rounded the corners of the main brick building and looked at each other. There was nothing. No doors on the building, no windows. Just brick on one side and the Potomac River on the other.

Matlock slowed and descended over the open speedboat. He looked it over closely. There was no one aboard. He noted two small antennas, one on the bow, another on the stern.

"Goose chase!" he transmitted to Chauncy. "No one aboard. Remote control decoy."

"Find the cab!" said Chauncy. "Look for it at the airport."

After a few minutes, Matlock got clearance from ATC to transit the traffic pattern at Washington Reagan National Airport. The Yellow Cab was at the end of the queue, waiting in line for another passenger.

Two of Chauncy's men arrived a few minutes later. Yes, the driver had come from Marina Towers. Yes, he dropped off a passenger before looping around and getting in the taxi line. Yes, the photograph was of the same person that he had taken to Marina Towers.

Lima, Peru: March 12, 1999

Wanda touched down at night at the Lima International Airport. He taxied into a hangar at the far end of the runway and was met by three of Espinoza's men. They escorted him out the back door to a helo pad, and in a few minutes he was in a helicopter on his way to one of Espinoza's largest processing plants, high in the hills below the snowy peaks of the Andes.

After an hour flight, the Bell Long Ranger circled the landing spot, exchanging light signals with people on the ground.

Espinoza met him exuberantly, asking how his trip was.

They were jeeped to a headquarters building. Espinoza wanted him to see some of his operation and then brief him personally on what had to be done.

The plant was immaculate. Raw coca leaves by the ton were stored in underground silos. By conveyer they came into the factory and were deposited into giant vats. The machinery looked like a Jim Beam distillery, with stainless steel evaporators, condensing tubes, separators, and fifty people around in white coats, monitoring each stage of the process. Then, instead of bottlers, there were dryers, shake tables, sifters, and baggers. The bags of pure cocaine were then conveyed through a tunnel to another building.

"Where does it go from there?" asked Wanda.

"My little secret," said Espinoza. "But if you would like a kilo bag, call it a pre-paid bonus."

"Cash only, as you know," replied Wanda.

"Then you will have it as a post-operation bonus, street value," said Espinoza.

"Yes," said Wanda. "That would sweeten things."

"Follow me," said Espinoza as he walked toward the door of the factory. "I want to show you something."

Soon they were staring down into one of the coca leaf silos.

"How full does it look to you," asked Espinoza.

"Don't know how deep it is," replied Wanda.

"Exactly," chuckled the General, "forty feet."

"Then it looks about one third full."

"Yes," said Espinoza. "This time of year in the past they were never less than two thirds full. Something is interfering with our picking operation. And I wanted you to help with possible solutions. Your services will be required, I am thinking, to eliminate someone. Let me brief you."

Espinoza then related to Wanda most of what he knew about Bloomquist. Wanda mentioned that a man, Brandon, had to be eliminated, and then neutralizing all else would be easy. They talked for an hour.

"How long have you worked for me?" asked Espinoza.

"Eight years," said Wanda.

"*Si*," said Espinoza. "And I want you around for the next three months exclusively for me. There are several jobs that may be required. But the first one now, from what you've told me, seems to be to eliminate Brandon."

"Brandon is good," said Wanda. "It will cost you more."

"What exactly do you mean?" asked Espinoza, irritated.

"Brandon has been alerted. An alerted quarry is much more difficult to find, much less defeat. Extra precautions, planning, people, and equipment will be required. My expenses will be higher. Figure twice the normal fee for Brandon, plus another for keeping me on retainer for three months."

Espinoza thought a minute, blew a puff of cigar smoke out, and knew that this would probably be well worth it at ten times the normal fee.

"The full triple sum will be in your account tomorrow," said Espinoza as he held out his hand out to seal the agreement.

The Pentagon: March 12, 1999

"And so we finally meet," said Pitman to General Johnston in his ornate Pentagon office.

"Fine office. Paintings. VCRs, four. TVs, six. But telephones, one with twenty buttons. Tell me, general, what do you do for a living?"

"I protect the country, Mr. Pitman."

"Really," said Pitman. "And how do you do that?"

"By doing my job," said the general.

Pitman drew a list of names from his coat pocket and handed it to the General.

"Is killing Air Force officers and U.S. civilians part of your job?" asked Pitman.

104

"Please sit down, Mr. Pitman," said Johnston. "There are some things you don't understand."

They both sat on a plush couch. Pitman eyed the five rows of colored ribbons on Johnston's blue uniform. There was not one star on any of them for repeated similar endeavors and not one combat V for valor in a combat zone. Pitman categorized these types as "flat salad officers," often ticket punchers. The awards were for showing up or being a token something or another . . . not unlike a recent high-ranking flat salad U.S. officer who got caught falsely advertising a combat V on his chest of ribbons. *He*, thought Pitman, *'flat-lined' his 'flat salad' career with a bullet from his handgun. Johnston reminds me of this type, like the warden in the Shawshank Redemption. Get away with it until you get caught, then do yourself in. These types rarely faced the music of their own cheating on society.*

Pitman was glad he had taken extreme precautions and decided that General Johnston would not be required to face his own music publicly.

"There is a machine that can rule the world," said Johnston. "It is more important than nuclear bombs. We had it, then gave it away, back to the Russians. But we are the only ones who know how to operate it. And it is necessary to keep this information secret. I know about your man who went to Wright Pat. Obviously, from your list, he found out more than we thought. But these deaths were necessary. This is a thing of monumental proportions. It has to be protected at all costs."

"Protected?" asked Pitman, raising an eyebrow.

"Yes," said Johnston. "At all costs."

"Sorry, General," said Pitman. "I did just hear you say that and should learn to make my questions more specific. Protected from *whom*, General?"

"Why, from the rest of the world," said Johnston.

"And what protection did the Air Force Officers on this list have the right to? Perhaps protection from you?" offered Pitman.

General Johnston squirmed and said, "Interesting point, but you are missing something. You cannot get out of here alive unless I say so."

Pitman twitched the big toe on his right foot and a small blade emerged from the front of the sole of his right shoe. He coughed while stretching it under the coffee table toward General Johnston's calf.

"Tell me about the machine?" asked Pitman.

"There is probably only one of these machines. The Russians gave it to us for a while, during the Lend-Lease agreements of World War II. They did not have the capability then to evaluate it. In tactical warfare, Mr. Pitman, surprise is worth at least fifty percent of the equation. We cannot let any future foe know of the essence of such power. We had to eliminate any possible source of information."

Pitman coughed again while thrusting his foot forward and nudging Johnston's calf. He apologized politely, changed his body position, and moved a few inches further away on the couch. The super-sharp, super-thin blade had gone painlessly and un-noticed into General Johnston's leg for a hundredth of a second. To an observer, it was just someone sitting near another person, and having a short cough, then moving away.

"The list?" asked Pitman, pointing to it.

"Well, as I said, no one could have this type of knowledge on that level. It would compromise our efforts to protect this great country."

"These young, dedicated, educated, talented, and hard-working military people are this country," said Pitman. "Not to mention many civilians killed on the side. It seems you are but a petty power monger who kills what has made you."

"Call me what you like, Mr. Pitman. It makes no difference. You are a non-player. I only agreed to see you because I wanted to know what you knew. Now that you are no threat. . . . "

"No threat?" interrupted Pitman, a little surprised at this conclusion.

"Yes," said Johnston. "You see, this is, as mentioned, what we call a 'secure' office. You will be taken through a hidden door. And you will disappear. It is only one of our methods."

"In that case, I thank you, General," said Pitman while looking at his watch. "I had no reservations a minute ago. Now I have *double* no reservations. And you will have a heart attack within, oh, I would say the next minute or so."

Pitman again flicked his right toe and pointed to the thin, silver blade that had just poisoned General Johnston.

General Johnston reached for the button under the side table.

"Go ahead, push the button. I was going call for help anyway," said Pitman.

Johnston pulled his hand away, wondering by what audacity Pitman would have pushed the button himself. Then he felt the sharp pain in his chest and winced. Pitman said that he had signed his death warrant when he summarily killed innocent members of his own society.

"But there is an out for the time being," added Pitman, holding up a small syringe.

"Antidote?" asked Johnson.

"Antidote," said Pitman. "Were you responsible for Aeroflot?"

106

"How long an antidote?" asked Johnston.

"You will have a heart attack and die or seem to die. We will recover you from the morgue before you wake up and put another body in your place, and you will tell us everything else you know."

"Okay! Okay!" said Johnston, clutching his chest.

Pitman reached over, stuck the syringe through the General's uniform and into his chest and squeezed the tiny plunger.

"Now you will wake up in four days, regardless. If you do not answer this question, you will wake up in a coffin under six feet of dirt. Think about it. Now, were you responsible for Aeroflot?" asked Pitman.

"Yes, Aeroflot," said Johnston. "Our machine had to be field tested."

"How?" asked Pitman.

"With one of our pilots I had slightly drugged. He, like the others, thought he was flying our most advanced simulator. . . . This one was ordered to fly through an airliner . . . all simulated, of course. We needed proof-of-concept to bargain with the Russians. But he's gone. They're all gone. No proof. Will I wake up above ground?"

"In a way," said Pitman. "After further answers, you will get a new identity. A new face. New teeth. No fingerprints. And a new job as an unknown sheepherder in the far Outback of Australia. You will have no communication, no transportation. There will be a bounty on you if you try to leave. A small coded wire will be planted deep inside your thigh muscle tissue. You won't know it's there. But we will always know where you are in case we need follow-up information. You will have to learn to eat different types of animals and insects to survive for long. . . . "

Johnston fell back in his chair, unconscious, still clutching his chest.

Pitman pushed the button on the speaker phone to Johnston's secretary and called for medical help. Two Air Force guards entered with side arms cocked and aimed.

"The General seems to have had a stroke or something," said Pitman, glancing toward the open door at his two backup men. "And if you don't just relax, your brain housing groups will be blown apart."

The guards turned and saw the two Pitman operatives in fine business suits pointing small machine guns at their heads.

* * *

Colonel Bobarski realized, at being informed of the death of General Johnston, that he would be in trouble if he didn't do something quickly, if he didn't take the initiative. He immediately walked over to Johnston's office in the Pentagon and watched as the ambulance gurney was wheeled down the wide corridor. Then he went into the General's office. The place was full of high-ranking brass. One was trying to track down the General's wife. Another was looking through his briefcase. Colonel Bobarski went to the secretary's desk and looked at the appointment calendar. Someone named Pitman was the last visitor. Then he went to the aquarium in the corner. It was a twenty-gallon apparatus with two dozen pink anabantid gouramis in it, schooling around green aquatic plants that gently waved in the current generated by the bubble-filtering pump. When no one was looking, he reached in and scooped up the top gourami, tethered to the bottom by a thin monofilament line. It was a plastic one, perfectly matched in color to the live ones. It held the micro-laser disk of all the documents relative to Groom Lake, Wright Pat, and the Russians. He put it in his pocket and left.

Georgetown, Washington, D.C.: March 12, 1999

After dinner, Allie left the dishes and went up to her study. She had photographed the bracelet, and then had the negative blown up into a three-foot-by-four-foot print which she taped to the wall in front of her desk. Pitman came in with a tray of hot tea, set it on the edge of the desk, stood behind her, pulled her long hair to the side, and began rubbing her neck and shoulders. She moaned softly and looked up at the photograph. Some pieces suddenly clicked into place in her mind. . . . Bloomquist, the Incas, the highjacking, and the possible treasure of Peruvian art were connected. *Bloomquist couldn't have set up an airliner with a bunch of terrorists*, she thought. *There was someone else. There had to be.*

"What do you see in the photograph, Andy?" she asked.

He said, "For the tenth time, my dear, it is a picture of a cat and some stars in the shape of a cross. The cat has little ears and is wearing a dunce cap or an object of that shape.

Allie got up, walked around the desk, and pulled the giant photograph off the wall. She turned it upside down, retaped it to the wall, sat back in her chair, grabbed Pitman's hands, and placed them back on her shoulders.

"Now what do you see?" she asked.

He squinted, closed one eye and then the other, and said that it could be a cat with big ears sitting on a dunce cap instead of wearing it.

"Are you sure it's a cat?" asked Allie.

"Pretty much a cat either way," he answered. "One way, it has little ears and a fluffy tail. The other way, it has big ears and a smaller tail. But either way it is a cat. Yes, definitely a cat. Does it mean anything?"

She opened the atlas on her desk and turned to Peru. Then she took a felt tip pen and outlined something. When she finished, she showed it to Pitman.

"Recognize anything?" she asked.

"I don't believe it!" exclaimed Pitman. "It's almost an exact copy of the photograph. A cat!"

He leaned over and kissed her on the cheek, then asked, "What's your analysis, mega-brain?"

"Well," began Allie, "as you see, I outlined Lake Titicaca on the map. The name translates to mean either puma, cougar, or jaguar, all cats. So I think this image on the gold bracelet is some sort of map. And we will soon find out something else that this atlas doesn't show."

"Like what?" he asked.

"Just a hunch," she said. "Can you dig through that box of charts from the U.S. Geological Survey I bought? There should be one that details the terrain around this lake."

He started flipping through the neatly packed and folded papers while she began pouring tea.

"I think this is the one," he said, extracting a chart from the box.

"Fold it to the north part of the lake," she said.

He put the map in front of her. After a moment of staring she grabbed his hand and squeezed.

"What is it?" he asked.

"Andy, look! That dunce cap in the bracelet photograph is an equilateral triangle. Three sides of the same length, three sixty degree inside angles."

He looked again at the photograph while she let go of his hand and began drawing lines on the map.

"Yes, something," she said as he looked down at the atlas.

"And here is the same triangle you have drawn on the photo of the cat-o-the-lake," he added.

"Yes, this is amazing, Andy. There are three mountains here, just north and east of the top of the lake. They are each about the same height: 14,675 feet; 14,383 feet; and 14,714 feet. I have connected their peaks on the map. One of the sides of the triangle runs through a town called Rosaspata."

Pitman's eyes went to the photograph on the wall, then to the map on the desk, then to the wall, and back again.

"It is a perfect match," he said. "Those peaks connected together make the same equilateral triangle sitting on the head of a cat or underneath its rump."

"Yes," she said. "And now I'm at a dead end. I have no idea what these stars are."

"Well," he said, "I may be able to arrange for someone to explain stars and other things."

"And who might that be?" she asked.

"Perhaps a lead to the next Sapa Inca," he said.

Allie felt a little left out.

"What is it you haven't told me?" she asked.

"Only that two of the party on the plane to London that died there were the Sapa Inca and his heir," he said.

"And there is another Inca to replace that one, though probably without the solution to the bracelet," she said with finality.

"Yes, and the surviving Inca from London, Tamac, is the linchpin for the credibility required to find the new Sapa Inca. I have a feeling that Bloomquist's bracelet may convince him. Just a feeling."

"Yes," she said. "It makes sense."

Pitman rubbed her shoulders, fingers probing to the bones, getting to the painful root of stress. Then, with relaxed hands, he massaged her neck muscles.

"Also," she added, "see the small dot in the center of the triangle on the photo?"

"Yes," he said. "A small dot."

"Now look at it with this magnifying glass."

Pitman peered closely. It was not just a dot. It had concentric circles within its circumference, one of which looked to be minutely inlaid with a repeated pattern of equilateral triangles with bars on them and interlocking circles.

"Saucer?" he asked.

"Flying saucer, probably," she said.

* * *

Pitman was delighted with being able to keep his promise so soon. He radioed Tamac's contact on the single side band radio and said that the bracelet was on its way. It would be delivered by a man named Henson, a special courier from the state department, at the Ariba Restaurant in Lima just outside the airport at midnight. The man seemed pleased and said he

110

would meet him, asking what he looked like, and inadvertently used Pitman's name when thanking him. Henson was an old friend of Pitman's and often travelled in South America while off duty to visit an illegitimate daughter from his youth who lived in Paraguay. He said he would be glad to deliver the "package" in Lima on his way back.

Lone Pine, California: March 12, 1999

Jane gave the Eagle and his wife a hug on the tarmac after exiting the business jet at the small Lone Pine airport. The Eagle's wife, Dorothy, drove her to Brandon's farm. Everything looked great in the house. And the Mojave desert air gave her a vitality that never happened in D.C. or New York. They talked outside while feeding the dogs and horses. The Eagle was doing more dancing and pool playing than eagling, mentioned Dorothy. Jane didn't comment. It was good to be back. Before retiring, she opened all the windows and drew all the curtains back.

"And what about my earrings you said you would make?" she asked.

"Still looking for a certain type of turquoise," said Dorothy. "But that will happen . . . probably while you are still alive."

The next morning, after her modem work, they saddled up the two Andalusians and went for a ride. That evening Jane played the piano for ten minutes, then went to bed. Though it was just twilight, she wanted to keep her body clock on eastern time.

* * *

Borgia liked the evening better. During late night, people were too aware of dangerous things. Evenings were the best times for abductions. They were awake then, feeling safe. There was much less talk or resistance during evening kidnapings. His driver dropped him off a quarter mile away.

He knocked loudly and she got up, wondering. He stood outside the door and asked about a loose horse that had gotten out of his pasture down the road. Jane looked at the new hat. Then the new boots. Then the new jeans.

"Come in," she said. "Would you like some coffee? I've not seen any loose horses, but one of ours got out last year, and I had a hell of a time finding him."

He sat down at the kitchen table. She walked away to get coffee from the pantry. When she returned, he was staring into the barrel of a Ruger 357 Magnum.

"State your business, mister," she said.

111

Since she was standing too close to him, within arm's reach, Borgia correctly figured her to be a novice. Quickly he grabbed the pistol and bent it away, out of her grip, from her palm before she could fire.

After looking at his watch and pointing it back at her, he said, "You will tell me what you know of Brandon. Don't make problems. We will be comfortable, in the living room."

He motioned her to the couch in front of the fireplace.

"Could I have some water?" she asked.

He looked out the window and talked into his cellular phone. She heard him say that he would be "back tomorrow."

After it was completely dark outside, he told her it was time to talk. Her mouth was dry, her anxiety building. She was pissed.

"So, what do you want to know?" she asked.

"Where he keeps his files," Borgia said.

"In the pipe on the wall," she said motioning her head toward it and saying, "Do you know how to tell a redneck? By their uniform. Very disciplined. They have to wear their jeans low enough over their pot bellies so that in the back at least two inches of the crack in their ass shows. They also have to have green teeth. But they are nice people. Nice try, but you are not a redneck."

Borgia pulled the peace pipe down and inspected it closely. He pulled the stem from the bowl. Inside the shaft was a roll of old two dollar silver certificates.

"What's this?" he asked.

"Exactly how much your ass is worth after tonight. Fertilizer money," she said.

He lost his temper and slapped her too hard. She passed out. He got a beer from the refrigerator, sat back down waiting for her to wake up, and looked out the window for his accomplice to arrive and take them to the airstrip.

* * *

General Espinoza read through the transcripts of all state monitored telephone radio messages for the day. The references to Pitman and a bracelet caused him alarm. It could be an icon to their movement, a holy relic. He decided to get rid of the thing once and for all. He paced the floor for a while, then called Wanda.

"I want you to eliminate a flight," he said.

Wanda said he was still on retainer.

"I will give it a shot. But," he advised, "I am on to Brandon, and this delay will give him a few days. He's dangerous."

"That's okay," said Espinoza. "Here are the specifics."

The next day, Wanda wore mechanics clothes on the tarmac of the airport in Asuncion. He had a tool belt strapped around his waist and a clipboard in his hand as he entered the airplane an hour before takeoff. The refueling crew was busy on the ground and the cleaners and caterers were inside, busy at work. He stepped into the cockpit and nimbly unscrewed the panel of the INS, the Inertial Navigation System, on the center console. He disconnected the plug to the knob used in selecting the longitude, followed the wires to the condenser, which he disconnected and rotated five degrees. Then he reconnected both condenser and knob and screwed the panel back in place. *Neat job*, he thought, as he pulled some putty from his pocket and squashed it invisibly behind the mounting of the magnetic compass over the instrument panel. The putty contained magnetic filings that would cause the compass to read a few degrees off heading. He watched carefully as the compass slowly turned seven degrees toward the north.

Georgetown, Alexandria, Virginia: March 12, 1999

Tamac was healing nicely at Brandon's safe house under Chauncy's protection. He had requested that Pitman fly in an Incan "healer" from Peru. Her name was Illaquitak. She had trouble getting some pouches of herbs through customs, but after a careful inspection, the immigration people found no evidence of living plant matter, drugs, or micro-organisms and let her through. After a few hours of herbal treatment, the swelling in Tamac's face was almost gone, and he was feeling much better.

The Pentagon, Washington, D.C.: March 12, 1999

Colonel Bobarski re-read for the tenth time all the information left by General Johnson in the pink gourami. His contact with the Russians was successful, and he was ready to leave. They were to pick him up in an hour two blocks from his house on Prince Street in Old Town, Alexandria. He would be flown out that evening. His research on Pitman had proved somewhat successful. The man was high up in the CIA and was probably behind the phantom Lieutenant Jones who visited Wright Pat for a weekend. Pitman most likely possessed the only other documentation relative to the machine. But it didn't matter. There was only one machine around, and it was in Russia. He would tell the Russians nothing about Pitman. General Johnston had died of a heart attack. And now Colonel Bobarski was literally worth his weight in gold.

Asuncion, Paraguay: March 13, 1999

Henson scampered aboard the South American Airlines DC-10 clutching a gift from his daughter, and his diplomatic pouch close to his chest despite the handcuff and chain tying it to his wrist. He sat back and waited for what seemed a long time before he heard and felt the plane going to full power.

As it lifted off the runway, Henson promised himself two drinks during the flight. The Captain called for gear and flaps up. When the checklist was completed, Henson saw the no smoking light go out and reached for a cigarette. The Captain then turned off the seat belt sign, and Henson started looking for the flight attendant.

They were headed for La Paz, Bolivia, the last stop before Lima, Peru. The night was clear, and the flight climbed to altitude and cruised along the airway. A half-hour before landing, the Ground Proximity Warning System, or GPWS, flashed on for an instant as the plane descended through twenty-five thousand feet.

The Captain noted both the light and the absence of a normal audio warning. He decided to stop the descent, level out at twenty-three thousand feet, and check his route just to make sure.

"I would like to see the airway charts," he said to the co-pilot.

He passed them over.

"Well, we're on heading, on course," he said.

"That's the way I read it," answered the co-pilot, as the captain continued the descent.

"*The timing is perfect*," thought Henson as the flight attendant brought him his second drink. *Twenty minutes to landing.*

At twenty-two thousand feet, the GPWS light again flashed on, and as the Captain reached to turn it off, the audio mode blasted in the crew's ears, "Whoop! Whoop! Terrain! **Pull up! Pull up!**"

The Captain grabbed the power levers with his right hand and slammed them full forward while pulling back on the yoke with his left. The aircraft's nose started up and the craft quickly began climbing at a four degree flight path angle. Three seconds later, the bottom of the nose gently kissed the snow on the five degree up-slope of a snow-capped mountain.

In the time it took for the nerve signals from the pilot's buttocks to reach his brain, the aircraft had gone from a gentle slope of snow to a much steeper up-slope of ice at twenty-three thousand, two hundred forty feet above sea level. The high speed caused the nose of the plane to smash in against the prehistoric ice and granite uplifting, which pushed the cockpit air back into the fuselage. In a tenth of a second, the forward lavatory had crunched rearward thirty feet through the first class section. The air pressure in the rest of the plane was then so high that the entire main fuselage burst apart like a hard slapped paper bag.

The Captain, co-pilot, flight engineer, and several passengers in first class were instantly mashed into a mass of unrecognizable protoplasm. The rest of the flight crew and passengers were blown out sideways, momentarily alive, onto the snow and ice. Almost half of them then suffered death from impact or blunt force trauma. The other half survived their wounds for a few seconds, then quickly succumbed to exposure from the cold and lack of oxygen.

Henson was blown out the left side of the plane, still strapped into his seat, and tumbled a hundred yards, breaking most of the bones in his body. He came to rest laying on his side, absurdly still clutching his drink glass in a death-grip, and gasping at the stars. The cold Andean wind blew over his face, and in a few moments the aircraft wreckage, and passengers, were buried under a fresh blanket of blowing whiteness.

Camped at sixteen thousand feet, an Indian alpaca-herder wrapped himself in a warm blanket and noted the sound of the jet. Then he felt a slight tremor in the ground on which he lay, and sat up, listening intently. Earthquakes were not unusual in the Andes, but they were seldom singular, normally rumbling on for several seconds. Then the sound of the jet engines abruptly stopped, followed by a dull audio thud in the thin air. The Indian didn't know that the seismic tremor from the impact would reach him before the sound of the crash. But he knew that a passenger jet had ceased to exist, and he made preparations to pack several of his alpacas, depart for the lowlands, and report the incident to the local, ancient, Incan authorities.

Lone Pine, California: March 13, 1999

A lone Indian named Walks-In-Rain Thompson on a bluff overlooking Brandon's ranch house watched the strange man walk up and called the Chief on his cellular phone. Chief Dancing Eagle gave him instructions and immediately left the Sage Bar with four dollars of pool winnings in his pocket. This time he took the side road to Brandon's place. A thousand feet away, he slammed on the brakes of his pickup and viewed the premise with

115

night-vision binoculars. All looked calm. There were no strange vehicles around. He swept the scene again, focusing in through the living room window. "The pipe," he said out loud. "The pipe is not on the wall."

He grabbed his medicine bag from behind the truck's seat and started toward the house. Halfway there, he first heard, then saw a car come down the main entrance road. He focused his binoculars on Walks-In-Rain, who swung his binoculars toward the Eagle. When the Eagle saw Walks-In-Rain looking at him, he put his binoculars down and gave him instructions in sign language.

Borgia signalled his driver with a penlight and woke Jane up with a splash of cold water.

"Time to get rolling," he said.

She groaned, "What do you want?"

"I want Brandon's computer codes, you know, to the machine in his study," he said as his accomplice carried the computer and all the disks piled on top out to the truck.

"He doesn't tell me his codes. And I don't know what files you're talking about."

Borgia slapped her again.

Then he stopped suddenly, looking at his chest. Two arrow points jutted through his torso. There was little bleeding.

A knife slashed down through the window screen between the two small holes made by the arrows and in stepped Dancing Eagle.

"That's right," said the Eagle. "One kidney gone. One lung, gone. But you have one of each left for now. And now it's time for us to, what is the term, 'get rolling'?"

Moscow: March 13, 1999

Colonel Bobarski was legally dead in the United States. The Russians had done a perfect job, even down to duplicating the dental work on the corpse, which had burned up in Bobarski's West Virginia cabin. And the Colonel was safely ensconced in a small comfortable dacha outside Moscow with papers and money for quick transportation anywhere in the world.

With the information provided by Bobarski on flying the machine, the Russians quickly started operating it. And though all Americans who had were dead, and though the Russians would have done things differently by keeping one or two pilots alive, they appreciated the thoroughness of the maintenance of secrecy.

Also, regular reports were being received from Wanda. Though

Pitman and Brandon were no longer important, they would let Wanda's contract run its course. Brandon especially had caused too much damage in the past.

Alexandria, Virginia: March 13, 1999

The plane crash prompted Pitman and Allie to go to Brandon's safe house and see Tamac immediately. They had to talk to him about the lost bracelet. Chauncy let them in, and they sat in sofas around the coffee table.

The two Peruvian associates flown in by Brandon at Tamac's request stood by the door. Pitman started the conversation.

"Tamac," he began, "we have some bad news. The bracelet of your ancestors has been lost. An airplane crash high in the Andes killed all aboard. It is higher than even Incas can go without oxygen. I am sorry. Now you do not have a token of our good faith. And you have no original record to guide you to your wealth. But we may be able to help anyway."

"The bracelet of my ancestors, then, has been returned to our sun god in the mountains," said Tamac. "This is as it should be."

"Yes," said Pitman. "But there are people who may have photographs of this bracelet, as we do. If they decipher the signs on it, then your people may lose the entire treasure."

"What do you suggest?" asked Tamac.

"I suggest you first tell me everything about what has transpired so far concerning these artifacts that have been sold in England. Then look at the photographs we have of the bracelet and see if there is something you can see."

"And your motive for this help? Is it still drugs?" asked Tamac.

"Yes. Mainly drugs that are undermining our society, our very existence as a people. Some of these drugs are grown in your country."

"Yes," said Tamac. "We want to eliminate this drug business also. It keeps our people in the bondage of labor by the Spaniards. We know they will not leave our land without a war or compensation. They have modern military weapons, we do not. But they understand money. Our plan is still to buy them out. But if they get to our ancestral treasure first, then we will not have the means to buy. And what else?" he asked.

Pitman looked at him with questioning eyes.

"You said 'mainly drugs'," said Tamac.

"Yes," said Pitman. "There is something else. There may be a space ship there with your treasure."

"We call it the Itstalcumpambas, the gift from our sun god," said Tamac.

117

"That is why much of our treasure has been taken there for centuries, to honor our god. It is part of our folklore, our heritage, though few through the centuries have actually seen it. It was there eons before my people became what you would call a civilization. Tradition has it that it was left here by other gods who flew away in something just like it."

Tamac sat very still for a minute, then got up and stared out the window. Finally he turned and said, "Our plan, Mr. Pitman, is to get our country back. Perhaps the gift from our god can help, perhaps not. But the treasure certainly can help now. And that is where our focus is. The Sapa Inca took some works to England for auction, to get money to buy land and to help finance our cause. He was accompanied by two of our three Rememberers. But he and his son were the only ones who knew where the treasure is, and they are both dead. We have looked at everything we know about it and have come up with almost nothing. Only one Rememberer is left, and she only has part of the solution to it. The treasure may well be lost."

"Well," said Pitman. "What if I were to tell you that my wife has deciphered some of what was on the bracelet?"

Tamac looked at Allie with wide eyes and asked her to relate what she knew. Allie told of the cat being the same shape as Lake Titicaca and of the three mountains that make the perfect triangle. Tamac was impressed and alarmed at the same time.

"If this much can be figured out by a stranger," said Tamac, "then we are truly in dire straits."

"My wife is gifted, Tamac. It is doubtful another can determine as much in the same short amount of time," said Pitman. "But given enough time, it could be deciphered by others."

"Then," said Tamac, "perhaps Mrs. Pitman could help with the rest of it, given more information. I may be able to offer some assistance now. I have been following what your country is attempting with this drug business, and am convinced that our interests along these lines are mutual. Perhaps we can provide some information for Mrs. Pitman."

The Pitmans looked at him in a different light. The man didn't talk like a peasant. His face, after the healing, had a special quality of serenity and command. He talked with authority. Allie suspected he might be more than he let on.

"I would be delighted to hear anything," said Allie. "I love puzzles."

"Do you know exactly what a Rememberer is, Mrs. Pitman?" asked Tamac.

"I believe they were people of yours who kept the records of the empire on strings—produce, population, laws, things like that," she said.

"Yes," he answered. "And also the history of our people. Illaquitak, here, is our last one of the three who held part of the secret. She will speak to you. Please show her your photographs of the bracelet and darken the room a little."

Allie watched the nurse walk over and sit down and, while Chauncy got up and closed the curtains, she studied the woman's teenage face and jet black hair.

"How old are you, may I ask?" asked Allie as she turned on the tape recorder and pulled out the photographs from an envelope. The woman slid her chair closer to the coffee table to look at the pictures and said, "Sixty-three."

Quickly she leafed through the photos, was convinced they were of the real thing, then sat back in her chair, and closed her eyes while pulling a small *quipu* from her jacket pocket. For a full minute she ran her thumbs and forefingers through the knotted strings. An eeriness was felt by all as they waited in the dim room, and listened, trance-like.

"I am Illaquitak," she began in a low voice, as if at a seance. "I am a Rememberer. My people are from an ancient past, a past beyond the flood and the ice. We walked on earthquakes and volcanoes. We were, and are, astronomers, mathematicians, engineers, hunters, farmers, voyagers, priests, architects, fathers, travelers, mothers, and kings. Our story has been learned and repeated by each generation. This is part of our story you seek.

"The sparrows attacked the eagle in the square at Cuzco, the navel of the universe, near the lake of the jaguar. But the eagle did not die. When night came, and the sparrows were asleep, the eagle flew to the stars. It will return with the sound of heavy water on the day of reckoning, a day of total equality. I am Illaquitak. I am a Rememberer."

She opened her eyes and looked at Tamac, then at Allie.

"That's what we have, Mrs. Pitman," said Tamac. "I've heard it a hundred times."

Allie looked at her notes and said she would do what she could.

"Well," asked Pitman. "Where to from here?"

Tamac said that he wanted to return to Peru as soon as possible. If Mrs. Pitman came up with anything, she should not, under any circumstances, relay it except in person, in Peru.

"Fine with me," said Allie.

"All the airwaves," continued Tamac, "and telephone lines in Peru are

119

monitored by the military. Messages couched in short conversations are fine. But no solutions."

"A code word to that effect, and a predesignated place for her to meet you would be helpful," said Pitman.

Tamac thought for a minute and said, "The word will be 'blade', the place will be the northernmost shore of Lake Titicaca."

"Good," said Pitman, "and arrangements will be made for your return when you desire." He handed Tamac a piece of paper with his private telephone numbers on it.

"Also," added Pitman at the door, "there is a certain General Espinoza in your country, and your new U.S. Ambassador named Bloomquist, who are under suspicion as being in the middle of this whole thing. You should be wary of both of them."

"We have known of, and have tracked, Espinoza for years," said Tamac. "But thanks for the information on Bloomquist."

"Any idea when you want to leave?" asked Pitman.

"Tomorrow," said Tamac.

* * *

Chauncy called Pitman.

"You know that tail you wanted on Jess? Well, I was wrong and you were right. There is someone on his ass, perhaps two people. Very clever. Very invisible. It took three more of my men to confirm it. He was set up here in Washington."

"Set up for what?" asked Pitman.

"The big sleep, or abduction first, probably," said Chauncy. "The tails were only to get his schedule. Distant tails. Binoculars, telescopes. Nothing up close."

"Any clue on who it is?" asked Pitman.

"Not who, just what. These people are smooth, pros. Don't have much on the second one. The first walks like a big woman, fat face, talks like a man. Goes to the best restaurants, stays in the best places. Pays cash for everything, probably to keep from using credit cards. The second stays out of sight. They've got Jess. And we can't find him."

Pitman thought about taking the men out now. But then he wouldn't know their source. Besides, Brandon could probably take care of himself.

"Nationality?" asked Pitman.

"Sorry, boss. They're both white or Hispanic. That's it."

"Thanks, Chaunce. Keep 'em in sight. If you see anything dangerous, move in."

"Rog."

High Sierra Mountains, California: March 13, 1999

The Indian sleeping drug on the arrows put Borgia under within thirty seconds. The Eagle tied him up.

"How are you?" he asked Jane.

"Thirsty," she said.

He got her a glass of water, and while she was drinking it he went through his medicine bag, pulled out a pair of dikes, and quickly snipped the heads and tails off the arrows in Borgia's torso. He unscrewed a small jar and applied an oily poultice on the four ends of the two arrow shafts.

He lifted the fat man onto his left shoulder.

"Where?" asked Jane. "What?"

"Dorothy will be over in a few minutes and will drive you to the Inyokern or L.A. Airport. I'll have some answers in a day or three, and I'm borrowing Manny and Spike. The foal and dogs will follow along. We'll be in the mountains. I don't much like the way this person treated you. Walks-In-Rain will call the sheriff to pick up the one outside. He'll be awake in a few hours. Fly back commercial. Okay?"

"Fine," said Jane, rubbing her cheek, thinking, *Not frigging fine at all!*

Georgetown, Washington, D.C.: March 13, 1999

Allie fixed some tea, went to her study, and looked at the giant photograph of the bracelet. She pulled some papers from a file she had labelled *Inca Notes*, and asked Pitman if he got anything out of what the Rememberer had said. He hadn't. She looked at the woman's words a long time. Pitman began rubbing her neck.

"The eagle flew to the stars. It will return with the sound of heavy water on the day of reckoning, a day of total equality," she said.

"Total equality," she mumbled in concentration. "Why total?" she wondered. "Why not just equality? Perhaps the end of the world, Judgement Day."

She looked at the bracelet for equality. The three mountain peaks made an equilateral triangle. The Incas were architects. Then she perked up and said, "**The** day of reckoning, and **A** day of equality! Like there were many days of equality, but only one day of reckoning. And they were also astronomers. Andy, will you please get me your copy of Dutton's Navigation?"

"Sure," he said. "It's in a box in the attic. Back in a minute. Haven't opened it for years."

He returned beating dust off the cover, handed it to her, then began rubbing her shoulders. She opened it to a star chart.

"You see Andy, here is a U.S. Navy map of the night sky in the southern hemisphere. And here is an Inca diagram from the wall of the Temple of the Sun at the Inca mummy morgue, Coricancha, in Cuzco. The four stars that comprise the Southern cross are in the same relative position in both the Navy chart and the Coricancha wall drawing. But the Cross in the photograph of the bracelet shows it slightly rotated or askew relative to True North when compared to the orientation of the other two."

Allie patted Pitman's hands from her shoulders, got up, and turned the photograph on the wall upside down. Pitman pulled up a chair and sat down.

"Would you like a drink?" she asked. "I have to think away from this for a while, then sleep on it."

"Yes, I would," he said.

She came around the desk and walked out the door. He got up and followed her down the stairs to the living room. There he sat in his big chair and thoroughly enjoyed the show again. He thought about it. Over the years he had never once missed watching her inspect two glasses, carefully pour whiskey in one and water in the other, and then slosh them together. Finally he concluded that he hadn't the foggiest idea why he enjoyed it so much or why it was such a catharsis to him. He had friends who felt wonderful after each of a thousand times riding the same horse over the same trail. They couldn't explain it. It was just what it was. And he was smart enough not to think too much on it.

Allie handed him the drink, walked to the couch opposite the chair, and began to sit down. Then she rose and walked back toward him, took the drink out of his hand, sat in his lap, and said, "Kiss me."

Pitman, seeing the scholarly twinkle of awareness vice submission in her eye asked, "Is this another sexual thing?"

"If I'm right, in a day or two you can take your next roll in the hay to the bank!" she said, placing his cheeks between her hands and kissing him firmly on the lips. "But first, I want your analysis of this country Peru."

Pitman reached for his pipe with his free hand, thought quietly for a minute, then began the history lesson according to Pitman, the history buff.

"Patents," he said.

"Patents?" she asked. "What the hell does that mean?"

"Perhaps that was the wrong place to start," he said. "First go forward a few decades. Then back up a few from 'patents', and I will come to the point."

"Any philosophic?" she asked.

"None," he said.

"Then do continue," she answered, settling into his lap. He stuck his pipe into his mouth, lighting it with a butane, then started.

"I will use an example. The entire world, not just the free world, but the Communists and ex-Communists and all the other second and third world countries today have access to machines that fly in the sky and that can take them almost anywhere else on the planet in a day. A hundred years ago, most everyone had the same access, except it took a life savings and a year to get to the other side of the world. Spain, France, and Portugal had the wealth to make the investment toward technological advancement. But they did not.

"If it were not for the form of government of the United States, none of these billions of people would have airplanes or radios or television or refrigerators, higher yield crops, or inoculations against disease. Not even the French. Louis Pasteur was treated like all the glider and airplane inventors in France: as curiosities, not investments. Spain took trillions of dollars in the equivalent of modern currency from this hemisphere, first enslaving the people here, the Indians, then exterminating many races through overwork. And they spent four hundred years not investing a dime in capital improvement. I hate to pick on Spain because they are getting their act together today. But they are a good example of a people who could not separate the functions of religion from the functions of government. When this cannot be done, then the bottom line is an inability to separate fact from belief. In the history of the world, when a government is solely based on a belief in any being, then facts take second place to the belief of whoever is in power. What they believe to be the facts become the facts-to-keep-their-power. And they *believe* that they will eliminate anyone who does not do what they want them to. And so they do. As the Bard of Baltimore, H.L. Menken said, 'The problem with Protestants is not that they want you to believe as they do. It's that they want you to do as they believe.'

"Unfortunately, in several of the Mideastern countries, isolated from but using in an arrogant way the destructive elements of the two-way street of technology, the ones with the power have also become the belief and the sole interpreters of the belief. And the people who disbelieve are summarily killed."

Allie squirmed, again asking, "You're sure you're not getting into your philosophic?"

"Not yet," said Pitman. "But thanks for the warning. Patents. The Saudis are the only ones in that part of the world who have consistently recognized relative worth from the beginning. Other smaller countries there have taken their lead. But the bigger ones have blown it. They all like televisions, automobiles, tall buildings, electric power dams, and roads. But they've mostly been middle-men for thousands of years, trading their geographic position for money, producing almost nothing of value to other peoples, taxing the trade gateway between East and West. After Vasco de Gama bypassed them, they had a bit of a bad time. Some Arabs, in 1756, went to the desolate and uninhabited land of Kuwait to try to start over. Then the United States discovered oil and the use of it. And, because of our patent laws, people came forward with ideas that could make them wealthy, their efforts protected. Entrepreneurs invested capital. Airplanes suddenly became worth inventing. Automobiles allowed a vast freedom of movement. And oil became the mother of invention, improving the quality of life for many billions of people.

"Most of the middle-men in the Mideast however, except for the Saudis, saw this wealth as a way to power, not as a way to wealth for all their people, but just for them. They couldn't get it out of the ground. They couldn't refine it for use. They couldn't pump it into their camels or make tents with it. They even couldn't find it. But they could use it to buy tons of the technological stuff that would increase their personal power without costing them any capital investment. They are doing the same thing with their black gold of oil that the Spanish did with their metallic gold in countries like Peru . . . like the Soviet Communist leaders did with the slave-labor from numerous countries through the threat of organized murder. Same equation—extract the wealth, produce nothing for the populace, and keep the population in check while working them at a subsistence level through force. But above all, they will not allow enforceable laws that could enable anyone else outside their minute power-clique the opportunity to improve their lot or especially to become wealthy. No enforced patent laws. That's Peru today. A *junta* posing as religious, pious people, keeping the populace down while extracting the wealth. Now, and for years, that other religion,

Communism, has been making an attempt at the wealth there, for 'all the people'. One hypocrisy for another. No enforced patent laws."

Allie kissed him on the cheek and said that he had another minute. She had to get to bed or be worth nothing in the morning.

"That's it," said Pitman. "That's my story on Peru. The Incas have had it. After five hundred years of getting along in order to exist within their own non-dependent culture, they are now being physically threatened by this drug-greed business. They want to control their own destiny now, since the alternative is death . . . sorry honey, did I go past my time?"

"Thanks. You were perfect," she said.

Old Town, Alexandria, Virginia: March 13, 1999

Chauncy stayed at the power plant in Old Town, listening to the progress on the radio. It all seemed to fit. There were no tracks in the mud flat on the shore of the Potomac River, no swirls of brown leading to the trees where the boat left. "Yes," said Chauncy. "Definitely a decoy."

When the report from his men on the taxi came in, Chauncy gave orders to immediately buy it and have it driven to his farm as soon as possible. "Don't let anyone in the back seat. And Matlock," he added, "pick me up back here when it's on its way."

"Rog," said Matlock, as Chauncy watched the distant chopper break off its high hover and begin flying along the highway. Then he walked the length of the long building, looking for climbing ropes, chinks in the bricks, anything odd. An eerie feeling came over him on his second pass. He inspected the ground. Just gravel.

* * *

The taxi was in a meadow behind his farmhouse when Chauncy arrived. It was nondescript. An old Chevy. Chauncy and Matlock looked the outside over carefully, noting nothing unusual. When Matlock reached for a door, Chauncy grabbed his hand, saying "Not yet, Mat."

"What do you have in mind?" asked Matlock.

Chauncy said it was a hunch, a feeling. "I don't like being jerked around," he added. Then he whistled a high shrill tone.

When Matlock saw the old bloodhound saunter off the back porch dragging his ears, he knew what might be up.

"Why do you call him Ball Peen?" asked Matlock during the eternity it seemed to take the dog get to them.

"Because since he was a pup, when he's on a scent, you can't sway him off the trail even by beating him over the head with a ball peen hammer."

"Nice trait," said Matlock.

Chauncy first had the dog smell the right rear door handle. Then he pulled him back, opened the door, and said, "Zat it, zat it, Ball Peen?"

The dog first sniffed the floor of the taxi, then the rear seat, whined a little, then backed out of the car, sat on his haunches, and howled loudly toward the sky.

"Good boy," said Chauncy.

"I reckon we'll be flying Ball Peen back to Old Town," said Matlock.

"Right on," said Chauncy as he cut a patch of rear seat upholstery from the old taxi with his pocket knife.

* * *

Matlock landed in the power plant parking lot. Chauncy gave Ball Peen a sniff of the upholstery. The dog led him at a good clip through the fence to the back of the power plant. Chauncy unclipped the leash, half expecting him to go through the hole in the fence toward the water. But back and forth he went, along the brick building, sniffing and whining the whole time.

Matlock videotaped the dog and the surroundings as per Chauncy's normal operating procedures. After ten minutes they left and flew back to Chauncy's farm.

The report on the speedboat was in when they arrived. Chauncy pulled the papers from his fax machine and handed each page to Matlock as he finished reading them.

"Well, what do you think?" he asked.

"Remote control all the way. No prints," said Matlock. "Obviously a diversion. No solutions."

Chauncy became more and more depressed at being stifled and the thought of Brandon, of all people, held captive. He went to the refrigerator.

"Want a beer?" he said to Matlock.

"Sure," said Matlock as he connected the final wire from his tiny video camera to Chauncy's TV.

The video showed the dog running along the brick building, halting, running further, coming back, never once turning toward the river.

"That's an unusual angle," said Chauncy.

"Yea," said Matlock. "I don't need to look through the eyepiece to take recordings. Usually just hold it by my side while looking things over."

126

They watched the videotape twice while talking about all the particulars they could think of concerning Brandon's disappearance.

Suddenly Chauncy coughed, inhaled beer, coughed again, and gasped for breath while Matlock beat him hard on the back. Beer foam ran out of his nose as he settled back into the chair.

"You okay?" asked Matlock.

Chauncy took a final recovering gasp, wiped his nose with a handkerchief, and said, "Sorry Mat. Could you play that last minute back in slow motion?"

"Sure."

They watched the dog float by the brick wall at an easy lope, his huge ears looking like Dumbo the Elephant, winging him along. He stopped and abruptly turned toward the wall, losing his balance for an instant. Then he backed off, looking confused, and continued by the building, sniffing to pick up the scent anew.

"There!" exclaimed Chauncy. "Back it up."

They watched the scene again.

"Did you notice anything?" asked Chauncy.

"No," said Matlock.

"Then play it again, and freeze it when I say 'now'," said Chauncy. "Now!"

Matlock stared at the frozen Dumbo and the brick wall. Then it came clear.

"Good eyes, Chaunce," he said. "The Peen had a whole nose when we got back here. But obviously half of it disappeared into a brick wall for an instant. We couldn't notice it at the time because his ears were blocking our view. But the camera was held lower."

"Holograph?" asked Chauncy.

"Definitely a holographic entrance," said Matlock. "Top of the line stuff. I'll crank up the chopper."

* * *

Brandon sat in the cold room strapped into a chair under the white light that seemed to be the standard prop for KGB-type 'interviews.' He recognized the face of his interrogator from a previous mug-shot viewing of Russian Embassy personnel. Though he couldn't place the name, the graying hair combed straight back and the cruel, wide, unsmiling gash of a mouth were the familiar idiosyncrasies he had noted earlier. The man was an ex-Soviet General, new to the United States in a kind of mercenary role, helping the new independent Russian state with its cash problem, hiring out to the highest bidder in an 'official' capacity.

Probably one of those Russian horses asses, thought Brandon, *who still thinks that might makes right.*

The General pulled up a chair, sat down, stared at Brandon, then nodded to someone else off to his left side. Like a shadow, a figure came out to the edge of the light and swung a hard rubber pipe into Brandon's face.

"Now that I have your attention," said the General, "I hope you see that time is of the essence. You will answer my questions or you will be dead. Is that understood?"

Brandon spit several pieces of chipped teeth out, then searched the rest of his mouth with his tongue for more fragments before answering.

"How much money do you have on you?" he asked the General.

"Ah," said the General sarcastically. "It is always a matter of money with you Americans. You think it is always worth something to others. How much were you thinking of giving for your ransom?"

Brandon moved his feet slightly forward against the bindings. The minute he had been strapped in, his big toenails had tripped small levers on the insides of his cowboy boots that opened small containers of acid built into the tops of his boot backs. The liquid slowly ran down and soaked into the straps that held his ankles. It usually took four or five minutes for it to eat through strands of rope, a little longer for wire; less time to weaken them enough to be broken.

"You're not listening," said Brandon, "I asked how much money *you* have on *you*."

Brandon's feet imperceptibly moved forward from the chair legs a fraction of an inch. His muscles tightened. He could feel the strands, one by one, start to stretch and weaken. Adrenalin pumped into his bloodstream. He was now ready.

"I am asking the questions," said the General, "Do I need to have my man here get your attention again?"

"The nearest I can figure," said Brandon, "is a minimum of two caps, maybe a root canal also. I'd say three thousand dollars should make me happy enough not to kill the two of you."

"What are you talking about . . . caps, root canals?" asked the General.

"Dentist fees," said Brandon. "Your man just chipped at least two of my teeth. If you pay me for the damage now, I might go easy on you."

Brandon had two other options. But the acid seemed the best for now.

He would save the two tiny projectiles under the skin of each of his wrists. They were connected with micro-circuits to the finger tendons that went up into his forearm and could be fired through his skin by cocking the wrist back and extending his middle finger up while clinching the others. It had taken much practice to master the technique before the surgical implants. Also, the fabric in his shirt, pants, and underwear were interlaced with unnoticeably thin kevlar threads. He could survive virtually all knife wounds, and most gunshots below .45 calibre.

The General started to say something, then gave a sigh of disgust and again nodded to the man with the rubber pipe. Brandon concentrated, his brain absorbing every photon of dim light around him, calculating future movement. Out of the shadows stepped the figure.

Like a coiled spring, Brandon stood and unwound. His right foot snapped out of the ropes, knee almost to his chin. Then, in a single coordinated movement, he spun around and extended his right leg out full length. The chair, still strapped to his arms, swung behind him. The back chair legs struck the General across the head and knocked him onto the floor, while the last four inches of foot extension did its calculated job. The heel of Brandon's cowboy boot smashed through the shadow's solar plexus and into the heart, rupturing the aorta and popping a ventricle. Then Brandon turned to the General, who was struggling to rise, and kicked him hard in the temple, causing an easy death. Then he sat back down in the still-attached chair next to the General, retrieved a tiny knife with his teeth from the seam of his pants by his left knee, and quickly cut his arms loose.

In a few minutes of searching along every nook and cranny, Brandon knew he was sealed in a tomb. There was no obvious way out. The only door had no handle. After covering the four solid metal walls and the metal ceiling, he found only a three-inch air vent, and then he knew that it was all a set up for everyone's elimination, nothing else. He bet that the vent contained a microphone and transmitter and that all conversation was being sent to a remote station to be recorded. Wanda would come back in a few months and see, out of curiosity, how all three died, and to see if Commander Brandon had had a "nice death." Brandon almost threw up at the thought. Then he began scraping and tapping at the walls and floor with his fingernails. He checked how much acid he had left in the different compartments of his boots and clothing to eat through the metal or concrete. He could only give it one shot and decided on the concrete floor. Once through that, he had enough energy stored in his 13 percent body fat, to dig his way out in a day or two.

He picked a spot where his knuckle-rappings seemed to indicate a thinner layer of cement near the same wall as the door. He considered using the plastic explosive in his boot sole, but decided against it. The room was sealed, and the overpressure from an explosion could cause a brain hemorrhage. Besides, he didn't want to draw attention, and he had time.

After applying the acid in a one-foot diameter circle, he waited and meditated, conserving energy. After a few hours it had eaten through, and Brandon began stomping with his boots and prying with metal chair legs. In another hour, he had leveraged and broken enough concrete to make a three-foot hole through the cement floor. Then he started digging.

In a few hours, after carefully spaced periods of rest, Brandon was down three feet and digging toward the wall. Suddenly he stopped, and concentrated. He could barely hear the throb of helicopter rotor blades through the steel walls.

Chauncy! he thought.

From the air, Chauncy looked at the spot from the video of the bricks where Ball Peen's nose had disappeared.

"Mat," he said, "can you fly down close to that place first, between the side of the building and the electrical transformers on the other side of the alley?"

"Yea," said Matlock.

Chauncy saw, for an instant, the bricks disappear and become a large metallic door. Then as they passed, the bricks reappeared.

"Land over there in the parking lot," he said, "and follow me at ten meters with Uzi and plastic satchel charges."

Chauncy looked around at the huge transformers and soon saw what appeared to be a small TV camera mounted high on one of the stantions. With his side arm equipped with a silencer, two identical sounds disturbed the weekend silence of the place: 'Pffft. Pffft.'

Then he looked at the brick wall. Miraculously, a section of bricks had disappeared, and was replaced by a dark iron door. He walked over and rapped on the door. Brandon rapped back in Morse code, "SOS, B."

There was a handle, but no lock or key hole. Chauncy tried the handle. Matlock crouched low with his Uzi at the ready.

The door slowly swung open, and Brandon stepped out with a slight smile on his face, as if to say *What took you so long*, his eyes painfully adjusting to the sunlight. He put his finger to his lips to tell Chauncy not to talk, and they went back inside. Brandon borrowed Chauncy's pistol and flashlight. Chauncy inspected the two dead people while Brandon took careful aim at the air vent and fired into it. Then he shined the light inside. A shattered mini-mike lay on its side, its connecting wires severed.

Within two minutes they were all on the helo and headed to Chauncy's farm. "So, who were those guys?" asked Chauncy.

"Wanda's idea of humor," said Brandon. "We were all to be eliminated. Those two also, after they had done their job on me. And I thought I was sick. Now he will know we have his number, Chaunce," added Brandon. "I have a feeling this Wanda character will want to make it a quick and final thing with me the next time he tries."

Lima, Peru: March 13, 1999

Wanda stayed in his Gulfstream after returning from the mountains. Naomi was driven by Espinoza's men to shop for food. She did all the cooking aboard the Gulfstream. Wanda spent most of the time in the communications cabin behind the plane's bedroom, coordinating business via fax/modem and satellite telephone.

From his men in Washington, D.C., he read the sound-activated recording transcript of Brandon's "last words" as it came off the fax machine. He immediately called and had the original audio recording sent over commercial telephone lines. It arrived within ten minutes.

From the conversation, there was little torture, mostly just a bunch of smart talk by Brandon about teeth, followed by some sounds indicating a short struggle. There followed many sounds of tapping, scraping, and what seemed to be digging. Then there was the sound of the door opening. Then the microphone went dead. He called Espinoza.

"Brandon escaped what I had in mind," he said. "If I am unsuccessful here in Peru, your money will be returned."

Espinoza, always the businessman, said, "If you are unsuccessful, you will most likely be dead. Return half the money now, and I will provide you with any people and material resources you may want to use, according to your plans."

"The funds will be wired to you within the hour," said Wanda. "I may need two Peruvian Air Force fighters, one with your top pilot, the other with me in it, to do the job quickly if he gets out of Mexico."

Espinoza again said that everything he needed would be provided, and he could delay Brandon for a few days at any of the possible fueling stops in southern Mexico.

Chapter Seven

East of the Urals, Russia: March 16, 1999

The saucer drifted out of a Russian hangar. It was a clear day. Pitman watched the space satellite video of the operation with intense interest.

First the saucer-shaped craft slowly circled the remote airfield. Then it accelerated off screen at an incredible speed. The satellite camera reacquired it as it quickly returned to the general area of the airfield. A Mig-21 fighter took off. The saucer flew wing on the Mig for several miles, then backed off. First the Mig's canopy came off and was pushed back by the airstream. Then the ejection seat came out. From the satellite camera in space above, the pilot and his seat looked like a black dot. The dot was pushed back also. When the seat separated from the pilot, the dot became two dots. Then the pilot dot became a much larger white dot as his parachute opened.

The Mig continued along on autopilot. The saucer then flew in a wide arc toward the Mig, turned sideways, and accelerated directly into it. It could not be described as a crash. The saucer neatly sliced the Mig in half just aft of the cockpit. The front end plummeted toward the earth. The rest of the plane burst into orange and yellow flames, then exploded into a white and black ball of smoke. Then the saucer descended and propelled itself in a straight line directly toward the hangar from where it had come. It went inside, and the hangar doors closed.

"Fantastic!" said Pitman.

Georgetown, Washington, D.C.: March 17, 1999

Pitman noted her airy attitude the next morning at breakfast. He waited until they had cleared the table, then could stand it no longer.

"Care to tell me what you figured out on the bracelet?" he asked.

What makes you so sure I solved anything?" she asked.

"You've been flitting around the kitchen like a damn Tinker Bell all morning. And I don't remember marrying an air-headed bimbette," he said.

"Very good. I may indeed have some star dust to sprinkle on this. See Andy," she said suddenly sitting down and grabbing her coffee cup. "The four emeralds on the bracelet probably represent the stars of the Southern Cross. But they are different for two reasons. First they are upside down on the bracelet because these people, these Incas, were at the top of their world. The cat is sitting on the triangle, not wearing a dunce cap. The bracelet can be viewed from two directions, that of an observer standing in front of the wearer, or the wearer looking at the bracelet. We have been looking at it as if standing in front of the wearer. But the Inca, the Sapa Inca, could look at his bracelet and see the map of the earth and stars. From his dead-eye view, the Southern Cross is the same as the one shown on the Navy chart.

"The second difference is that the Southern Cross on the bracelet is skewed, rotated. If the edge of the bracelet were a line of geographical latitude, then Lake Titicaca, the jaguar, and the three mountains that make up the triangle are aligned perfectly. So we have to consider that they knew, very accurately, where north and south were and are. And it makes no difference that our north was their south."

She got up and refilled her cup. Pitman wrote down most of what she had said and started evaluating. So far it made sense. But again, he realized, it might be too much for Andy Pitman. He had watched his wife's mind work before. And every time it was with profound respect. Not that he had ever felt insecure because of it. But this time he was feeling stupid. He brushed that thought aside and rationalized that this was the first time in his life that he had felt even a tiny degree of old age in his brain.

"One of the mummy morgue wall paintings in Cuzco makes sense with this," said Allie. "It depicts the Constellation Crux, which contains the 'Southern Cross', which is oriented relative to the sunrise to indicate Fall, or more specifically their vernal equinox. The bracelet shows the Southern Cross with an orientation several degrees different relative to the sun.

"I submit, Mr. Pitman, that the stars on the bracelet of the dead Incan Emperor comprise the Southern Cross in the Constellation Crux, and that this Cross is oriented or rotated in the position in the southern sky that

133

corresponds to when the period of daylight is equal to the period of night—the vernal equinox in our hemisphere, the autumnal equinox in theirs—'a day of total equality', as per Illaquitak the Rememberer. This equinox would be during the month of March, March twenty-first, according to both my protractor and the almanac."

Pitman put his pencil down and said, "That's only five days from now. Any idea which little lake it might be?"

Now it was her turn to be impressed.

"What lake?" she said.

"There are several small lakes around the triangle made by the mountains," said Pitman. "One of them might be important."

"How so?" she asked.

"The month of March marks the end of the dry season in the mountains there. Mountain lakes usually lose some water during dry times. No replenishing from melting snow, plus evaporation from the higher temperatures at those altitudes. Perhaps one lake would reveal something on the bottom with a lower water level . . . something that could not be seen during any other time of the year."

"Andy," she said, "you're just never going to grow old, are you? How do you know so much of the southern hemisphere?"

"Flattery again, my dear. Remember, we met in Rio, which is in the southern hemisphere. And I wasn't down there for my health. What do you want now?"

The dual-pronged pang of both sides of love for him arrowed into her heart at the remembrance . . . the dig that she wasn't there for her health either, the reference to the romance that wasn't supposed to be romance. *Some kind of universal balance, like gravity or Newtonian physics*, she thought, *that had surfaced in spades during the Chiang Imperative.*

"I now know which little lake it is Andy. With your explanation, it is the one on the map that is exactly on the north-south side of the triangle of mountains. The one at the same relative distance from the bottom of the triangle as the triangle is from the bottom of the cat, and that the cat is from the South Pole, the bottom of our Earth, the top of theirs. I think these Inca people knew a hell of a lot more about geography and astronomy than we realize. The lake is called Lake Moho. And it is shaped like a bone."

High Sierra Nevada Mountains, California: March 18, 1999

Dancing Eagle sat by the small campfire in the mountains and waited for Borgia to wake up. The fat man stirred, then sat up painfully.

"Yes," said the Eagle. "You have two arrow shafts inside you. Not too serious now. Could be in a while. And you can't walk in the meantime. Of course I can remove them and put you in a hospital. What were your instructions with the lady Jane?"

Borgia looked around and winced. He was trained in only modern technology, not this Indian crap. This wasn't part of his contract with Wanda. And he knew he would die if something wasn't done soon.

"A simple abduction," he said. "Needed to get to Brandon. And information, files, anything I could find."

"Who," asked the Eagle, "are you working for?"

"Wanda. International assassin type. Very secretive. I just do small jobs. He pays very well."

"Where were you to take her?"

"Nowhere, a motel in town, for two days. I was mostly after information."

The Eagle rummaged through his medicine bag and retrieved a cellular phone. After two minutes with Brandon, he had the picture. The man on the other side of the fire would be freed to take a message to Wanda.

After punching the off button, he asked, "You want to make the trip down the mountain awake or asleep? Could be painful."

"Awake," said Borgia.

The Eagle again rummaged through his bag.

"Drink this, unbutton your shirt, and lie down," he said, handing Borgia a small flask of whiskey mixed with herbs.

"You are good at following instructions," said the Eagle, watching him chug the flask. "Here is what will happen. I will remove the shafts. There will be a little bleeding, but you will be able to move afterward. I'll call for an ambulance to meet us at the road. In an hour you will be in a hospital. Tomorrow you will report to this Wanda person and tell him that *Brandon will give him an easy death if there is no further attempt at the lives of any non-players.* Got it?"

Borgia repeated the line.

"Good, and now I'm going to remove the shafts. I will grip the ends and count to three."

The Eagle removed the poultice on Borgia's front side and stuck the two blobs on his stomach. Then he gripped the protruding shafts with his strong thumbs and index fingers.

"One, two," then he pulled. They both came out in an instant. Borgia was waiting for the number three. When it came, it was all over.

"Three," said the Eagle while plugging the holes with the blobs of poultice.

Lima, Peru: March 18, 1999

Wanda listened to Borgia's message on his answering machine. Now Brandon was doubly warned. All personal aspects had to be taken out of the equation. The playing field had to be purely environmental. The odds were better. If Brandon was delayed en route, Wanda had direct routes to Hermosillo, Mazatlan, Mexico City, Acapulco, and Tapachula already installed in his onboard navigational computer. He could fly quickly to any of those fuel stops and take care of the business with local help on the ground. If Brandon got into Peruvian airspace, Peru's top fighter pilot would make the first pass. Then, if need be, he would make the kill himself. Not much of a contest against an unarmed civilian propeller plane.

Chapter Eight

Mazatlan, Mexico: March 19, 1999

Espinoza's lieutenant arrived at the airport in time to see the Lake Renegade taxiing for takeoff. As he drove to the small operations building, Brandon and Allie were rolling down the runway. The lieutenant went into the building and checked their flight plan. Then he called Espinoza.

Tapachula, Mexico: March 19, 1999

Brandon and Allie's gas stops at both Hermosillo and Mazatlan went without incident. Their next leg in Mexico took them to Tapachula, a small town near the southern border. Here they were met by an army officer in uniform who informed them that they had to go through customs in the sole building on the airfield. It looked more like a two-story shack, thought Allie. Brandon first walked over to a man standing by a fuel truck, handed him a hundred dollars, and pointed to the plane. The man brightened up and said, "*Si, Señor.*"

Inside the building they found only stifling heat, flies, a telephone hanging on the wall, and four people playing cards at a small table. Brandon asked where customs was. One of the card players asked to see their passports. Allie handed hers to Brandon and he, after inserting a fifty dollar bill in each, handed them to the man. He perused them carefully, passed them around the table, and said that it would take about three days to clear them.

Brandon noticed the army officer making a phone call.

"Well, let's get our bags," he said to Allie.

She wondered what he meant. Certainly it was not to get their luggage.

They walked out to the plane. Brandon told Allie to put a bag out on the wing, then to get back in and flip the switches for starting.

"When I say 'go,' crank her up," he said.

Then he walked to the other side of the plane and handed the gas man another fifty dollars, while pulling the hose out and closing the cap. He handed the hose to the man, made an X in the ground with his foot, pointed to it, then to him and said, "*Usted aqui. Comprendo?*" The man nodded and stood on the spot, holding the hose.

Brandon casually walked back to the other side of the plane, stopped to tie his shoe, then said, "Go!" while grabbing the bag and jumping in.

The engine caught on the first rev as he tossed the bag onto the back seat.

"I've got it," he said while pushing the throttle to full power, and placing the flaps full down.

Allie noticed a jeep with four soldiers in it racing toward the end of the runway. Incredibly, she soon realized that Brandon wasn't even going to use the runway. There was enough flat dirt around it, and they were airborne in a thousand feet, screaming over the trees. He turned south and climbed, retracting the gear and flaps.

"That was, well, unusual," said Allie.

"Not for these parts, if they don't get a bribe. Otherwise it is not uncommon for them to shoot you down after take off. But these guys got a good bribe and still tried to detain us," said Brandon looking at the gas gauges.

"Do you think the delay back there was the beginning of some sort of setup?" asked Allie.

"Damn right," said Brandon. "They've been on to me for a couple of weeks now. Someone paid a lot more than a hundred dollars for the delay. We'd have been installed in some flea-bag hotel while a pro was flown in. As far as I can tell from past information, I am the only mark. But if you got in the way, they would take you out also."

"How would they have done it?" asked Allie.

"Probably a sniper, maybe two, and at least two spotters. They'd have covered the hotel entrances from a half-mile away. Someone would be constantly looking through telescopes equipped with night vision. High-powered rifles would already be bore-sighted for the distance, altitude, and temperature with cross hairs on the doorways or any windows they thought I might be behind. There would be time for one good shot. It would be enough. Then they would be airborne before any police arrived. Nice neat job. Some unidentified half-Chinese gringo killed. No locals apparently involved. No one to interrogate. No evidence. The local economy improved a bit."

Brandon glanced at the gauges and said, "We've now got enough fuel to get to Costa Rica. Is your little satellite microphone transmitter still on?"

Allie looked in her shirt pocket, checked the dim lights on the tiny device, and said that it was and seemed to be working properly.

"Then, hello Pitman!" said Brandon. "If you didn't get the part in the customs building, we will need passports."

Pitman had been half-listening to their conversation. It was a one-way transmission device, and he couldn't send them a message except through Brandon's wallet/fax. But he had nothing to say for the present. His arrangements would be obvious.

Pitman made several calls. The U.S. Military Attache would meet their plane at El Coco Airport in San Jose, Costa Rica. Brandon and Allie landed and received credentials which carried the weight of diplomatic immunity in Costa Rica.

They then flew to Panama and checked into the Howard Air Force Base BOQ, looking forward to a good night's sleep. Keys to an old jeep and their new passports were waiting for them at the desk, hand delivered from Pitman by a State Department official on a regular military night courier flight.

After a good dinner at the O'Club, Brandon said he had an idea that might help. They drove into the city and purchased, at a supermarket, three fifty-gallon plastic water jugs, several lengths of different types of plastic hoses, and five tubes of hard drying silicon glue. Then they went back to the plane.

The jugs fit neatly onto the back seat. After an hour of cutting hoses and containers and applying the silicon, they headed back to the BOQ.

"Think it will work?" asked Allie.

"We'll see how the glue has dried in the morning," said Brandon. "But even if the seals aren't perfect, all we really have to do is keep a window open and not smoke. We can throw each container out when empty. Should increase our range by at least twelve hundred miles, which means no gas stops until we're past Lima. Think you can take it for fifteen hours?"

"Probably," she said. "Though it's reaching my limits."

"Understand," said Brandon. "Let's each try to sleep while the other is flying."

Cordillera de Huanzo Mountains, Peru: March 20, 1999

The next day, after filling the water bottles with fuel, Brandon taxied to the longest runway at Howard.

"In case we're too heavy?" asked Allie.

"If we're not off and climbing by the six thousand foot marker, we still have room to land and stop," said Brandon.

He took them low out over the Pacific Ocean and under radar coverage. Twelve hours later they bypassed Lima by two hundred miles and came in at the little bay of Bahia San Juan, near the town of San Juan Demarconia. They landed on the water shortly before dark, got fuel from a dockside jet boat dealer and some coffee and tortilla cakes. Then they used the bathroom. The sea was unusually calm, and Brandon decided, instead of spending the night there, to fly out and land about ten miles from shore.

"That Tapachula escape was lucky," he said to Allie during the short flight. "I think we should take no chances if we can help it."

The plane came to a stop on the water. Brandon checked the maps again to make sure they weren't parked on a shipping lane, then climbed out, opened the nose hatch, and threw out a sea anchor—a small parachute device to keep them from drifting very much due to wind. He then cut the silicon seal away from the Renegade's central fuel tank, snapped the legal cap in place, and tossed the last water bottle overboard.

After folding their seatbacks down, Allie handed Brandon the tape recorder and tape of her conversation with Illaquitak, the Rememberer. He listened to it many times before nodding off. They slept comfortably in the plane, bobbing on the ocean. Before light, they took off to the east, toward the Cordillera de Huanzo Mountains.

* * *

The air force chief in Peru had been Espinoza's 'man' for almost two decades. General Valesquez had been given instructions to eliminate any aircraft of U.S. registry that looked suspicious; and that any flying east of Lima, by definition, looked suspicious.

The General was awakened at daybreak and informed of the small plane that had landed at Bahia San Juan the night before. He cursed violently, then gave permission to dispatch the two Peruvian Air Force jet fighters. Wanda was the pilot of the second one.

* * *

Allie handed Brandon a cup of coffee in a styrofoam container shortly after lift off. At first light she opened her paper sack of tortillas and they small talked about the beauty of the country while eating. He studied the map for a few moments, handed it to her, and decided to fly an indirect route to their destination, tracing it on the map with his finger. Allie asked him why not go directly over the mountain passes on the way to Lake Titicaca. He said there were powerful people who wanted them out of the way, and since there were fighter planes parked less than a hundred miles away and they were in a small defenseless kite, being caught in the open by one of them was tantamount to being a clay pigeon; the mountains provided a certain amount of cover, and he knew how to fly in mountains.

"Besides," he added, "this little engine has a fine turbo-supercharger for flying at medium altitudes. It will make it possible to maneuver next to high ridges."

She asked, "What kind of cover?"

He said the first type would be escaping from their radars and the second type would be turning at close quarters.

"I understand the first," she said, "but not the second."

"The second is like a mongoose fighting a cobra. The cobra has poison fangs. The mongoose has quicker reactions," he said pointing to the areas of rough terrain around them. She interrupted him and pointed ahead, saying, "Two small specks, shadows, just went across the valley in front of us."

He dropped his empty plastic coffee cup on the floor between his legs, snapped the throttle back, and dove the aircraft into a nearby canyon. White smoke from a missile streaked by them.

"What's the radius of this box canyon?" asked Brandon.

"What do you mean?" replied Allie.

"What's the distance between the one canyon wall and the opposite wall? How wide is it?" he asked while looking behind for the fighters.

Allie read the map.

"At the lowest altitude it looks like about a mile," she said.

"There's one of them," he said while weaving the plane and cutting the engine power again.

"Why are we slowing down?" she asked.

"Need to let him catch up," he said.

She thought him crazy and asked, "Why let him get close?"

"Those missiles don't work in ground clutter. Peruvian jets don't have 'look-down, shoot-down' equipment. No third world countries do. He'll use guns. The sure thing," said Brandon."

The Peruvian Air Force jet fighter followed the small Renegade low into the canyon. Brandon waited until it was barely within gun range. Then, before slamming into a cliff, he reefed into a sharp turn and headed in the opposite direction. The fighter could not turn enough inside the canyon, then tried to climb out as it slammed into the cliff a few feet from the top.

Allie felt her plane shake from the explosion and looked back to see a bright orange fire ball erupting from the wall of rock. Then she looked at Brandon. His eyes peered intently for the other plane.

"Boxed in," said Brandon. "See if there's another box canyon close by . . . like this one, only bigger?" he added.

Allie read the map in earnest.

"There's one to the east, over this cliff to our left, a few miles ahead. We'll need to climb about a thousand feet to get over and into it."

"How wide?" he asked while pushing the throttle full forward."

"Looks to be about three miles at the far end."

"Good," he said. "Enough room for him to turn, and the wind is from the northwest."

Brandon switched the radio to the international hailing frequency, called "Guard," and transmitted, "Was that your wingman, Wanda?"

No mistakes with me, thought Wanda before answering while maneuvering for the sure kill. "Nothing personal, Commander, but you and Mrs. Pitman will be eating granite boulders long before I run low on fuel."

Good, thought Brandon, *it is now a personal thing.*

Allie put the map in her lap and thought that this strategy made less sense this time than the last. A bigger canyon? She relaxed her anxiety by watching his face and eyes. He reminded her of a mongoose all right, timing things perfectly. His head moved forward to look at the towering walls of the canyon, then back to the fighter. His hands turned the aircraft slightly every time he looked back in order to get a better, an exact, view.

She gripped the map tighter as they approached the dead end of the second canyon. When it looked to her that there was still plenty of time before having to turn, Brandon said, "Got him!" while reefing the Renegade next to the towering cliff to the north.

"This looks like a good place. Plenty of room for him to turn here," said Brandon.

"Why," she asked, "is it good that he can turn here, and also good that there wasn't enough room for the other to turn back there?"

"Because now, if he didn't think there was enough room, he would never come in, no matter how pissed he is that his wingman got smoked. But there is enough room as far as he knows. And, as I said, their radar missiles don't work this low over the background clutter of rocks and cliffs. Not enough heat from us for heat-seekers either. He'll go for the sure thing again, just like his wingy . . . guns. Looks like he's absorbed it all and is rolling in now."

Allie refrained from asking more at the time. She had learned in her youth to fly fighters, Aircobras and Mig-21s in Russia, but there was nothing in her training that approached this type of airplane warfare.

Brandon weaved the plane slightly to keep the jet in sight and descended lower into the box canyon. The jet followed, gaining steadily.

"Yes, I think he's got it," he said looking back, adding in a cockney accent, "By Jove, I think he's gawt it!"

Allie felt a pang of nausea in her stomach. Wanda turned exactly on line with the Renegade and climbed a few hundred feet above it for a better, safer, shot. Wanda knew that Brandon would soon have to climb into his bullets. He couldn't go for the flats. There was no escaping it. And Brandon knew it also.

"Okay," said Brandon. "We have one here who knows what he's doing, so there still may be trouble, though I doubt it. Cinch your parachute straps tight. If I say 'go', unbuckle seat and shoulder straps, grab the D-ring with your right hand, open the door with your left, kick out, and immediately pull the ring."

Brandon took the plane down the valley at ten feet with throttle full open, gaining speed while angling still closer to the northern wall of the canyon, his wingtip missing by only a yard. Wanda flew high, weaving, angling for the sure gun shot. Brandon craned his head around, watching, concentrating.

"You watch the ground and pull the yoke back a little if it looks like we're going to hit the ground. I'll work the rudder," he said to Allie. "Right now I have to look back to keep this guy in sight."

When Wanda came into gun range, Brandon grabbed the controls and abruptly jerked the Renegade up and into the fighter's line of fire.

"Bait," he said to Allie.

Wanda smiled as he pulled up and pressed the trigger.

"Goodbye, Mr. Brandon," he said into his oxygen mask radio mike.

Two 23mm bullets sliced through the thin metal of the Renegade's tail, doing no damage to the controls as Brandon pulled harder into a vertical climb.

Wanda pulled up to follow, applying full afterburners and wondered for a moment how the little plane could out-climb him. He felt his wings buffet slightly from an accelerated stall condition. Too late, he nosed back down and half-turned toward the safety of the valley. His jet slammed into granite at over two hundred miles an hour and exploded.

Allie felt the second shock wave of the morning shake her pet airplane as the Renegade continued straight up into the blue sky. She hung in her seat belt, stunned, as Brandon winged over for a look back at the crash. Then he leveled out and cruised on politely toward their destination.

"You only saw two shadows?" he asked.

"Only two," she said, finally releasing her grip on the map. She had seen things close to this with her Andy. But not this. Brandon, in a civilian piston-powered four-place, slow, light plane had just defeated two military jets. And he didn't show the slightest elation or depression or feeling.

"Why did they. . . . How did you?" she finally spat out.

Brandon took another look at the fireball behind him, pulled the map from Allie's lap, and said, "Got any more sandwiches?"

On the way to Titicaca, he explained to her that the first pilot had just screwed up.

"He got sucked into a lower altitude where the radius of turn required was less than what his aircraft could do. The second pilot, Wanda, hadn't screwed up, as far as he knew. The pure-jet types," he continued, "are high-altitude pilots for the most part. Sure, they low-level through mountains. But that gives them little knowledge about mountain flying. Helicopters are really the best way to learn, preferably with someone who knows from experience . . . not from test pilot type flying. Wanda knew he could turn in less than two miles at those speeds. He had probably done it hundreds of times. But never on the west side of a canyon when the winds are from the west or northwest. You see, when the high-altitude wind blows over cliffs that border valleys that lead to lowlands, those air molecules go down rapidly on the one side of the valley and a little up on the other. Any more coffee?"

Allie poured from the thermos into the styrofoam cup and said, "That doesn't answer my question."

Brandon took a sip, looked again behind him, then at the map, and said, "The first guy I boxed in. He couldn't turn like this aircraft can. Wanda didn't fall for it. He followed us into a wide canyon. This is a straight-wing airplane. He had a swept-wing airplane. He could go faster. I can turn sharper, either left and right or up and down. So I maneuvered him into the down-draft side of the canyon, the west side. And then I climbed out of trouble.

"He had a half-second to shoot. But that half-second put him in a position that he couldn't fly out of. When I felt the two hits on this Renegade, I knew we would either have to bail out or we had made it. Either way, we would be alive, and he would probably be dead. You see, we were going straight up when he fired. There was plenty of altitude to bail out.

"If he knew mountain flying, he wouldn't have gotten into the situation. But they both had to get down close to our altitude and use guns. Peruvian jets don't have radar missile guidance systems that allow tracking another aircraft with the ground close in the background. As I mentioned, it's called a 'look-down, shoot-down' capability. They don't have it. So their choice was to wait for us to climb to a higher altitude, which we wouldn't do. Down low, they would run out of fuel long before we would. So they had to come down and use guns.

"He was probably wondering why his powerful plane, with a healthy engine, could neither climb nor maintain altitude as the down draft from the cliff slammed him into the rocks. Or at least his airplane hit the rocks and exploded."

"What do you mean by that?" she asked.

"A crashed fighter is just that. It doesn't mean he was in it when it crashed. If he was quick enough at recognizing the situation, he had about a second to eject. Still it is doubtful he and his parachute could have avoided the fireball."

Allie was impressed with the explanation. The most perfect survivor, aside from her husband, she had known. A warrior in the healthy sense of the word. One who sought no notoriety for feats. A man who had just saved her twice from certain death if she had attempted this flight herself. But, aside from those impressions, this was the first time she had ever, in ten years, heard Jess Brandon complete more than a few sentences. Unconsciously she put her hand on his shoulder.

He turned and said, as if reading her mind, "Mrs. Pitman. What is it you want to know?"

"I want to know how you won just now. Not the technical things. The reasons you gave were good and accurate, but they weren't the real reasons."

"If you will give me good vectors to Titicaca, and refill the cup, I'll tell you what I know," said Brandon, impressed with the question.

She looked at the compass and said to climb to fifteen thousand feet and head zero seven eight. "Between the two peaks at ten o'clock," she added.

"The answer to your question, Mrs. Pitman, is that except for the English-speaking people, Western Europeans, and Israelis, no other educational and governmental systems in the world allow independent thought while flying military aircraft. If it's not in the published procedure of these other countries, or being dictated by some general sitting in an armchair, it's not possible to do. These late pilots were trained for high-altitude jet fighting. They knew nothing of the air at low altitude or mountain air or fighting light planes. These things weren't in their manuals. They were trained by a dictator mentality, where truth is manifested by power. It's pretty much like what the Red Baron said in World War I, 'The difference is made not by the crate the man is in, but by the man who is in the crate'. And language is a part of it. One could describe an interesting and exciting story concerning even blimps, like Clancy did with submarines. The young human mental makeup is attracted to such things of valor and intrigue."

"Blimps?" she asked.

"Do you know the history of blimps?" he asked.

"Deflatable airships is all I know," she said.

"They were first used as observation platforms for European armies. During World War I, there where two types of lighter than air craft—dirigibles and limps. Dirigibles had metal structures and kept their shapes when hydrogen gas was removed. Limps collapsed after deflation, being made of rubber. The U.S. Navy needed observation platforms over the Atlantic Ocean when the German U-Boats were providing such a menace. I believe the 'A' class 'limp' was the Firestone contender for the government contract. The 'C' class came close, a European contender. Goodyear, with the 'B' class limp won. Hence, 'Blimp'."

"So what's the excitement story?" she asked.

146

"The excitement story is how something so slow can be attractive to the human mind. I mean, with competitive pilots nothing is good enough. You fly jets, but they are not swept-wing. You fly swept-wing, but they are not supersonic. You fly supersonic swept-wing, but they have orange training command paint jobs. And so you similarly have a blimp pilot making an approach to an aircraft carrier. The landing signal officer—the LSO— on the deck of the carrier watches him do a few rope-and-go's to a nearby destroyer. Then he watches him do a bag-over, then a hiss-out before his final approach. The LSO doesn't like this manatee approach to naval aviation and gets on the radio. He knows that dropping ballast will make the strange machine go up. And when the blimp is on final approach, the LSO says, 'You can do all the strange maneuvers you want, but on approach, when I call for power, I want to see SAND'! This is an example of a bad LSO, by definition bad because he never flew blimps.

"So what about the jets?" she asked.

"I was apprehensive about those two jets at the time. But it quickly became obvious that they had no knowledge of low level mountain flying, or what light aircraft can do in this environment. They considered this plane like a blimp compared to their armed, supersonic jets. And though there are unforeseen variables that can happen during any engagement like this, there were essentially none this time, and those two jet pilots were pretty much sitting ducks."

Chapter Nine

Lima, Peru: March 20, 1999

General Espinoza was sweating in the cool, air-conditioned room. Wanda and the other jet had not returned and had made no contact. He put down the phone and turned to Bloomquist.

"We have two fighters missing. They went after a goddamn civilian, single-engine airplane. And I aim to get to the bottom of it. What do you know that you haven't told me?"

Bloomquist sat his large frame down in a plush chair and suddenly felt tired.

"General," he said, "as I said before coming down here, I think this man Pitman is behind the TWA airliner, your disaster outside London, and the Sapa Inca. The courier that died in the crash was sent by him. He was CIA, and they are directly involved in drug interdiction. But my sources say that Pitman is still in Washington."

"Can your government provide me with satellite surveillance of the area a few hundred miles outside Cuzco, without the CIA being involved?" asked Espinoza.

"It can be requested of the Defense Intelligence Command through the State Department. A routine update of all air traffic in the area every hour. They can then fax it down here direct on our secure machine."

"Good," said Espinoza.

Delta Flight 462 To Washington, D.C.: March 20, 1999

Jane tried to get her mind off her near-abduction. She watched a movie on Delta Flight 462 headed for Dulles. *This relationship with Brandon might not work*, she thought. His occupation had now almost gotten her killed. If it hadn't been for the Eagle, she would probably be history. He mentioned quitting after this, and she tended to believe him, but this time she had been placed at risk. It was now a physical thing. She needed to know what he was doing. It wasn't fair otherwise.

She pulled her purse from the floor of the plane and retrieved a wad of credit cards. Impatiently she swiped her MasterCard across the phone mount on the seat back in front of her. After thirty seconds she was talking to Andy Pitman.

"Jess and Allie are on their way to Peru and should be back in two or three days," said Pitman. Then he decided to tell her some things about the business, now, even if on an unsecured commercial telephone connection. He could detect the frustration and near-panic in her voice. She had been put in a bad position and had to be leveled with.

"I know how you feel," said Pitman.

"I just bet, Pitman," said Jane, the bitterness surfacing.

"So I'll give it to you straight," he said, ignoring the sarcasm. "Dancing Eagle and his wife used to work for me. Now they are mostly retired. When they do work, they do it voluntarily. We are always testing our adversaries. One of the most useful things to know is if they are the kind to harm civilians or take hostages. It puts them in several categories which are much easier with which to deal. It establishes them as unsophisticated and desperate. Desperate people make mistakes and are easier to eliminate. We find out much during hostage-taking attempts. Sometimes kidnappers can become hostages and information givers themselves. It can be an important feint in this kind of conflict.

"You were being monitored and protected by invisible people all the while you were at Brandon's place. There was little chance of any major harm coming to you. But there was a chance. And for that you deserve to know what's going on. But look at it this way—you helped Brandon with what is probably his last job. Maybe you helped him survive it. I'll brief you on the entire operation in detail when you get back."

Damn right he will, she thought as she banged the phone back into the mount in front of her. Then she leaned back and realized she was strangely less angry. Soon, at over five hundred miles an hour, she slept like an exhausted infant.

Lima, Peru: March 21, 1999

Bloomquist used the computer and modem in Espinoza's office, reviewed his current financial situation via the Worldnet, and fought off the panic. Sweat rolled down his temples. He had to have hard cash and a lot of it, soon. His shell game would soon catch up, and instead of him leveraging, he would be leveraged out of business. *Perhaps it is good the Renegade got through*, thought Bloomquist. *Mrs. Pitman is no fool. She has connections with the Incas. Perhaps she could lead me to the treasure, and my problems would go away.*

Lake Titicaca, Peru: March 21, 1999

Allie descended the Renegade toward the surface of the clear waters of Lake Titicaca. At a hundred feet a flock of bright pink flamingos flew in front of her flight path. She yanked the yoke hard back while twisting it clockwise and applying full power. Then she circled around for another try.

"Flamingos?!" asked Brandon. "Here? At this altitude? At these cold temperatures?!"

"Supposedly they're quite common here," she said.

On the second try she eased the throttle and yoke back at a hundred feet on the radar altimeter and let the aircraft slap itself onto the glass-like water. She slowed to a stop, then at 2,000 rpm started a turn toward the north, toward the nearest land.

Standing on the shore were three Incas in peasant garb.

"We won't be taxiing onto the shore," said Brandon as she reached for the gear handle. Allie turned the engine off and opened her door. Once the plane's bottom hit ground, he opened the side window and tossed the Incas a line. Then he and Allie stepped off into shallow water and waded ashore through green reeds, small sharp rocks, and some sand. The three Incas remained silent until Brandon said the word "blade."

"Greetings Mrs. Pitman, and you must be Mr. Brandon, who saved Tamac's life," said one of them. "I am Umu. We have transportation a quarter-mile away."

Brandon shook hands and said he would be ready in a few minutes. He waded back to the plane and shortly returned carrying the aircraft's battery.

"Could you hide this somewhere nearby?" he asked.

One of the Incas took it from him.

Brandon again returned to the plane with the tow rope coiled over his shoulder, opened the cowling, scooped several cupped hands of water from the lake, and poured them on the engine. Then he went inside and unscrewed a petcock on the floor behind the pilot seat. Water gushed through it. He got out and pushed the airplane further away from shore, holding onto the long tow rope.

Allie and the others watched in amazement as the plane slowly sank and disappeared from view. Brandon came up to them and handed the end of the tow rope to Umu saying, "This needs to be buried in the sand."

Umu handed it to one of the others and said that it would be done and they should be on their way. Allie asked if the cold water of the lake could crack the block of the warm engine, if that was why he cooled it a little first.

"Correct," said Brandon.

After a twenty minute hike, they came to two four-wheel drive International Scouts hidden by freshly cut reeds. A few minutes later they were on their way to the mountains.

Lima, Peru: March 21, 1999

Espinoza looked at the photograph of the plane landing on Lake Titicaca. Another satellite photograph, an hour later, would confirm its final position there. After that it would be dark and they would be looking at infrared photographs. In the meantime he made arrangements for a squad of troops from the Peruvian Army to mobilize and head toward the north shore of the lake. The caravan of three army Hum-v's and two trucks left Cuzco within the hour. The next photograph came in on time. But it showed no airplane.

Espinoza paced the floor while Bloomquist sipped a glass of wine. *Perhaps the craft just dropped off someone*, he thought, *then went somewhere else.* He was in radio contact with the troops and would stay in Lima until he had more information. Then he would fly to Cuzco and follow from there. The first infra-red photograph also showed no aircraft. But it did show two vehicles at the base of the high mountains that weren't there before, or if they were there before, weren't hot.

Cordillera de Huanzo Mountains, Peru: March 21, 1999

Brandon rode shotgun in the first Scout with Umu. Allie was in the back seat of the second sitting behind the two others. *These guys seem pretty serious*, she thought.

After a few miles one of them turned to Allie and began talking.

"I am Viracocha and this is Ayar, also representing the Sapa Inca. And how are you, Mrs. Pitman?"

151

She said she was fine, and asked where Tamac was.

"He is taking care of other concerns. We will stop shortly for something to eat, and then you can relate to the three of us what you have deciphered. We are equipped, with waystops, to go almost anywhere in Peru and are presently provisioned for a week."

"Sounds good," said Allie.

As if on signal, the vehicles pulled off the road and, side by side, headed for a group of small trees and brush. Allie and Brandon exchanged glances that said everything looks okay. The lunch fare was taken from the tail gate of the first Scout. It consisted of corn cakes, dried bean paste, some jerked meat, and water. Allie thought it the most sensible food she had eaten in years and felt invigorated afterward.

Umu then began to ask her questions. It was obvious he was well informed of what Tamac knew. Allie took the photograph of the bracelet from her pocket and a star chart of the southern hemisphere. In less than two minutes she was finished. Umu comprehended all of what she said and for the first time, smiled.

"We are indebted to you Mrs. Pitman, and to Mr. Brandon. It fits with our folk tales. And you are correct about the water levels being at their lowest at this time of year. We will investigate Bone Lake."

He paused for a moment, then said, "You should know that the Inca people have always considered that to be in debt is to live as a dead person. Therefore the Sapa Inca has insisted that should this search be successful, and though your country's immediate interests will have been satisfied, we would still be indebted to you personally. He wants you to take whatever you two can lift at one time, which we will help carry back to your plane, should we find anything. That way all debts will be paid in the shortest time possible. I must warn you, however, that there may be some danger involved."

Allie looked at Brandon and had her answer. He nodded that he was for continuing on.

* * *

They drove all night, going higher and higher into the mountains. By morning they were at the lake. She looked around its steep rim, noting the dry, different colored shoreline where the water had been higher earlier in the year. But she saw nothing unusual. The Incas untied a large package from under the canvas on the roof of one of the Scouts and placed it on the ground. It was an inflatable rubber boat, which they unrolled and connected to a compressor hose from the Scout engine. In a few minutes it was blown up. Umu attached a five-horsepower outboard to its transom, and the three Incas lowered it down the steep cliff-face with ropes. When it was in the water, Umu climbed down and called for Brandon, Allie, and Ayar to do the same. Viracocha stayed with the vehicles.

The lake was dead calm and crystal clear. Umu asked Allie if she had any suggestions. Allie kept thinking "total equality," and said to head toward the northeast shore, the relative position of the dunce cap on the jaguar. During the ride Allie marveled at the mountains, the breathtaking majesty of them. Umu checked out his walkie-talkie with Viracocha, told him to camouflage the Scouts with some of the high-altitude grey-green bunch grass, and to spray water on the engines and exhaust systems until they were cool.

The northeast shore was bleak except for a small waterfall pouring into the lake. They motored past it and seeing nothing unusual, continued north, staring into the depths. After a few hundred yards, Allie asked Umu to go back to the waterfall.

It was curiously simple, about ten feet wide and twenty feet high. Umu drove the boat back and forth, looking at Allie. Finally she said, "Turn off the motor."

Umu cut the switch, and they sat there drifting in front of the fall.

"Listen!" she said.

They all listened, noticing nothing. But her sensitive ears had picked up something.

"Sound of heavy water!" she said. "Just as the Rememberer remembered it."

Umu asked what she was talking about.

"There's more sound coming from this fall than the water falling here is providing. There is a deep rumbling of bigger waters. Listen!"

Now Umu could hear it also. It was as if the waterfall was providing two sounds. He pulled an oar from the boat and paddled closer. The deep sound became louder.

"Let's go behind it," said Allie.

Brandon pulled another oar out and assisted in the rowing. Ayar, on the bow, peered ahead intently as the boat edged around and behind the fall. Then, in one swift motion, the current sucked the boat into almost total darkness. Umu and Brandon backpaddled furiously to no avail. Allie moved to start the motor, as the boat suddenly jerked around, almost throwing Brandon out, and came to an abrupt stop. Ayar stood on the shore of a large pond inside a cave, holding the boat steady against the bank with the bow line. Thirty feet further inside the cave the pond water cascaded down a steep cliff into a black abyss, thundering furiously.

Umu said something in Incan to Ayar, and the man nodded a 'you're welcome'.

Both Brandon and Allie were still catching their breath as their eyes became more accustomed to the dim light. Then, when they could see how close they had come to disappearing down a virtual black hole, they had to catch their breath again.

Umu handed each of them a large flashlight and motioned for them to go ashore. Ayar tied the boat securely to a nearby stalagmite that had a large groove around the base of it.

"Looks like this has been used many times for similar purposes," said Umu, shining his flashlight on the ancient column.

"There might be a path around here leading further into this cave," he added.

They looked over the flat, sandy surface with their flashlights. There didn't seem to be a way out. Then Umu said, "Over here!"

He was standing next to a rock that was almost as big as a house. On the side of it, barely visible, were not steps, but toe-holds cut into its side. Behind the boulder was a one-inch wide line of a glowing green substance that led off into the dark recesses of the cave.

"There is a path up here," said Umu. "We'll follow it."

"Just a minute," said Brandon, as he began cutting a ten-foot circular ditch in the sand with his knife by the pool where they were standing. He then buried the boat rope in it, and placed a small boulder at one end to hold the boat, unhooking the other end from the stalagmite. Then he re-moved the outboard motor cover, attached a small device to the electric starter and throttle, and placed it in reverse gear.

"What are you doing?" asked Allie.

"Contingencies," said Brandon as he replaced the cover.

Then he placed a small grenade under another stone by the shore, and buried a spare pistol in the sand next to it.

Umu nodded approval, saying that they should now be going. Umu went first. When at the top, he threw a rope down and called for the others to follow.

"This looks very promising," he said as they gathered at the beginning of what was definitely a wide path cut out of the stone surface of the cave, with a glowing green line of what looked like glass in the middle of it. Umu chipped a piece of it off with his knife, studied it for a second, then put it in his pocket.

Lima, Peru: March 21, 1999

Espinoza carefully studied the satellite photos from the past twelve hours. The first one showed bright infra-red signatures from the still-smoldering Peruvian jets . . . big splotches where they crashed, and a smaller one of a helicopter fifty miles away and heading toward them. He followed the two vehicles from the north shore of Titicaca into the mountains, where they disappeared a few hours before sunset. *The north shore where the light plane disappeared*, he thought. That was probably the place of rendezvous. If the vehicles headed back there, then the plane could be expected also. He would plan to intercept them there.

The Mediterranean Sea: March 21, 1999

The USS *America* turned into the wind and began launching aircraft. At the same time, the USS *Kennedy* landed its last aircraft of the twelve-hour cycle of flight operations. The Mediterranean seemed to glow bright blue in the sunshine.

Twenty minutes later, strange radio transmissions were heard on the bridges of both carriers and all the support ships in the two battle groups.

"Jesus, what was that?"

"Romeo Alpha, are you painting anything on your scope?"

"Arm all missiles! Hot guns!"

"Two six, break! Break!"

"Can't turn enough!"

"Two good chutes."

"What the hell!"

Then it was completely quiet for nearly a minute. No pilots answered their radios. The skippers of both carriers were at a loss. An eerie silence then seemed to ooze from the radio speakers on the bridges of all ships in the fleet.

"General quarters!" both carrier skippers ordered at nearly the same time. The claxons clanged as the airwaves quickly became saturated with transmissions from survival radios. Nearly eighty pilots, navigators, and radar operators had hit the water within a few minutes of one another, climbed into their rafts, and began transmitting. It seemed like chaos.

Then another incredible thing happened. The *Kennedy's* planes were parked neatly on the flight deck after their cycle of flying had ended. Its captain looked in awe as he watched a 'saucer' fly down one side of the deck at a moderate speed of about two hundred knots. It clipped off the vertical stabilizers and rudders of twenty-six aircraft. Then it turned around and flew up the other side, doing the same to another thirty-two aircraft. All the planes on the flight deck were now non-operational. The saucer seemed to stop and hang off the bow for a few seconds, as if to think of what else it could do. Then, in one swift motion it accelerated down the port side, abruptly turned to fly over the aft end of the ship, and clipped the top tail rotor blades off the two helicopters parked there.

No AA missiles or guns in the battle groups could be brought to bear. Nothing hostile or unidentified was seen on radar. The *Kennedy* deck crewmen were the last to see it as it accelerated straight up and out of sight. The entire fleet was made impotent in less than two minutes.

The saucer next headed for the seventh fleet in the Pacific and soon ravaged it in the same manner.

Two hours later, the White House received the ransom call. . . .

"Desire two hundred million metric tons of wheat in two weeks at Minsk and one hundred billion in gold. Further negotiations will begin after delivery. Minister of Defense, Democratic Republic of Russia."

Shock permeated and paralyzed the entire U.S. government hierarchy.

Lima, Peru: March 21, 1999

Bloomquist became increasingly perturbed with Espinoza. The man was doing all the planning without consulting him.

The next morning, Espinoza studied the latest satellite photo which picked up the two vehicles heading toward the lake and immediately activated his arrangements to fly to Cuzco. Bloomquist insisted on going along. Espinoza thought it a good idea for the future ambassador to be implicated in this operation. *It could be an especially useful tie that binds,* he thought.

Cordillera de Huanzo Mountains, Peru: March 21, 1999

Allie and Brandon followed Umu along the path of glowing green glass with Ayar taking up the rear. The sound of the two waterfalls was soon left behind. The going was often uphill and slow. After a mile, they came to a tunnel. Umu said he would go first and call to them if everything was okay. After three minutes, they heard him and followed. At the end of the tunnel was what looked like a solid wall of stalagmites but with the green line leading into it.

"Over here," said Umu.

They followed the line and the sound of his voice around some large stones and then immediately were at the entrance of a gigantic room, perhaps ten acres in area. They couldn't see the ceiling. Instead, a glowing white light illuminated the room through cloud-like vapors a few hundred feet up. It looked like they were standing in a long-extinct volcano where the opening at the top was far up and hidden in perpetual clouds. Allie first noticed next to her a full sheave of corn. Seven-foot stalks made of tiny bits of turquoise and emeralds that held dozens of ears of golden maize with thin, silver wires of tassels that waved gently in the slight breeze made by her movement into the room.

Then Allie looked around and took it all in. The saucer-shaped object faintly glowed at the center of the cavern. Into the walls of the room were carved thousands of shelves cut into the rock, each loaded with shimmering and glistening gold and silver art pieces. There were acres of objects on the ground, solid gold hoes, spades, and other hand tools. Large reed boats of gold, five-foot piles of gold nuggets that had been waiting for the artisans five centuries ago. Gold llamas, alpacas, and vicunas of all descriptions with ruby, emerald, and sapphire eyes. Golden macaws, parrots, umbrella-birds, and cock-o'-the rocks. In one section there was an acre of half-rotted remains of old woven baskets under four-foot piles of gold insects, shellfish, and reptiles of hundreds of varieties. Solid gold model cities, with streets, houses, temples, and nearby mountains glistened from two acres in the far corner of the cave. Nearby, twelve solid gold life-size maidens glowed in naked perfection, their sandals even showing slight wear.

Allie leaned against the wall of the cave. It was the treasure trove of many kings. Never had she imagined such a concentration of art and wealth. Each piece was worth a small fortune. And there were tens of thousands of them. Then, at the far side, she saw an entire forest-garden of flowers, ferns, and trees, all gold and silver with blossoms of pearls and emeralds. And in the middle of the forest stood the huge Sun God symbol, a disk of gold fifteen feet in diameter with rays consisting of thousands of priceless gems.

Umu interrupted her concentration and reminded both her and Brandon to choose as many pieces as they could lift, and they should be going soon.

Brandon slowly walked around the vehicle. There were no visible seams, no rivets, no point of entry. He noted a single symbol on its top side, above the sharp saucer edge directly in front of him. It looked like a sideways pitchfork with three tines, a trident. One step further around the craft, and the trident disappeared. Now he saw two interlocking circles directly in front of him. Another step, and the circles went from sight, seemingly replaced by a triangle with a bar on its top. These three symbols were repeated five times as he circuited the vehicle.

He touched the faintly glowing surface. It was not warm or cold, but seemed to match his hand temperature. He put his cheek to it, and it still seemed neutral. He scraped his pocket knife along its surface several times. Not a scratch. Then he shined a flashlight along its surface at his eye height while walking slowly around it again. Half way around, at an angle, he saw five slight finger-sized indentations in the underside of the saucer edge. He walked toward them and they disappeared. He walked back and looked again, memorizing their position. He walked back and felt for them. Yes, he could barely feel them. All five. Almost unconsciously he placed his fingers and thumb into the slight depressions. Nothing. He pushed and tried to turn his hand clockwise. Nothing. Then he tried to turn his hand counter-clockwise. With no friction or resistance at all, his hand rotated the depressions ninety degrees, and the circle or 'finger-pad' of depressions lifted slightly from the skin of the craft.

Then there was the sound of air being expelled out of the vehicle. He noticed movement to the right of his hand, and a door, oval shaped, seemed to split up in pie pieces and recede into the sides of the opening. He removed his hand, stepped to his right, and peered inside. It was lit, but there was no coming on of lights . . . no light bulbs or laser illuminators. It was a universal light, from no source he could see. It was as if all the material inside glowed of its own accord.

Brandon stepped inside. There were five places to sit—two in front of a console and three behind them. He walked to the right front seat and sat down. There were arm rests, but no seat belts or restrainers of any kind. There were seat backs and head rests. He leaned back, and the seat material seemed to form exactly to his shape, kind of like laying on a waterbed, he thought. Other lights seemed to come on, one from above and from the sides. He peered up and around, but could still see no bulb or source. The inside walls sloped smoothly up from the flat, clean floor. On each side and between the three rear seats were four cube-shaped boxes about two feet high and a foot square on the tops. They were the same color and texture as the floor, and seemed part of it, as there was no seam between them and the floor of the craft, an no apparent openings or hinges. In front of him was a console, sort of instrument panel and a wide blank screen. Above that, and completely around the vehicle, was a three-foot band of dim light. He

158

followed it around with his eyes, and noted Allie, Umu, and Ayar in one corner of the cave. It was a window to the outside.

He watched Allie place her hunting jacket on the ground and start to pick out things from around her. She chose dinner plates, jewel-encrusted necklaces, miniature gold animals, and some small ears of corn with golden kernels and silver leaves, and placed them in the large pockets and pillow-sized bird compartment in the back. She zipped all compartments closed, grabbed the corners of her jacket, and lifted nearly fifty pounds.

Brandon looked back inside the craft. On the right side armrests of each of the two front seats there were half-sphere shaped protrusions, about the size of oranges. They each had five deep finger depressions in them. He slowly grasped the one on his armrest with his right hand and the instrument panel and screen lit up. It felt as if his hand was holding an overripe tomato. On the top of the screen were figures exactly like some of those he had seen in the Roswell photographs. There was a triangle, a rectangle, and two interlocked circles.

On the bottom right of the screen were several colored 'ink-blots,' six of them. Each had from two to seven bright white dots in them. He studied each blot. Parts of the fifth one looked familiar. He could make out South America and most of North America, but Baja California and part of Florida were missing. Australia was a slightly different shape, and New Zealand was missing. Ceylon was missing. Africa, Europe, Antarctica, and Asia looked about right. There were large islands in the middle of both the Pacific and Atlantic Oceans. *Lemuria and Atlantis?* he wondered. There were three white dots on this 'map' of the land masses of the Earth. One was plainly near the west coast of South America, where he was sitting. Another was in northeast Russia, Siberia. And the third was on the island in the middle of the Atlantic. He concluded that these ink-blots were maps of the land masses of six different planets, and that the white dots represented the locations of crafts similar to the one he was sitting in.

He tried to rotate the 'ripe tomato.' Nothing happened. He pushed forward and back and to the sides. Nothing. Then he pushed directly down. The 'cockpit' room glowed in red light. He eased off, and the room turned blue, then green, then white. Slowly he squeezed his fingers together, toward making a fist, while pulling up on the tomato. Effortlessly and silently the craft lifted off the ground. At about a yard up, he slowly spread his fingers, and the craft stayed where it was in the air. He re-grasped the tomato and pushed it down slightly, and the craft settled back to the surface of the cave. He tried it again, and at about two feet up, he rotated his hand slightly left and right. He could see Allie going left and right across the window, staring toward him with her mouth agape. He rotated his wrist slightly clockwise, and the craft tilted to the right. He leveled it and again slowly pushed down on the tomato. Again the craft gently landed.

It was a machine of untold significance, he thought, as he let go of the tomato control and watched the instrument panel again go blank. It was definitely from another civilization and far beyond any technology on planet Earth. Also, he knew he could fly it.

Allie also knew the significance of it.

Brandon exited, closed the door, and walked around to Allie. The Incas stood in shock.

"And what might the plan now be?" she asked.

"Have to think about it," he said. "But for now, we continue with our original purpose."

Brandon selected things he thought Jane would like and so picked out many of the same type items as Allie. Then he added two beautiful emerald and gold rings and felt as if a great weight had slipped from his shoulders. *Jane would like one of these*, he thought. *And I would like the other.* Then nearby he spied a small gold-headed fish with opal eyes and silver scales. *Yes*, he thought. *Dancing Eagle might like this.*

He put the pieces into the compartments of his hunting jacket, then lifted it—a good hundred pounds of treasure—saying he was finished.

Umu, now recovered from the shock of seeing what he saw and not believing it, said, "Very good," and then placed about half of what they had each gathered into his and Ayar's knapsacks for the walk out. Tamac's offer, he knew, was specific—what they could lift, not what they could carry.

Brandon and Allie threw their burdens over their shoulders by the jacket sleeves so they could be easily dropped at the first sign of danger.

It seemed an easier walk back to the pond in spite of the extra burdens. Though Umu seemed pleased so far with the results of the trip, he mentioned several times that the first priority was to get everyone out safely. He said he sensed danger that had not been there during the walk in.

They climbed down the footsteps carved into the giant boulder and reached the edge of the pond. Brandon was the last down and dropped his heavy jacket to take a breather.

The first thing everyone noticed was the inflatable boat from the other Scout tied up next to the one they came in. They started looking around for Viracocha, when out of the shadows stepped a figure pointing a pistol at them. When he came into the light it was evident that he was horribly disfigured. The entire left side of his face was burned black and puffed out. One eye was swollen shut. Nearly all the hair on his head was burned off and sticking to his skull in greasy splotches. His left arm hung limply. It was Wanda.

"I thought I saw a chute go into the fireball after your unfortunate, ah, accident?" said Brandon.

"Yes, it was a close thing," said Wanda, painfully, through half a mouth.

"And how did you get here? I already know why," asked Brandon.

"Quite," said Wanda. "I had a standby Puma helicopter in the area. Vectored him in with my survival radio. Got all the satellite information from Espinoza's office. Flew out here. Have to finish the job. "

Brandon flipped the micro-remote switch in his hand, and the boat engine started at full throttle reverse. Wanda glanced behind him as Brandon pushed the rock holding the rope aside, shoved Allie to one side, and flipped the rope with his right toe from beneath the sand into the air. Umu and Ayar hit the ground. Brandon dove for the spot of sand where his pistol and grenade were buried.

Wanda looked back toward Brandon and fired once randomly as the rope looped around his legs. He didn't seem to notice as he took careful aim at Brandon. The boat accelerated toward the abyss. As he squeezed the trigger, he was yanked off his feet. He fired the entire clip blindly while being dragged into the water. Then he let go of the pistol and began paddling furiously with his one good arm. There was a final gurgling yell as the boat cascaded over the waterfall into the terrible darkness, dragging him behind.

Umu, Ayar, Brandon, and Allie slowly got up, as if in a dream. Brandon told them what to expect about Viracocha.

The boat ride against the current out of the cave could have been done with two or three strong paddlers. The five horse-power engine made it a snap.

They found Viracocha lying by the Scouts, his throat slashed. Umu wrapped him in a blanket and put him in the back of one Scout. In a few minutes they were somberly heading toward Lake Titicaca as the sun approached late afternoon.

* * *

An hour north of the Lake, Umu asked Brandon what he wanted to do.

"I don't know, Umu. We can pull the plane from the lake, let it drain for a while, put the battery in it, and take off. That may be the best thing to do for now. Let's get everything and everyone else safe first."

Umu asked if the plane's engine could still run after being underwater. Brandon said he doubted that any water got into the cylinders, that the air filter would keep most of it out at that shallow depth.

"It's fuel-injected," he added. "A closed system. No carburetor. Sealed electronic ignition. Sealed radios. Some water may have gotten into the exhaust manifold, but that will blow out quickly enough. No, I think it will be okay, Umu. A little damp inside for a while. Some of the instruments may not work right away. But the heater and high altitude will help. Should be as dry as a bone a half-hour after we're airborne."

"Amazing," said Umu as he keyed the mike on the Scout's radio and began talking in Incan.

* * *

Just before dark, Espinoza and Bloomquist met the squad of troops on the road to the north shore of Lake Titicaca. The latest radio report from Lima on satellite photos confirmed that the two vehicles were now less than an hour away. Espinoza decided to remain a mile away, hidden behind thick brush, until the airplane showed up. He wanted to get everyone and didn't tell Bloomquist that he had decided to kill them all, and to hell with the Inca treasure. This interference with his business had really gone on long enough.

* * *

The two Scout drivers, Umu and Ayar, approached Lake Titicaca cautiously, going around the area slowly as the they looked for tracks in the sand. Then they parked next to the water. One of them dug the plane's tow line from the sand and tied it to the trailer-hitch of the lead Scout. In five minutes the plane was sitting on the shore draining water.

Espinoza looked through his night goggles and couldn't believe what he saw. The plane had materialized from nowhere. When the water stopped dripping, Brandon went inside and closed the petcock. In another ten minutes he had the battery reinstalled. Allie emptied the two Inca knapsacks, inspected several objects, and refilled their jackets with them. Brandon then heaved them onto the rear seats of the Renegade and strapped them in with seat belts.

Umu handed Allie a sack of food and a skin of water, which she placed on the jackets in the back. The radio in one of the Scouts crackled to life in the strange language. Umu said something into the mike and hurried back to the plane.

"You two best be on your way," he said. "There is big trouble about."

At that moment the pristine silence of the high lake was shattered by a long burst of machine gun fire. Out of the shadows walked Espinoza and Bloomquist with several soldiers.

"And so," said Bloomquist to Allie, his eye patch twitching. "We meet again. Care for another hand of poker?"

"What do you want?" she asked.

Bloomquist started laughing to himself while pointing toward the plane.

"The pieces I saw you put in the coats are beautiful, Mrs. Pitman," he said, holding up the night-vision goggles that hung around his neck.

Allie felt sick. She saw Brandon slip a knife into his hand, seemingly from out of the side of his leg.

Then Bloomquist said, "Mrs. Pitman, I am only a collector and can pay you handsomely for what you brought. The important thing is that they have been found."

Espinoza spoke in Spanish to his men, and they lined up in the formation of an execution squad.

Bloomquist said, "What are you doing, General?"

"Mr. future ambassador, you fool," said Espinoza. "You still don't see the big picture do you? You can have what treasure is here. Be satisfied with it. But these people have to die. I now know that this smattering of wealth that you have been so interested in is known only by this group. Even if they told us where the rest of it is, we could never get it out. The entire Inca population would rise up en mass. So just stand aside."

It was all over in three seconds. Espinoza turned to give the firing command to his troops in time to see all eight soldiers fall forward groaning, each with a spear point protruding from his chest. Even Brandon had no time to react. Espinoza stood in shock.

A Coleman lantern hissed, filling the entire scene with an absurd white noise, as if they were all on a camping trip. Espinoza looked around, wondering what had happened, as several Incas in ancient feathered warrior garb came out of the shadows. Suddenly, in terror, he pulled out his pistol, only to have his hand severed at the wrist with one swing by a club embedded with a line of razor-sharp obsidian stones.

Tamac walked up.

So he is the new Sapa Inca, thought Allie, as one of the warriors tied a string around Espinoza's wrist stump to stop the bleeding. Tamac said something in the strange tongue, and Espinoza was instantly pushed to his knees.

The feathered Indian leader turned and asked Allie if she knew what he had to do. Allie said no, that she didn't know. Espinoza, the Spaniard, the Hidalgo, the non-planter of fields, screamed, knowing very well what Tamac had to do.

Tamac had Espinoza gagged and told Allie that his ancestor, Atahuallpa, was garroted and it ended Inca rule for centuries, and so this Spanish rule must now end with this Spanish Hidalgo. He was a bad person, without honor, against nature.

"You see," he said, "one can be betrayed in a political or military sense, as Atahuallpa was, and it is understood. There was no personal dishonor. We would have accepted that. But Atahuallpa was also betrayed in a religious, a cultural, a personal way. And, to keep from being burned, which is unthinkable to an Inca, he was required to become a Catholic.

"When my ancestors hid most of the golden art back then, it was our tribute to the Sun God, a show of respect to him and his air-machine left to us as a token of his love. It would have been a sacrilege for the Spaniards to have any of these treasures. You see, we had no desire to fight an enemy who has no respect for his agreements. They are not people to us, but only entities to be either obliterated or endured. We made an ancient truce which has lasted all this time. Now, this drug business has driven a wedge in this truce. It has become a different thing altogether. The drug business could be allowed for a while. We even used the coca leaves ourselves for thousands of years to dissipate hunger and fatigue during hard times. But greed came into play. Greed past reason. The type that is against the ancient truce, against honor. Now they want to sacrifice our culture also. Now we must have our country back. The waiting is over. The reason has arrived. And so he must die the same way as Atahuallpa, by the garrote, and repay the debt of centuries. Hopefully his death will be the beginning of the end. I think you have a trite but accurate saying for it: 'What goes around comes around'. We would choose your word, 'karma'."

Tamac nodded, and the rope was looped around Espinoza's neck and twisted tightly, tourniquet-like with a stick. After a full minute, Espinoza's bulging eyes burst a few small blood vessels and his breathing stopped. The garroter announced the moment of death in the strange language, and the Sapa Inca, with his Inca rules now again intact, walked over to Brandon to thank him.

"Thank you for your help Mr. Brandon, Mrs. Pitman. Mr. Bloomquist has, in his own way, been a friend to my people and our way of life and has paid handsomely for some of our art. This has helped create the market we need. But I suggest that his association with these drug people be exposed.

He is a harmless person if kept out of positions of power, but we will do with him whatever you wish."

Bloomquist was in shock. His entire life was focused on being President someday. Could his life's work be over? He wondered, looking at Allie. She checked the lights in her shirt pocket on her remote communicator.

"You are only an appreciator of art," she said. "And there is no way now that you will ever be President, probably not even Ambassador. This has all been recorded via satellite back to ten places in Washington D.C., Virginia, Arizona, Michigan, and Nevada. Tamac is right. You are harmless and should be a one-eyed librarian, only with the patch covering your bad eye. Besides, I don't want a President or Ambassador who cheats at cards. You had a winning hand all these years. Now it's time to fold."

CIA Headquarters, Langley, Virginia: March 21, 1999

Pitman listened to the satellite transmission from Allie's microphone in her shirt pocket and felt greatly relieved. He, more than anyone, knew that intricate and dangerous operations such as this are not over until the last nail is in place. He checked the movement of the reels on the recorder and opened his desk drawer for blank cassettes. Copies would be sent of all recordings concerning Bloomquist to the members of the Senate who confirm Ambassadors. There would be no confirmation hearing, he thought. Bloomquist's name would be withdrawn by the President, probably within the next two days.

Then he typed a message to Brandon on his satellite fax/modem. Brandon had to be filled in on the latest.

Brandon felt the pulsing vibration from the tiny remote relay in the watch pocket of his jeans. He pulled his wallet from his back pocket, flipped it open, and read "Urgent from P" on the top line of the paper-thin liquid-crystal screen. He excused himself from the others and sat down in the sand nearby, scrolling through the message.

"Russian craft has disabled U.S. Mediterranean Sixth Fleet and Pacific Seventh Fleet. Eighty-two aircraft destroyed in flight. Tails of one hundred five 'clipped' off while sitting on decks of four aircraft carriers. Craft seems impervious to impacts with objects of smaller mass. Missiles not effective against it. Caused Aeroflot disaster. Demands of Russians received. Negotiations with Russians in progress. Pitman out."

Chapter Ten

Lake Titicaca, Peru: March 21, 1999

"Tamac," said Brandon, after reading Pitman's fax during the minute of silence after Espinoza's death. "I want to return to the cave of your ancestors. Umu said we could take what we could carry, on your orders. There is something else there I want and can carry."

"Yes," said Tamac. "The messenger from the sun. Umu told me what he saw in the cave. When I attended UCLA I read about King Arthur. This ship is like the English Excalibur sword. Most people think that stories like the great flood and Noah are true because they are mentioned in your Bible book. And that the stories about King Arthur and Merlin are also unique to your culture. Yet many cultures much older than yours, like mine, also have these same stories. The reason they have lasted throughout the ages is not because of your books or my culture. They have lasted because they represent universal truths. These things have actually happened and will happen again. We know it. This ship has been our Excalibur sword for many millennia. Legend has it that it once flew. Of course it is obvious that it had to have flown to the spot where it now sits. There is no other way into the cave for something that size to get there except from above. But we did not know how to fly it. Only gods or super-humans could. Is this sun ship any less believable than a sword stuck in a rock which could not be extracted by any known human at the time? Illaquitak said this would be a day of equality, the day of reckoning. It is the equinox. We have reckoned with the past sins of the unwashed Spaniards. You have extracted the sword and now have the right to rule here. We will transport you back to the cave, and then, in a fine ceremony, proclaim our subservience."

"I don't want to rule anything, Tamac. I just want the ship, the sword. Give Bloomquist a vehicle and free passage out of the country. And keep Mrs. Pitman's airplane. Shortly after leaving me at the cave, if everything goes well, you will see your sun ship land here to pick up our things and perhaps Mrs. Pitman. We will then go away and leave you to resume buying your country back with the wealth in your cave. And in the process, you will kill the drug business here. The message will be clear to all, that Tamac rules here, that Tamac is the Sapa Inca, and your people will see Brandon no more."

"And so it will be," said Tamac.

* * *

Brandon discussed his new plan with Allie. She was all for it.

"It's not set in concrete," said Brandon. "You can return at your leisure."

"In for a penny, in for fifty pounds," said Allie.

* * *

On the drive back to the cave, Umu asked what Brandon would do with the machine.

"Just have it for now," said Brandon. "I have information that the Russians have a similar one and have already done much damage with it."

Umu seemed concerned and asked, "If two indestructible machines were to battle one another, then what is the point?"

During the rest of the drive, Brandon told Umu everything about Operation Blue Book, Roswell, Groom Lake, and Wright Paterson Air Force Base.

"So, these machines are vulnerable," concluded Umu.

"Yes," said Brandon. "But we don't know exactly how they can be destroyed."

Brandon waved goodbye as Umu's inflatable motorboat sped him through the waterfall out of the cave entrance. Then he eyed the boat Umu left tied up on the stalagmite and full of provisions.

Brandon hiked back to the volcanic cavern. He walked around the ship, looking for anything different. It still glowed faintly. A messenger from the gods, or someone, he thought, wondering how old it was.

"No telling," he said to himself. "Probably older than any of these treasures."

He looked at the depression in the dirt a few inches next to the base of the ship, made before his previous short take-off and landing. It seemed heavy enough to make the same mark. But it wouldn't make the side flakes. *Dirt creeps*, he thought, *like plastic and glass creep. In this environment, with slight changes of temperature, the dirt will take millenniums to creep the quarter inch or so.* He looked at the heavy golden segmented bases of the model of the city Cuzco. They each had to weigh tons and had been there for many centuries. But it would take a microscope to detect any creep at all.

This ship has been here for at least a thousand years, he thought. *Perhaps several thousand. The ink-blot map indicated continents as they looked tens of millions of years ago, but that could have been when the last map was drawn, not how old the machine is.*

Brandon twisted the dial with his fingers to open the door. This time there was no air sound as it receded like an iris into the sides of the ship. The air pressure difference between inside and outside had equalized when he first opened it. Earth's atmosphere must have been denser when it was parked here, thought Brandon. If instead, air had been sucked into it when he first opened the door instead of blowing out, then Earth's atmosphere would have been less dense back then. But then the pressure difference could also be explained by different altitudes. If the atmosphere was the same then as now, an increase in the elevation of the mountain itself from crust upthrust would also explain a higher pressure now inside versus outside this perfectly sealed vessel. Brandon shook these thoughts from his mind. He could speculate on such things later.

He stepped inside and operated the similar finger device on the wall to his left to close it. After again sitting in the right front seat and looking around from habit for some sort of seat belt, he placed his fingers onto the control.

Maybe it compensates for g-forces and turbulence, he thought as he slowly squeezed his fingers together. The ship rose a few inches. On the screen appeared several smaller pictures or views. In the middle he could see the blue glowing mist at the ceiling of the cave. He squeezed more, and rose toward it. *There was a way in*, he thought. *There must be a way out.*

As he pressured his hand left and right and forward and back, the top view changed accordingly. He rotated his hand, and the wrap around window showed that he was slowly spinning inside the cave. He relaxed the rotation pressure, squeezed more, and soon saw the hole in the roof through the mist on the middle of the screen. Then in a flash of a final grip, the top view was bright sunlight, and the forward view in the wrap around window was a breathtaking look at a hundred miles of the snow-capped Andes Mountains to the north and south. He wondered exactly how he had gotten there. The opening to the top of the cave was full of misty clouds. Perhaps the machine recognized the general direction desired, what was possible, and missed all dense objects.

Brandon flew down the east side of the Andes toward the jungles in the upper Amazon River basin. On the way, he stopped by a mountain peak and slowly tried to fly the right edge of the saucer into it. At the last second, a few feet away, the machine veered off. He circled around and tried it at a higher speed. This time it veered off further away, while maintaining the general direction of flight afterward. At very high speeds, it changed direction a little when miles away.

He tried the same thing at a lower altitude with the tops of trees. At first, the machine didn't change direction at all. He flew directly into branches, and then into the trunks of small trees, clipping them all off neatly at about a hundred miles an hour. He picked out a thicker tree trunk, and flew toward it at a slow speed, perhaps twenty miles per hour. The craft veered off.

Brandon backed off a few miles, then flew toward and through it at several hundred miles per hour, then circled back. The thick trunk was neatly severed, as if cut by a giant chain saw. He didn't even feel a bump.

Evidently, he realized, the machine *could* recognize the density of all objects that were in its flight path and also calculate its kinetic energy relative to those objects. If more dense, at slow speed, the craft would avoid them. If less, it would just fly through them, depending on the speed. *Kind of like it figures kinetic density*, thought Brandon, though he had never heard the term. He decided to try water and dove on the Amazon river. At high speed it again veered off. At about two hundred knots, it entered the water, then veered from the bottom. He slowed to a walking pace, then stopped. He could see a school of piranhas, and toward shore, a large electric eel. Slowly he surfaced, and the jungle reappeared on the shore lines.

Brandon then flew back to the top of the snow-capped Andes. It took about five seconds. He stayed there a moment, then rotated around until he saw Lake Titicaca. As he pushed his hand forward, the lake got bigger. He pushed his hand firmly forward, and the lake flashed past him. He stopped, turned around, and approached it again. He was getting a good feel for the amazing machine.

Allie watched the ship flash past at an incredible speed and disappear into the distance. There was no noise. Then it came back at a slower and slower speed, descending on its way toward her and gently landed fifty feet away.

Brandon came out with a smile on his face.

"This is quite something!" he said.

"I should say so!" said Allie.

"Want a ride?" he asked.

"Sure," she said.

"Okay," he said. "We'll leave your plane here for Tamac. Let's load our goodies in this and go."

"Great," she said, walking with him toward the Renegade.

Brandon turned on the battery and side-band radio.

"Eagle, Brandon here, come in," he transmitted.

In a few seconds the Eagle responded.

"Yes, yes, everything's fine here," he said.

"Have the doors open on the big barn on the hour, and clear out the tractor, bailer, and trucks. Empty it of all heavy equipment. I want a twenty by twenty foot area in the center open. Understand?" said Brandon.

"Yes, yes. Clear everything out, have the doors open at eight o'clock, right?"

"Right, and stand by to close the doors after I arrive. This aircraft looks like a big dish."

"Yes, yes. A big dish. I'll be here."

"Thanks, Brandon out."

Lone Pine, Moscow, and Beyond: March 21, 1999

"So, let's go," he said to Allie while turning off the radio switches in the Renegade.

Allie walked into the ship as if she were in a dream world, looking around in amazement as Brandon loaded their things.

Brandon had her close the door with the inside finger-pad so she would know how to get out on her own and to see if there was anything special in only his 'Excalibur' fingers. There wasn't.

After she removed her hand, she said, "Anywhere to stash these?" pointing to their treasure on the floor.

"Leave them there. Somehow this thing compensates for gravity and turbulence."

They sat in the front two seats. She looked at all the glowing lights around the screen and asked if he knew what they meant. He said he only had a couple figured out so far and explained how the one hand control worked and that two of the vertical lights on each side of the screen were logarithmic altimeters to the nearest surface underneath, and nearest to the craft.

"I did some experimenting," he said. "The white bands move up and down. One indicates the distance to the nearest planetary surface from the ship, the other is pointed directly down and indicates the distance to the planetary surface nearest to the bottom of the ship. When both bands are at an equal level, then we are level with the horizon of the nearest planetary surface for landings and such. If we roll the craft and point its bottom toward the sun, one band will stay the same while the other will go up, showing a level, I would guess, of about ninety-three million miles. Pretty neat."

"What about fuel?" she asked.

He pointed to a thin, horizontal band of light about two feet long just below the middle screen. A half inch of it at the left end glowed pink. Then it faded into green for about an inch, then blue for the rest of its length. Above each end of the line was a representation of a star constellation.

"I think that's the fuel gauge," he said.

She looked at it closely.

"And what if they used the color blue to mean empty?" she asked. "We would almost be out of gas."

"See these constellations?" said Brandon, pointing to the two of them embossed in the metal above each end of the band of light. "They're both the same, except that one is rotated about ten degrees from the other. I would guess that they represent constellations so far away that their apparent orientation relative to this galaxy, if I remember my astronomy, would take about nine million years to rotate those ten degrees. Kind of like a back-up fuel gauge in the sky. So, if pink is what's left, in relation to the length of the line, I'd say we have around nine hundred thousand years of gas left. If the blue length of the line represents what's left, I'd say there is about eight million, one hundred thousand years of fuel in the tank. What do you think?"

171

"Makes sense," she said. "Except that if the ten-degree rotation cycle is on its second lap around our galaxy, or actually three hundred-seventy degrees in circuit, then we could have about two hundred fifty million years of gas left."

"Useful information for Mayflies like us," said Brandon as he looked at his watch and asked, "Would you mind it if we went to Lone Pine? I could drop you off in Virginia or Maryland in about a minute. But I'd like to keep our exposure time to a minimum for now."

"Lone Pine is fine," she said.

Brandon squeezed and pulled. He counted one one thousand, two one thousand, and the craft left the atmosphere.

"Well, what say?" he asked while steadying into a hundred mile high hover over Argentina.

Allie said it was quite impressive, but that for now she would like to get back.

He pushed, quickly descended, and asked her to look for some landmarks between the clouds. She spotted part of the Amazon River, and he veered toward the west and descended further down.

At about ten thousand feet in his estimation, he headed north in the dark. They picked up the lights of Yuma Arizona in a few seconds and he slowed down. She noted many much thinner, bands of white light on one of the 'altimeters.'

"Yes," he said. "It looks as if it picks up everything around in the air. Those must be other aircraft. I would guess the higher up the lines, the further away. The thicker the line, the bigger the plane. And I notice now that there are little dots around each line, which probably give some sort of bearing information. If those are aircraft, they are probably going into and out of San Diego, L.A., Las Vegas, San Francisco, Salt Lake City, and Denver."

Though he knew it was dark outside, the wrap around viewing screen showed the terrain clearly. *Perhaps some sort of infra-red and low-light TV compensator*, he thought. He found the Grand Canyon and continued north over the desert.

Approaching Utah, with the Great Salt Lake in the distance, he let further down, headed southwest, and followed familiar highways through southern Nevada and California. The towns of Beatty, Stovepipe Wells, and Furnace Creek flashed by before coming across the upper Mojave Desert and China Lake to Lone Pine. Dancing Eagle stood by the big barn door as he floated in and set down.

"Oh. This is great!" said the Eagle, as Brandon and Allie stepped out of the hatch. "Now all we need is some government people snooping around!" He quickly rolled down the metal barn doors, then gave Allie a hug.

Brandon smiled and said there were some things to unload. The gold and silver objects were set on a side work bench. He selected the gold-headed fish with opal eyes and silver scales and handed it to Dancing Eagle.

"Is this a bribe?" asked the Eagle.

"Yes," said Brandon. "I need to smoke the pipe."

Years before, when the Eagle had made it for him, he said that Brandon should not smoke it until he felt ready, but that in the meantime having it was also good medicine. When the time came, he added, the ancient ceremony would be performed—that of blowing smoke toward the four corners of the earth.

"I'll saddle Manny," said the Eagle, "and pack you some things."

Brandon told Allie he wouldn't be long and to make herself comfortable as they walked through the barn's side door to the house.

He left on horseback and in a half-hour arrived at a place called the Alabama Hills, below the High Sierra Nevada Mountains. It was a beautiful area, full of gigantic boulders and bare-rock formations. It had been used extensively during the 1920s and '30s as a backdrop for Tom Mix, Gene Autry, Hoot Gibson, John Ford, Bob Steel, and John Wayne cowboy movies.

He climbed to a high rock, stood straight, and filled the pipe with Indian tobacco from the Eagle's pouch, called *kinnikinnick*. He then lit it and went through the short ceremony while looking over the Owens Valley to the north, The White Mountains to the east, the Indian Wells Valley to the south, then to the towering peaks of the High Sierras to the west. He thought of the lucky balance of power in the world this machine now provided. Both machines had already been first used for destruction—this one on two trees in the Amazon jungle; the other on the Aeroflot airliner and the planes of the U.S. Sixth and Seventh Fleets.

What a shame, he thought, *to use such wonderful gifts from the past for such purposes.* The discovery, celebration, and sharing of them with all the scientists in the world should have been the immediate usage. Perhaps that goal would be a good mission for him to undertake later. But for now, he couldn't share and needed to collect his thoughts.

He knew from Roswell that these machines could be destroyed. But how? He reviewed in his mind all the diagrams of that wreckage pattern from 1947. The craft had approached an open valley. However a small spire of rock stood in its path, perhaps unseeable from inside. The automatic kinetic-energy compensation software worked for the forward, knife-edge of the saucer shape, but maybe not for the underbelly at high speeds.

He took a last suck on the pipe, realizing that there was much danger ahead, and stuck his index finger into the bowl to make sure it was out. Slowly he slid it into the rifle sheath that was attached to the saddle, mounted up, and rode back to his barn. He needed to discuss things with Allie.

The Eagle took the reins of Manny as Brandon dismounted, pulled the pipe from the rifle sheath, sniffed the bowl, and handed it to Brandon, saying, "Keep this with you. It is now very strong medicine."

Allie listened to Brandon quietly until he was finished. Then she said, "I read the fax from Andy. I read the ransom demands from the Russians. I understand extortion on a large scale. If these two machines are indestructible, can't be reproduced with our foreseeable technology, and have only been used for destruction so far, then an attempt has to be made to destroy one or both. As you said during our flight to Peru, it is not the crate the man is in that makes the difference. It is the person in the crate. You are the person in the crate. And from what you have related, I think you should try to destroy the other machine and then go from there. You have already had more power and money than nearly everyone on the planet. And you have not abused it or used it for negative purposes. I think this planet could risk you being in control for a while. Give it a shot."

* * *

The Eagle opened the barn doors.

"Be back in a while," said Brandon.

"Good luck," said the Eagle.

The ship backed out and then shot straight up and out of sight. Brandon looked at his watch and headed toward Moscow.

In less than thirty seconds he was descending toward the Kremlin, well-lit in the pre-dawn darkness. Also, he knew he could have made the trip in much less time.

Methodically, he flew into and severed the top off the first onion-shaped Kremlin dome. It crashed loudly into a small courtyard below, its gold leaf rippling and peeling off the wood frame in sheets of shimmering convulsions. A dozen passes later, all of them, the candy cane ones, the twisted ice cream tops, the phallic nipples of a long-dead culture, were all clipped off as neatly as well-cooked asparagus tips with the edge of a fork.

Brandon then hovered over the city, waiting and watching. Ten minutes passed. Then a light on the right column of the craft's screen showed a dot of a different color. Bright green. He saw the light rise, presumably toward him, getting brighter. He squeezed his hand, rotated his wrist, and pointed toward it. The Russian craft flashed by his viewing screen, and he followed.

In less than a minute, though it didn't seem possible, he saw the other craft against the background of the surface of the moon a few hundred feet below. Then he saw the Earth rise blue and white from the moon's horizon. It was no illusion. He backed off, rotated his wrist, and flew around the dark side in the opposite direction.

On the other side, he saw, pointed, twisted his wrist, and squeezed the fingers of his right hand together. His craft veered away from the underside of the Russian craft. Perhaps not enough closure speed, he thought, as the Russian craft now approached him. As it also veered away, Brandon squeezed his fingers again, twisted his wrist, and headed back toward the far side of the moon. There, he settled onto the powdery surface and waited.

The Russian craft again appeared as a dot on his instrument. Then it was visible a mile above, stark against the cold black clearness of the vacuum of space. Brandon carefully placed his left hand solidly on top of his right hand and squeezed the tomato with all his might, while steering directly for the underside of the Russian craft. This time his machine did not change direction.

Suddenly, white light from the viewing screen and wrap around window blinded him as he was thrown onto the floor. Though no noise was heard, he knew there had been an explosion of some kind. He lay there for several minutes, trying to collect his thoughts. Painfully, he finally got up with a badly bruised knee, sat again in the seat, and looked at the screen and wrap around window. There were stars all around. Nothing close. No Earth. No moon. He didn't know where he was.

Slowly he rotated his head around, first right, then left, and could recognize a spiral galaxy similar to the Milky Way. It was puffed up in the middle. And he knew Earth was on the outer edge of one of its spiral arms.

He squeezed the tomato and went from one spiral arm to another, looking for two giant planets orbiting around a mediocre sun.

Brandon was surprised at the many thousands of planets he saw, none seen before by even the Hubble telescope. After five hours he saw his fourth Saturn-like planet with rings around it. Then he saw another Jupiter-like orb and circled around it, noting the familiar red spot. His blue and white planet, and her moon, soon appeared from the other side of that sun. He said, "Too cool," to himself and thought about where he was.

"So I wasn't blown out of the Milky Way after all! There are many other galaxies with the same lens shape. But they are so far apart from one another that the chances of me being 'exploded' into the middle, or even close, to another by chance was probably small."

He let his elation waft him. He was home. He liked it here. It was his part of the universe, as was Jane who waited for him. He savored the Earth rising on his screen.

Then strange feelings of predestination came over him as he cruised forward, in control of the most powerful machine in mankind's existence . . . a machine that his kind hadn't built and didn't have an inkling of how it actually worked, like procreation and the workings of the human body and plants. Then he thought of the nearly complete ignorance of mankind's understanding of the essences of electricity, gravity, light, magnetism, death, genetics, and sub-atomic particles. It seemed as if the knowledge of all the important things that were useful to people were largely kept from them, wrapped in ever tighter shells of mystery . . . the few dropped scales from the eyes of knowledge garbaged up and obfuscated by the word 'faith', a form of gambling.

He slowed to a stop and stared at the Earth, thinking about the many things going on there, where the only observable flicker of activity from where he was sitting was an occasional flash of lightning.

Then, suddenly, most of the words of the Rememberer were repeated over and over in his mind: *My people are from an ancient past, a past beyond the flood and the ice. We walked on earthquakes and volcanoes. We were, and are, astronomers, mathematicians, engineers, hunters, farmers, voyagers, priests, architects, fathers, travellers, mothers, and kings. Our story has been learned and repeated by each generation. This is part of our story you seek.*